Praise for JESSICA SPEART's
Rachel Porter Mysteries

"Fresh and close to the bone.
[Speart's] characters breathe with the
endlessly fascinating idiosyncrasies
of living people."
Nevada Barr

"A fine, funny book. Chills and laughs galore."
James W. Hall

"The author portrays the stark atmosphere . . .
vividly . . . There are plenty of appealing characters,
not the least of which is Rachel herself."
Publishers Weekly

"[Speart's] mysteries take readers
to all sorts of interesting places . . .
She has a real flair for bringing colorful characters
to life on the page."
Connecticut Post

"Rachel's take-no-prisoners attitude is fun and exciting.
Plan to stay up all night!"
Glynco Observer (GA.)

Other Rachel Porter Mysteries by
Jessica Speart
from Avon Books

JESSICA SPEART

A KILLING SEASON

A RACHEL PORTER MYSTERY

AVON BOOKS

An Imprint of HarperCollins*Publishers*

AVON BOOKS
An Imprint of HarperCollins*Publishers*
10 East 53rd Street
New York, New York 10022-5299

Copyright © 2002 by Jessica Speart
ISBN: 0-380-82061-7
www.avonmystery.com

First Avon Books paperback printing: July 2002

Avon Trademark Reg. U.S. Pat. Off. and in Other Countries, Marca Registrada, Hecho en U.S.A.
HarperCollins® is a registered trademark of HarperCollins Publishers Inc.

Printed in the U.S.A.

10 9 8 7 6 5 4 3 2 1

Acknowledgments

Thanks go to Chuck Ward, District Law Enforcement Ranger with the Bureau of Land Management; COL. Commodore Mann, former USFWS Senior Resident Agent and presently the 95th TC Commander of the Montana Army National Guard; Special Agents Tim Eicher and Doug Goesman; wilderness guide Smoke Elser; Dr. Chuck Jonkel; Merriem Baldwin; and finally to Special Agent Rick Branzell, who gave so generously of his experience, time, and friendship.

A KILLING
SEASON

One

*G*rrrroowwwl!

The Ford 4X4 roared in protest as my foot flogged the gas pedal, and its rear end swung side-to-side in a manic Mae West shimmy. It had been raining hard for three days straight, turning Montana's red clay earth into gumbo mud that clung to my tires in a smothering embrace.

At times like this I cursed the very existence of HBO, with its taunting reminder of what my life in New York might have been. Damn *Sex and the City*—all eighteen new episodes—for flaunting chic Manolo Blahnik shoes, Versace dresses, and Fendi baguettes! Okay—so in reality, I had been an out-of-work actress without any money, meeting my friends at a local bar for beers, unable to get into Nobu to sip ever-so-trendy Cosmopolitans. Still, a girl can dream of living the high life and being swept off her feet by her very own Mr. Big, can't she?

My vehicle slid along the slippery dirt road as if boasting, *I'm not tractionally challenged; I'm independently motivated!*

As the pickup fishtailed, I snapped out of my daydream and concentrated on the hazardous path before me. It was scarred with ancient tire tracks created by a long history of vehicles that had unwillingly performed figure eights. There was little consolation in knowing that previous cars had clawed and fought to stay on the road; it was somewhere along here that Al Carolton had slid off the path and into a ditch, on a day much like this three months ago.

No one ventured up here without a good reason—a dirt road in the mountains of northern Montana, so ruggedly remote it nearly screamed for people to stay away. Even fewer had the chutzpah to flagrantly trespass through the sovereign nation known as the Blackfeet Indian Reservation.

I eased to a stop when I saw a tree wrapped with yellow crime tape. Rummaging through my pocket, I pulled out a crumpled piece of paper, rechecked the directions, and then wadded it back into a tight, compact ball.

Pulling up my rain slicker's hood, I reached for the door handle, then jumped out. My feet were immediately swallowed by a deep puddle of viscous mud.

The marked tree's bark was scarred by the angry bite of a steel chain, doubtless where Carolton had attached the winch to extricate his pickup from its muddy trench. Instead, the wheels had continued to spin, rock-and-rolling ever deeper into the muck. As if things weren't bad enough, the cable then became entangled on its spool. A total "Charlie Forest"—more commonly referred to among locals as a "cluster fuck."

What happened next had been gradually pieced together by federal and tribal agents a week later, when the body was found. Their best guess was that Carolton had given up on his pickup and tried to hike out—with disastrous results. The evidence? A backpack lying on the ground—at least, what was left of it. Other clues consisted of a bootlace with traces of dried blood, tatters of fabric that had once been a shirt, a bloodied sock, and small pieces of human flesh. A rifle lay slumbering peacefully nearby.

A few yards farther on, a series of thrash marks marred the earth. Panic must have held Carolton tight in its grip as he'd fallen, his glasses shattering into a crude kaleidoscope that sadistically refracted the image of his tormentor.

Frantically scrambling to his feet, Carolton had made a final, frenzied run for his life. Blood splatters recorded his desperate path of flight. He managed to reach his vehicle, where he'd crawled inside and hastily locked the door. What took place next required little interpretation. Copious prints encircled the pickup—but only two rear paws had gripped the dirt.

Unleashing its fury in a heart-stopping spectacle, the grizzly had risen up on hind legs, and then crashed back down onto the vehicle like a battering ram. The damaged pickup proved no more a challenge than a metal can, as the grizzly peeled off its door in a frenzy.

Claws as sharp as switchblades then furiously slashed through the seat, turning the vinyl fabric into thin slivers of confetti. The terrified man inside must have made one last effort to escape, but it was too late. The grizzly locked onto Carolton's ankles and dragged him outside, where the bristling pine trees stood silent witness to the last gruesome moments of horror. Carolton's wallet had been found under their branches, decorated with an intricate array of bite marks; the punctured credit cards had identified the remains.

The official report had methodically described a classic carcass scene. A bear had fed on the body—along with coyotes, ravens, and scavenging magpies. Those black-and-white birds had tipped the agents off; they'd bolted from the brush as the men approached, scaring the living daylights out of the search party.

Little was found of Carolton's dismembered body. What made it gruesomely eerie was that one leg remained not only untouched, but still fully clothed. A critter had partially buried the limb, probably to savor it later on.

Hair, saliva, and blood samples had been taken from the scene in hope of catching the perpetrator, but it was as if the bear had vanished off the face of the earth. Most likely, it remained on the loose and was still roaming the area.

As the rain let up, fog began to roll in, draping itself over the mountains like a shroud. I headed for the spot where Carolton's body had been found, and squatted down. A veil of apprehension seductively enveloped my limbs like a fine wool shawl, slowly gliding across my arms, chest, and throat. Death was peering over my shoulder, leaning in close, letting me know that he was still around.

I didn't need the reminder. My mother had recently died, quite unexpectedly—too abruptly for nagging issues to be resolved, too suddenly to say I was sorry for any unnecessary hurt I'd caused, etching guilt into my psyche, as resilient as a layer of permafrost. The U.S.

Fish and Wildlife Service had responded by granting me a one-month leave of absence to mourn, settle bills, and pack up memories. It had proven just enough time for another agent with more clout and seniority to decide he had a hankering for catfish and the blues. He requested to be assigned to my station in Memphis, Tennessee, and the head honchos quickly used it as an excuse to separate me from my former boss, Charlie Hickok. Individually we were each considered a pain-in-the-ass. Together we'd come to be viewed as a mind-boggling, out-of-control, bureaucrat's nightmare.

Hickok had been sent packing back to his beloved New Orleans, while I'd found myself shipped off to the cold, windswept plains of Montana just as autumn flirted with the notion of giving in to Jack Frost. Charlie had been unusually thoughtful, and mailed me a parting gift. I'd opened the package expecting to find a box of chocolates, maybe a colorful assortment of Mardi Gras beads, or a cheap bottle of booze. Instead, there'd been a gift certificate for an extra-large can of bear spray.

"Congratulations on landing your ass in one of Fish and Wildlife's more remote duty stations, Porter. It just goes to show we must have done our job right. By the way, rumor has it there's a grizzly bear hiding behind every tree. So keep your eyes open, your mouth shut, and watch out for your rear end!" the attached card had read.

From what I could tell, he wasn't far off the mark. My posting was smack in the land of the Unabomber, extreme militia, UFO sightings, bitterly cold winters, mysterious cow mutilations, and bad country roads.

Two popular local bumper stickers pretty well summed up the situation. "Montana—It's Not for Everyone" and "At Least Our Cows Aren't Mad."

On a more positive note, I was once more at a one-person station. Regrettably, the agent I was replacing was none other than Al Carolton—the unfortunate victim who'd been killed and half-eaten by a grizzly.

I was just beginning to obsess on whether the intact leg had been his right or his left, when the leaves behind me exploded in a frightening swirl of activity. Jumping up, I whirled around and pulled out my gun as graphic postmortem photos of Carolton fast-forwarded in my brain. Even worse, my hands began to tremble and my legs turned jittery as a pair of unseen wings brushed past my face. Their fluttering feathers virtually controlled the pounding of my heart.

The magpie laughed as it shot past, followed by a much louder sound. Crashing out of the brush was a short, stocky man who looked like a cross between an overweight Bacchus and a pissed-off leprechaun. Around his neck he wore a harness adorned with reindeer bells, which jangled with the urgency of a New York City car alarm. Bushy white eyebrows hung heavy as glacial ridges over his bloodshot eyes, and his beard contained enough twigs to make one believe a bird was using it as a nest.

"Just how long are you planning to keep us out here, anyway? It's not as if you're somehow going to resurrect the poor bastard, you know!"

Hal Ornish stood with his hands on his hips and scowled at me as if I were an errant student. A professor at the University of Montana in Missoula, Ornish was my latest addition in a growing list of unusual landlords. He'd surprised me last night by insisting on accompanying me on the five-hour trek to the Blackfeet rez. His decision clearly had little to do with his love for the great outdoors; he'd done nothing but fidget and complain during the entire ride.

"Besides, you should be creating a lot more noise. For chrissakes, sing a Girl Scout song or something, will you? Otherwise how's some wise-ass bruin gonna know that we're here?"

He removed a pint bottle of Wild Turkey from his jacket pocket. I deftly took a step to the right, to get out of the immediate line of fire. Clenched in his other hand was a .44 Magnum, which swayed like a tottering drunk as he struggled to open the whiskey bottle.

"Will you please give me that damn thing?" I motioned for the gun.

Ornish relinquished the firearm, preferring to concentrate on slugging down some liquid courage.

I knew that Ornish was nervous about being out in the wild, with good reason. He'd been attacked by a grizzly nearly fifteen years ago and bore the scars to prove it. A six-inch slash ran from his forehead down his face. A piece of his scalp had also been torn off and now sat in a jar of formaldehyde on his mantel at home, with all the glory normally given an Oscar statuette.

Hal pulled out a battered wristwatch—though the only way it would ever reveal the time was through divine intervention—and rubbed its damaged face with slow, steady strokes of his thumb. The hypnotic motion appeared to work like a sedative, for he immediately began to calm down. The bear had crushed the crystal with its teeth, halting the clock's hands at precisely six o'clock. Ornish had carried the watch ever since then as a good luck charm, believing it would magically keep all marauding bears at bay. Still, I wondered what the hell had prompted him to tag along in the first place.

Hal downed a second shot of Wild Turkey, and I was tempted to join him.

"Just think of it as an adventure," I said, as much to calm my own nerves.

"Right," Ornish snapped. "What you don't seem to comprehend is that adventures are what people experience when bad things happen to them."

I'd try to keep that in mind.

Ornish had a doctorate in human sexuality, and his "adventure" had resulted from an unorthodox experiment. Determined to prove that both animals and humans attract mates primarily through scent and sound, Hal had doused himself with elk estrus urine, headed into the woods, and given a lovesick call. But rather than attracting a frisky buck, Ornish proved to be a dinner bell for a hungry bruin. The grizzly grew annoyed when his Happy Meal wasn't very young and tender, and took its revenge by biting Hal on the arms, legs, and butt, and generally beating the hell out of him. Adding insult to injury, the offending grizzly had never been caught.

"I'll bet you a dime to a dollar it was Old Caleb who got that poor sonofabitch Carolton. He probably just wasn't as mean and tough as I am." Hal amiably poured a dribble of whisky on the spot where a small cross had been planted. "It's nice that you decided to pay your respects and all, but I gotta warn you, I'll be forced to take precautionary measures if we don't get out of here soon. There's no way in hell I'm about to let Old Caleb treat me like some walking T-bone again."

I doubted there was much chance of that—unless Old Caleb was partial to Wild Turkey these days. In any case, I'd looked around plenty, and there didn't appear to be any further clues as to why Carolton had been attacked. The only known witnesses to his death were the forest critters—and none of them was talking.

We returned to the 4X4, climbed inside, and proceeded to slip-slide back down the trail.

Two

Jagged mountain peaks ruptured the skyline as we finally emerged from beneath the evergreen canopy and hit level road. By now the sun had bullied its way through the clouds, and its rays danced upon golden aspen trees. Their bright leaves fluttered in the breeze like a swarm of monarch butterflies.

All this was home to Montana's largest Native American tribe, the Blackfeet Indian Reservation, which stretches across the eastern edge of Glacier National Park and down along the Rocky Mountain Front. The Blackfeet's bloody history was that of fierce Great Plains warriors. They remain the most militant tribe in Montana today—a reputation that's proven handy for keeping unwanted strangers off their land.

"By the way, we're going to make a stop when we get to Kiowa Junction," Hal informed me, checking out his image in the vanity mirror.

"What for?" I was beginning to feel like a chauffeur assigned to a secret mission.

"A friend of mine lives there, who I haven't seen in years." Hal focused his attention on a twig that remained stubbornly stuck in his beard. "I called and she's expecting us."

"I'm amazed you actually know someone here on the reservation."

So *this* was the reason that Ornish had decided to accompany me. Call me crazy, but I'd felt certain it was something besides my sparkling personality.

"Why the hell wouldn't I? After all, I've spent most of my entire life in this damn state." Hal was playing tug of war with his beard, and so far, the twig was the victor. "Fact is, the two of us used to be a pretty hot item way back when."

"This is an *adult* woman that you're talking about?"

Hal was just full of surprises. His main source of recreation seemed to be giving private tutorials to pretty young things, closely followed by eating, drinking, and attempting to become a contestant on *Who Wants to Be a Millionaire*. The news that he'd maintained contact with a woman over thirty was downright heartwarming.

"Well, it sure as hell ain't a man I was seeing!" Hal self-consciously pulled on the bill of his ball cap, which handily hid his bear-induced bald spot. Embroidered on the cap's front was the word COOTS in bold red letters. I was reminded of Henry Fonda in the film *On Golden Pond* whenever he wore it. I'd gone so far as to do my Katharine Hepburn imitation once, calling him an old coot in place of an "old poop." Ornish's response had been swift and irascible.

"I'm not some addle-brained old fool out looking for loons! The letters stand for Curmudgeons Openly Opposed To Technological Shit," he'd informed me.

Okay, that made sense. Not only did Ornish pride himself on being one of the most politically incorrect members on the teaching faculty, but he also reveled in shunning yet another "PC"—the personal computer. Hal refused to use his university computer as anything more than an oversized doorstop.

"I don't suppose you've got a scissors in this suit-case of yours," Hal groused, rummaging through my handbag.

"Help yourself," I dryly retorted, glad I had nothing to hide.

"For chrissakes, Porter! What do you belong to—a street gang in your spare time?"

He flicked open my Speideco knife, exposing its jagged blade.

"Yeah. We're called the Women Past Thirty Unite club. Our goal is to dissuade lecherous old men from having their way with young college students."

Hal shot me a dirty look that clearly read, *Who's old?* And *I'll damn well do as I please.* Then he started to hack away at the twig, using the knife like a machete.

"There! That ought to do it!" he triumphantly exclaimed.

Hal would have done better leaving the wooden perch in place; his beard looked as if *it* had lost the battle.

I drove past Babb and headed down toward St. Mary. Off to my left swam an ocean of prairie. Picture-perfect mountains loomed to my right, and I caught sight of a mountain goat peering down from his snow-covered perch.

The scent of mint began to fill the Ford, and I turned my head in time to see Hal spray another blast of Binaca into his mouth. This woman was obviously someone special.

He soon began to fidget as nervously as a twelve-year-old boy. Hauling out a scrap of paper, Hal studied his rough map and written instructions.

"Slow down. I think you make a left on the dirt road coming up."

We turned and drove less than a mile before the trail forked.

I hit the brakes. "Okay. Now what?"

Hal turned the paper upside down, as if that might help. All the while a herd of deer stood and stared, as motionless as statues. My guess was they were wondering what two palefaces were doing out here. I was thinking along those same lines when Hal puffed out his cheeks, loudly exhaled, and made his pronouncement.

"We head to the left."

Hal's choice was a bumpy lane littered with rocks. That, along with firsthand knowledge of his misguided sense of direction, made me swing the Ford to the right. Ornish begrudgingly grinned in acknowledgment that I'd probably made the correct decision.

We'd driven only a short distance when the trees drew closer, as if unsure whether to let us pass. Gnarled roots grabbed at the Ford's tires, slowing us to a crawl. I was certain I could hear the evergreens whisper among themselves, secretly conspiring against us. Their murmurs echoed in a coniferous corridor, whose cathedral ceiling grew increasingly dark and lush. I forged on, afraid to break the silence.

My breath caught in my throat as I glimpsed the road up ahead. Rows of slender cottonwoods lined the path, their graceful limbs decorated with strips of brightly colored cloth. A giddy breeze stirred and the fabric gaily waved to us in welcome.

Leaving the tunnel, we entered a field dotted with metal sculptures of bears in playful positions. A sturdy red barn stood beyond, as well as a large cabin of thick cedar logs. A column of smoke rose from its chimney. As we approached, the door opened and a tall, elegant woman appeared.

She was dressed in a rich angora sweater whose collar curled up beneath her chin. Pants gracefully swayed against the woman's legs in a generous swirl of fabric, and soft leather boots covered her feet in a shade as sinfully delicious as deep, dark, bittersweet chocolate.

Luxurious snow-white hair was pulled softly away from her face and sat piled atop her head in Gibson girl fashion. I couldn't take my eyes off the stylish figure that she cut. It was easy to see why Hal was smitten with the woman; I only hoped I'd look half as good at her age. But Hal's former squeeze was no more a Native American than I was Annie Oakley. Why was a Caucasian woman living on the Blackfeet reservation?

She raised her hand and shielded her eyes from the sun to look in our direction. Her gaze settled on Hal and remained there as the Ford came to a stop.

"Jesus, you got old!" she snapped at him by way of greeting.

There was a sprightly spring to Hal's step as he rushed forward and gave her an awkward hug.

"And you look as beautiful as ever." He beamed, reluctantly releasing her from his embrace.

The very air seemed to shimmer around her, though she hadn't so much as cracked a smile.

"Of course I do; I don't eat crap and sit with my rear end planted in front of a TV all night. Nor do I consider sprinting after coeds an Olympic sport," she tartly responded.

I grinned. The woman obviously had Hal's number. In fact, I was beginning to suspect that their relationship might not have had the happiest of endings. Then she focused her laser-sharp peepers on me.

"And who have we here?" she asked, with the slightest hint of disdain.

Oh brother. It wasn't hard to imagine what she was thinking.

"Just tell me you're not one of his former students that he finally managed to catch." Her warning extended itself all the way to her handshake, which gave my own a rock-solid squeeze.

If I *had* been involved with Hal, I might have considered jumping back in the Ford and heading out on the double.

"No, I'm simply a friend and his current tenant. My name is Rachel Porter, and I'm a special agent with the U.S. Fish and Wildlife Service."

That appeared to catch her off-guard; the woman's eyes flickered with a shade of apprehension. It was just enough to draw my attention before she quickly recovered.

"And this is Sally Starlight," Hal reverently introduced her.

"You forget, that was my name when I was single," she crisply corrected. "Now it's Sally Crossbow."

That helped explain what a white woman was doing here. She was obviously married to a Blackfeet Indian.

"How long has Frank been dead, anyway?" Hal lecherously questioned, beginning to stroke his mangled beard.

"Not long enough for me to be interested in anyone else. So don't go getting any funny ideas," she responded, promptly putting Ornish in his place.

Hal shook his head in amusement and chortled, as if he were just warming up for the game. "Damn, but you haven't changed the slightest bit."

Only then did the whisper of a smile cross Sally's lips. It quickly disappeared as a high-pitched cry pierced the air.

I glanced around, but there was no bird in sight that might have issued the call. The cry sounded once more, this time ending in a distinct *kee-kee-kee*. I nailed Sally as she nervously shifted her weight from hip to hip in a silent admission of guilt. She reluctantly met my gaze, and her shoulders rose and fell in a shrug.

"That's Mountain Chief. He's my latest addition," she revealed.

That was exactly what I hadn't wanted to hear—obtaining and keeping wild birds in cages is strictly against the law.

"What kind of bird is it?"

"A golden eagle. Would you like to see him?"

Sally didn't wait for me to answer, but strode toward

the barn. I followed with Hal trudging close behind, anxiously tugging at my jacket as I did my best to ignore him.

Sally skirted the building and headed around the rear, where a large wire pen stood next to a grove of willows. The bird screeched again and angrily eyed us as we approached.

"Apparently Mountain Chief wants his food now, rather than waiting till dinner," Sally said, trying to make light of the situation.

The eagle wasn't alone. Two other birds of prey were inside the cage with him.

A rough-legged hawk sat gazing off in the distance, its attitude as imperious as an ancient Roman senator's. It softly whistled to itself, the notes descending in scale. At the opposite end of the cage stood a northern harrier, whose russet feathers and disk-shaped face artfully blended in with the background. All three were juveniles, and each was missing a wing.

Sally threw chunks of carrion inside the cage and the trio of raptors went into attack mode.

"You're looking at Montana's version of drive-by shootings. A bunch of idiots has been running around taking potshots at birds of prey. I guess they're more challenging than plinking at road signs," she said in disgust. "Then you've also got your local yahoos who are shooting eagles and hawks for their feathers."

I suspected their plumage was being used for more than just religious ceremonies. I'd spotted numerous raptor feathers dangling from vehicles' rearview mirrors and fashioned into jewelry. If that weren't bad enough, eagle's talons were being hacked off and sold as decorative roach clips.

"I end up having to amputate a wing here and there to save some of the raptors. But you needn't worry; I'm a licensed wildlife rehabilitator."

That may have been true. But then, why had she acted so nervous and guilty earlier?

"By the look of things, I'd say these birds don't appear to be very good candidates for rehabilitation."

Sally zoomed in on me as intently as an eagle scrutinizing its prey. "I keep the ones that can't be placed back into the wild. Or would you rather I just destroy them and write it off as doing my part for conservation?"

"Hey, I'm not the enemy here," I reminded her, as we mentally circled one another. By now, two guys might have started to duke it out. As women, we accomplished the same thing without batting an eye.

Hal was smart enough to quietly stand aside until we'd finished sizing each other up.

Sally finally blinked. "Sorry. That's what happens when you live alone out here for so long. It becomes increasingly difficult to trust people."

I suspected it wouldn't have made any difference where she lived. From what I could tell, her instincts were dead on.

The birds continued to rip away at the strips of raw meat as I began to look around. A denser patch of woods stood beyond the willows, composed of windblown quaking aspen. Looming in the opposite direction were the jagged peaks and cliffs of Glacier National Park. It was off these snow-covered mountains that the wind barreled down, stunting every tree in its path.

As we began to walk back toward Sally's house, the bear sculptures once more came into view.

"Where did you get those?"

"My husband created them. Bears were his totem animal. Maybe that's why there are so many of them around here."

"You're talking about grizzlies?" I asked in surprise.

"Both grizzlies and black bears." She pointed toward Glacier National Park. "You've got a bear factory up in those mountains and a conduit that comes down along here, so it's to be expected. I believe in letting the critters pass through my land if they want."

"Let's get the hell inside." Hal nervously hurried toward the cabin.

Sally pushed the door open and we entered a large room, where a melange of aromas rushed to embrace us. There was the sweetly comforting smell of leather and deerskin, followed by the scent of rawhide. The pungent odor of burning wood mingled with the bouquet emanating from a pot of coffee brewing on the stove, while whatever was cooking in the oven smelled good enough to make my mouth water.

I was further seduced by the cabin's decor. Beautiful handmade furniture filled the kitchen as well as the living room. Ralph Lauren would have died and gone to heaven at the sight of so many gorgeous hand-loomed blankets casually flung over the backs of the plush leather couch and chairs.

But even more impressive was the artwork on the

walls. Every inch of space was covered with a different large poster, all touting the same stunning young woman. The femme fatale's costume consisted of nothing more than cut-out silver stars. All exclaimed, *Let Sally Starlight Transport You Out of This World in an Evening of Song and Dance!* Each ad boasted a different date and location—*Philadelphia, Pennsylvania! Tulsa, Oklahoma! Paris, France!*

I turned and looked at the woman standing behind me. Sally Crossbow was proving to be more interesting than I could have imagined.

"You were a performer?"

A ringlet had escaped from the powder puff atop her head, its tresses having been carefully arranged into a look of oh-so-casual perfection. The lock of hair slid beguilingly down her neck, reminiscent of a stripper removing an article of clothing. Sally lifted the rebellious curl and flirtatiously began to twist it around her finger.

"That's ancient history."

But she clearly reveled in the attention. The ringlet slipped from her grasp, as if naughtily misbehaving.

"Don't be so modest, Sally! Not only were you the toast of the town, but also the best exotic dancer that this state—hell, the whole world—has ever seen!" Hal said with unabashed admiration.

A throaty laugh bubbled from Sally's lips. "I *was* pretty good, wasn't I? I guess you could say I was the poor man's Gypsy Rose Lee."

Hal expertly picked up his cue.

"I deign to disagree. I believe it happened to be the other way around."

"Well, Rose *was* past her prime by the time I hit the

road. But one has to give the woman her due: she was certainly a class act. At least we had style back in those days. Exotic dancing was an art form. Not like now, when any girl with enough silicone in her chest gets paid to bump and grind on top of a bar. That's what helped kill vaudeville."

"Sally Starlight was your stage name, then?"

"My, but you *are* the sharp one, aren't you? No wonder you were made a special agent."

I gritted my teeth, thinking about helping Sally see a few more stars of her own, when she winced.

"Oh dear, I can be such a bitch! Please forgive me. My natural defense system kicks in whenever I'm around a pretty young girl these days."

"Flattery works every time. You're forgiven." I grinned and meant it. Truth be told, there were a few Victoria's Secret models that I wouldn't mind slugging myself.

"I'm afraid that I've just turned into an ornery old woman."

Hal nearly knocked me out of the way as he jumped to her defense.

"That's total nonsense! First of all, you're nowhere near old. You can't be. Hell, that would make *me* old, too!"

Sally's eyelashes fluttered demurely.

"If anything, you're more alluring than ever. You've ripened into a pretty hot tomato."

I was beginning to wonder if I should quietly slip away.

"You just tend to speak your mind, is all. And there's nothing wrong with that," Hal added.

Sally's lips relaxed into a smile. "You're an absolute scoundrel, Hal Ornish. This is how you won me over the first time! I think what we could all use is a martini."

Sally expertly whipped up three cocktails James Bond style—shaken, not stirred. She took a sip of her drink and then turned to me.

"I invented the name Sally Starlight, just the way Marilyn Monroe and Greta Garbo and Tina Turner created their identities. I was in the business of dreams, which automatically gave me the right to make myself into whoever I chose to be."

Sally dipped two fingers into her martini, plucked out an olive, and popped it into her mouth. "It just so happens that I was the Madonna of my day. In fact, I heard she found some old footage of one of my dance numbers and has ripped off all my moves to use in her next video."

Ooookay.

"By the way, I hope you're planning to stay for dinner, because I've already got a roast in the oven."

"Wild horses couldn't drag me away," I answered.

"And I've got the wine." Hal produced two bottles from his knapsack. "It's a nice Beaujolais."

Why, the sneaky old coot! I took a sip of my martini, secretly pleased with the way things had worked out. Hal and Sally continued to reminisce in the kitchen as I sank into a large leather chair, my senses surrendering to the tantalizing scents. Lulled by the buzz of gin and vermouth, I tried to decide whom I'd rather be stranded with—a young Clint Eastwood, or Harrison

Ford. Harrison was edging his way toward victory when a low rumble interrupted my thoughts.

Oh, please. Don't let that be my stomach making a nuisance of itself!

My wish was granted as the sound morphed into the sputter of an arthritic engine.

"That must be Matt," Sally said while checking the roast. "He has a tendency to just drop by."

She closed the oven and quickly stepped outside. Curiosity dictated that I follow.

An old blue pickup slowly approached us, wheezing and groaning as if relieved to come to a halt. A dog flew out of the driver's side door as it swung open. The critter appeared to be part chow and part coyote, with a coat the same golden color as the late afternoon sun. It dashed past me in a mad frenzy to greet Sally as a man emerged from the truck.

And what a man—his jet-black hair was so dark that it had a bluish sheen. Perfectly straight, it was neatly pulled back in a long ponytail. Dammit; that was the hair I'd always wanted for myself. I could almost feel my out-of-control curls grow even wilder with unbridled envy.

The fact that he had high cheekbones and a perfectly chiseled nose didn't make me feel any better. I was ready to write the guy off as someone who couldn't possibly have any depth, until I caught sight of his eyes and an involuntary shiver raced through me.

Almond in shape, they were darkly opaque with glints of yellow shimmering in each iris. His gaze met mine and I unexpectedly found myself having to look away. Maybe it had something to do with the fact that I was in Blackfeet territory, but I suddenly felt like an intruder.

He closed the pickup's door and approached the porch, eyeing Hal and me. His walk held the fluid sleekness of a cat on the prowl. It was as if he had invisible wings on his back, and soles of velvet attached to the bottom of his shoes. He'd barely taken his first step before he was up on the porch and standing beside me. My radar kicked in, aware there was something distinctly predatory about the man.

"This is Matthew Running," Sally said.

Running studied us intently, as if calculating whether we might be potential foes.

"Matt, meet a dear old friend of mine, Hal Ornish."

That seemed to get Hal off the hook. The muscles in Running's face relaxed as he held out his hand. "Hal Ornish, huh? I've heard about you."

Low in timbre, his voice bore a smoky quality, as if concealing a multitude of secrets buried beneath deep, dark layers. Its resonance worked like a transmitter, and my body its receiver. A buzz vibrated throughout my limbs, causing every cell to begin to thrum.

"And this is Rachel Porter. She's renting a room in Hal's house. Rachel's with the U.S. Fish and Wildlife Service, and is the special agent for this region."

That clearly whetted Running's interest. "How unusual."

There were those eyes again! What was it about them that made me so jumpy?

"What, that I'm an agent?"

I'd long ago realized that as a woman, I'd forever be

forced to establish my credibility at each new station, and with every person I met.

"No. That as a woman, you'd choose western Montana for your territory. You must like banging your head against walls."

"And of course a male agent wouldn't have to worry about that, would he?" I challenged.

"No, he would. It's just that men tend to blindly jump into things without thinking them through. Women are generally smarter than that."

Maybe this guy had more depth than I'd thought.

"Then I guess I'm the exception to the rule," I archly responded.

"Somehow I doubt that." Running laughed.

Even now his gaze held a predatory air, and I realized what I found so unsettling about it. He had the eyes of a wolf.

"I'm preparing an early dinner, Matt. Why don't you stay and join us?"

Running turned his head slightly, and his gaze swept the area before coming to rest on his truck for a brief moment. It was long enough to clue me in that something lay hidden beneath the tarp in the cargo bay.

"Are you sure it's all right?"

Sally gently touched his arm. "It will be fine. Don't worry."

"Thanks, then. That would be great."

I wondered what that exchange was all about as Running stepped inside the house with his dog.

Three

Hal poured four glasses of wine and Sally passed me a plate of cheese and crackers. Food is always a terrific icebreaker—at least it was for me and the dog. The pooch immediately jumped up and began to lick my face, doing his darnedest to convince me that I was his new best friend.

"Yeah, yeah. I know your type." I laughed and fed him a slice of Cheddar. "As soon as you don't get what you want, you're out of here."

I passed the plate on to Hal and the dog proved me correct.

"What's his name?" I asked, the sharp tang of Cheddar nipping at my tongue.

"Custer," Matt replied matter-of-factly.

I took it as an invitation to question him further. "That seems an odd choice."

"Not really." Running sipped his wine, allowing the moment to dangle. "That way he gets to live with the knowledge of who his real master is, and always knows his place."

"Matthew has a wicked sense of humor." Sally affectionately tugged his ponytail.

Yes, didn't he—along with an innate sense of how to keep me the slightest bit off kilter.

Dinner was soon ready. Hal helped Sally dish the food into bowls and we took our places at the table.

"Exactly what is it that you do?" I asked Running, spooning some potatoes onto my plate.

Matt picked up a slice of the elk roast and fed it to Custer before answering. "I'm your counterpart."

I looked at him, not quite sure what he meant.

Running's lips twitched in amusement. "You *do* realize that your agency isn't the sole authority for dealing with wildlife issues on the reservation, don't you? After all, we *are* a sovereign nation. I'm the tribal game officer for the Blackfeet reservation."

His tone let me know this was more than a casual exchange of information. Custer interrupted by sharply barking for another handout, and Running turned his hypnotic gaze on the pooch. The critter immediately fell silent, then sat on his haunches and quietly begged.

"Good boy," Matthew said, and gave him another piece of meat.

If Running was expecting me to behave in a similar manner, he was in for one hell of a surprise.

I'd been warned to expect resistance on the reservation. Not only was I a female wielding the authority of a federal agent, but the government wasn't very popular around these parts. The Blackfeet preferred to handle their own wildlife violations without outside interference, and this was especially true if a tribal member was suspected to be the culprit. Fish and Wildlife was rarely called in for help, and even when they were, getting information was difficult. That being the case, an unspoken hands-off policy was honored—unless endangered and threatened species became embroiled in the mix. Then the violation fell directly under FWS's jurisdiction. Should that happen, I had every intention of stepping in. And unlike Running's pooch, Custer, I wasn't about to be controlled or surrender.

"Well then, I look forward to working closely together," I said pleasantly and gave Custer some food off my plate.

Running turned his attention to Hal. "Do you mind if I ask how you got that scar?"

Ornish refilled his glass, more than happy to relate his tale.

"It was Old Caleb did that," he said, sounding like an inebriated Long John Silver. "You know about Old Caleb, don't you?"

As Running shook his head, Sally's fingers began drumming on the table.

"Well, you better learn about him real quick, being that you're the game officer for these parts. That bear is a psychotic man killer!"

"Here we go again. Don't be a total dipshit!" Sally slapped her palm down hard. "What happened was that your rear end was exactly where it shouldn't have been—parked smack in the middle of his territory. For God's sakes, you were standing right next to the bear's scratching post—on top of which, you even pretended to be his damn dinner. What did you expect? You're lucky he let you walk away alive."

Hal's bushy eyebrows twitched like two woolly caterpillars on a roller coaster ride. "I beg to differ! I'm the scientist here and I know exactly what happened."

Sally was swift and merciless. "I don't care if you're

Albert Einstein reincarnated, Hal Ornish. You have absolutely no idea what you're talking about when it comes to bears, whereas I live with them every day. Like it or not, you're a city boy. If you want to be safe, stay out of the damn wilderness!"

The woman must have had one hell of a dance act in her day; she contained enough passion to fuel a nuclear reactor.

Hal's eyebrows collapsed. "Goddammit woman, you just don't play fair. You become even more beautiful when you get angry. How am I supposed to argue with that?" He tugged on his cap, and the word COOT danced up and down.

Sally leaned over and fondly kissed him on the nose. "You're not, my dear. That's the whole idea. You're just supposed to agree with me."

It was clear that Hal was secretly delighted, even though he pretended to grumble.

I helped Sally clean up the dishes, and then turned to where Hal had settled down with another glass of wine.

"We'd better take off if we're going to make it home tonight. We've got a long drive ahead of us."

Hal's response was a disappointed groan.

"Thanks so much for dinner, Sally. It's been a pleasure meeting you," I said, wondering how gauche it would be to ask her for some beauty tips.

Ornish took Sally's hand and tenderly kissed it. "It's been far too long, my dear. I promise to call soon. By the way, I have a hunk of venison sitting at home in my freezer that's more than I can possibly eat. What say I bring it with me next time and we have it for dinner—just the two of us?"

Sally slipped her hand through Hal's arm. "Maybe it *is* time I had a little more company," she coyly conceded.

Hal appeared to float all the way out the door and onto the porch, where I joined him. I was just about to say good-bye to Matthew Running when a distinct rustling came from under the pickup's canvas tarp.

I glanced at Matt, whose expression remained studiously blank. The guy was a natural-born card player.

"Have I had too much to drink, or is there something going on in your cargo bay?"

My question was answered by a loud bawl. Then a second cry joined the chorus.

"I'd like to take a look, if you don't mind."

"And if I do?" Running responded, invoking the tribe's silent hands-off policy.

This was as good a time as any for Running to learn that I play by my own set of rules.

"It makes no difference. I still intend to see what you're hiding," I brusquely informed him. Walking over, I pulled off the canvas.

Two small grizzly cubs sat looking forlorn in a wire cage. I couldn't have been more surprised if Ringling Brothers Barnum and Bailey Circus had come marching down the drive. Especially since grizzlies have been protected under the Endangered Species Act since 1975.

Grizzlies roamed the Great Plains before the West was won. Their territory extended from Alaska down into Mexico, and from the Pacific Coast east to the Mississippi River. Their numbers reached in the hundreds of thousands. Then homesteaders, ranchers, and trappers blazed across the prairie, razing the grizzlies' ancient forest homes in the name of civilization.

Bears were shot, strangled, or poisoned in a victorious drive to tame the wild West. By the time it was over, fewer than a thousand grizzlies were left in the lower forty-eight states. They fled to isolated enclaves of vanishing wilderness, and today only a handful exist in Washington, Wyoming, and Idaho, slowly sliding toward oblivion. The creature's last stronghold is the high country of Montana, along the Continental Divide. This is where the species will continue to live, or will ultimately die.

I looked at the two wide-eyed cubs and knew they were frightened. The sight tugged at my heart. Not only were their coats pathetically scraggly, but the ribs in their bodies were showing. Each couldn't have weighed more than twenty-five pounds. Glaringly clear was the fact that they needed to be with their mother.

This was the time of year when bears are in a state of hyperphagia, or what's known as a feeding frenzy, when they view the world as one large garbage can. Days are spent chowing down on everything edible in a last-ditch effort to load up on calories before their long winter sleep. But winter was nearly here, and hibernation just around the corner. Left on their own, these cubs would never survive.

"Do you want to tell me exactly what the hell is going on?" I demanded, calling upon every ounce of self-control to hold back my anger.

Though grizzlies, wolves, and eagles had the highest priority at my new station, there was bound to be all-out war over my first arrest. I'd been hoping to pinch some low-life scum for shooting wolves or poisoning eagles; instead, I was about to nab the tribal game officer for the Blackfeet Indian Reservation. It appeared my career was now poised to explode, just when I'd thought it couldn't possibly get any worse.

Running's eyes narrowed, the yellow glints in his pupils dancing up a firestorm.

"These cubs have been running around loose in search of food, and getting into trouble. That leads me to believe their mother must have been killed. Recently they've even been rummaging through people's garbage. It was only a matter of time before they'd be shot, or left to slowly starve to death. Under the circumstances, I decided the best thing was to temporarily remove them."

Running's gaze never wavered, and I knew the man wasn't lying. Still, his actions ran totally contrary to U.S. Fish and Wildlife policy. Orphaned adolescents like these were considered no more than casualties, and left to die. Running had broken the law by picking them up. Either he was a man with conscience who also played by his own set of rules, or he was just plain mercenary.

Everything that lives and breathes can be used to make a buck. That goes from the stuff beneath our feet all the way up to the very treetops. There isn't a creature or plant in existence that isn't worth some amount of money. Running might even have intended to sell these cubs to a roadside zoo.

"And just what do you plan to do with them?" I inquired.

Matthew glanced at Sally, and she silently nodded. "These aren't the first cubs that I've found. There have been four others since early spring. Sally is feeding and fattening them up until the sows go into hibernation. Then we'll try to find a few sleeping moms and place the cubs inside the dens with them."

I could have sworn my mouth hit the ground. What did this guy take me for? A complete moron?

"In the first place, what makes you think the sow will accept them?" I asked incredulously. "And secondly, why hasn't this been reported to me?"

My emotions wavered between secret relief that he'd rescued the cubs, and white-hot fury. I'd never heard of such a thing being done before. On the other hand, it was just possible that their plan might work. Still, Running had deliberately left me out of the loop. Goddammit to hell! As if dealing with Southern rednecks hadn't been bad enough, I was once again faced with the gunslinging, macho attitude of cowboys and Indians.

"I don't care who you are, Running. I'll place you under arrest if I don't get some answers immediately."

The hint of a smile flickered across Running's lips. Now the guy was *really* beginning to piss me off.

"And just how long have you been stationed in Montana?" he dryly inquired.

Oh God, he was playing the old I've-been-here-longer-than-you routine.

"Nearly a month." I silently dared him to take the next step.

Running not only met my challenge, but upped the ante. "There's the answer to your question. You haven't even made a trip up to the rez to meet with me yet."

"It's not as if I received a welcome-to-the-neighbor-hood fruit basket from you, either," I promptly shot back.

I idly rattled the handcuffs on my belt, and discovered it instantly made me feel better. Perhaps *that* was the solution to my dealings with men. In my spare time, I could become a dominatrix. "And if my experience is your problem, then why didn't you bother to report this to the agent before me?"

"You know, I considered doing that," Running drawled. "Only it was just about then that he was getting some hands-on experience of his own. And you're aware of how well *that* worked out."

I mentally began to beat my own set of war drums. "Let me remind you of something you seem to have conveniently forgotten. As a protected species, grizzlies belong to the United States government and *not* to the Blackfeet tribe."

"Ah, yes. I keep forgetting how you whites own everything," Running replied in a voice as smooth as hot, flowing lava. "When the West was won, both the Indians *and* the grizzlies lost."

"All right! That's enough, the two of you!" Sally commanded, bringing the confrontation to a halt. "Rachel, why don't I show you where the cubs are kept, and then you can draw your own conclusion."

I hated being put in this position. If it were up to me, no critter would ever be killed or left to die. I glanced again at the cubs with their dopey expressions. Okay, so the world *wasn't* one big Disney film. But there was also no way I was about to turn them loose to meet certain death.

"We might as well bring these two along since we're going there anyway," I gruffly remarked. "Hal, why don't you help Running carry the cage?"

"Like hell I will! They may look cute now, but do you know what these two are going to turn into when they grow up? Massive flesh-eating carnivores that are schizophrenic, manic-depressive creatures!"

I couldn't believe the words coming from a man who called himself a scientist. Apparently, neither could Sally.

"Hal Ornish! You behave yourself and help Matthew with that cage right now. I'm not going to let these cubs die just because of your outlandish fear!"

Forget the beauty tips, forget the whips and chains—I wanted Sally's delicious sense of rage! I wondered just how far Hal would go to win back the woman he presumably loved.

"Sonofabitch. I can't believe I'm actually gonna do this," he sputtered and slowly walked toward the pickup.

The cubs began to whimper as the two men lifted the cage.

"Don't try to make me feel sorry for you, because it's not going to work!" Hal hissed.

"Shh!" Sally reprimanded. "The whole point is to keep the cubs as isolated from human contact as possible—they can't get imprinted on people. These cubs are like a bunch of street kids; they're probably going to have to learn how to be bears without a mom."

I was already impressed by her approach.

We headed toward the dense patch of aspen and silently began to make our way through, dodging branches and roots.

The woods finally thinned out, allowing me a glimpse of an enormous pen up ahead. Sure enough, four cubs frolicked inside. The quartet of pudgy babies cuffed each other as they fell over and crawled on one another's backs. Looking at them, it was hard to believe they'd been born hairless, toothless, and the size of chipmunks. The phrase *licked into shape* sprang to mind. It came from an old belief that newborn cubs were so soft, their mother's tongues had to mold them into shape. These cubs not only appeared to be doing just fine, but were well supplied with apples, roadkill, and water. Their bedding consisted of grass, moss, and leaves.

Sally held up a hand and the cage was lowered next to a chute that ran along the ground, connecting with the large enclosure via a trap door. Running unlatched the chute's entrance, placed the pen up against it, and opened the cage. The cubs inside refused to budge, afraid to face the unknown, until Sally prodded their rear ends with a stick. Then they let loose a startled squeal and barreled through the wire tunnel as Running pulled the lever and raised the other trap door. The pen's current residents quickly dashed over to examine their new roommates.

A nearby trolley revealed how food was sent in. I had to hand it to the woman; if the cubs were going to be successfully rehabbed, this was the way to do it. We quietly walked back out of the woods until we once again stood in front of her house. Sally and Running were probably smart enough to realize they already had me hooked, but I had no intention of letting this continue without my full involvement.

"I have an appointment back in Missoula tomorrow, so let's meet in your office first thing the following morning. We need to discuss what's been going on here," I told Running. "I also want you to show me the areas where the cubs were found."

Running folded his arms across his chest. "What for?"

"Because I plan to open an investigation."

"Into what?"

I was beginning to believe Running had an ulterior motive—to drive me crazy. "What do you think? Sows are obviously being killed! I intend to find out why it's happening, and who's behind it."

I didn't give Running the opportunity to object, but hopped into the Ford, and turned on the engine. Hal grabbed his knapsack and hastily jumped in the passenger side. Not a word was spoken until we hit the main road.

"That went well, I think," Hal offered. "Don't you agree?"

I answered with a roll of my eyes.

Four

Daylight had barely dragged itself through my window when something soft and silky brushed against my skin.

Purrrrrrrrr!

Hal's cat, Casanova, jumped up and joined me in bed, where he rubbed his head beneath my chin. Then he curled up on the pillow and emitted a loud meow, demanding to be petted.

Like master, like kitty. Stretching, I then rolled out of bed.

After jumping in the shower, I dried off and got dressed, all to an attentive audience of one. If I had a man half as interested in my every move as this cat, I wouldn't be spending my nights alone.

Having finished with my morning toilette, I high-tailed it downstairs to the kitchen.

Hmm. Figaro tuna or Friskies liver and chicken for breakfast? I began my daily search-and-rescue mission through the kitchen drawers, wondering why Hal couldn't ever keep anything in the same damn place. Finally finding the opener, I opened the Figaro tuna and spooned it into a bowl. Then I placed it in front of him and held my breath. Casanova barely deigned to take a whiff before bestowing a disdainful glance upon me and sauntering out of the room.

Looking around, I couldn't say that I much blamed him. I'd thought *I* was a lousy housekeeper before meeting Hal Ornish. Dishes were piled precariously in the sink, and samples of his weekly menu were hardened on top of the stove. Even *I* wouldn't go in the refrigerator, afraid of what I might find there. I was close to forking over the money to hire a housekeeper.

As if that weren't enough, a thunderous medley of snorts and snores shook the house. Hal was in fine form this morning. A newly opened bottle of Wild Turkey sat on the counter alongside a partially emptied glass. I was beginning to understand why it had been so easy for me to get a year-long lease here.

I grabbed my keys and was about to leave when Casanova flounced back into the room. Planting himself in front of the door, he blocked my exit.

"Okay, you little fur ball. But this is the only serving that you're getting today. I'm beginning to think you're addicted."

I unearthed a new box of Tender Vittles, tore open a vacuum-sealed packet, and poured its contents into a dish.

Casanova played the true gourmand by first sniffing the offering, and then flipping a nugget onto the floor.

"Enjoy your smorgasbord," I said and slipped out the door.

I'd taken up residence in the university section of Missoula, with its big trees and oh-so-proper houses. It wasn't that I felt particularly respectable at this point in my life; Ornish's rent had just been too cheap to turn down. Besides, I liked the area. The University was why Missoula had been nicknamed "the Berkeley of the Rockies." The town was a liberal bastion in a sea of conservatives. More Birkenstocks than cowboy boots were worn by its residents, who could best be described as an interesting array of fruits and nuts.

I walked to where my Ford was parked, and roundly proceeded to curse out the local cops. Damn, damn, damn! Tucked against my windshield was yet another lousy parking ticket. Snatching it off, I shoved it inside the glove box where it could schmooze with its other relatives. I understood that the street had to be swept, but why couldn't they just clean around me?

I turned onto Madison and crossed the bridge over the Clark Fork River, noting the usual brown schmutz that hung in the air. The dingy inversion, a by-product of exhaust from cars, pulp mills, and woodburning stoves, pressed down upon the town like the thin skin that mysteriously forms on chocolate pudding. Swinging left onto Broadway, I headed for my usual breakfast spot, the Oxford Saloon on Higgins Street.

A rundown 24/7 bar, the place has been around nearly as long as Missoula itself. There seemed little doubt that the joint still abided by the same outdated health codes. But if anyone ever dared mess with the Ox, they'd have found themselves tarred, feathered, and run out of town on the local rail. At six-thirty A.M., the place was packed with scruffy-looking cowboys, along with an assemblage of down-and-out derelicts. By eight A.M. the bar was in full swing. The result was a Western version of Hickey's skid row saloon from O'Neill's *The Iceman Cometh*. Except this dive had a little something extra—an enormous bison head hanging on its wall.

Contributing to the atmosphere was the *ching, ching, ching* of keno machines, which provided just the right amount of background noise. Surprisingly, a collection of rifles remained intact over the bar—especially when one considered the clientele who patronized the place. I had yet to figure out exactly what it was about the Ox that made it so special, but whatever it was, I always felt completely at home.

A bunch of black cowboy hats turned in my direction as I entered. As usual, I paid them no heed. Hopping onto my regular seat, I passed up the house special of brains and eggs, opting for a cup of oil-slicked coffee, a side of partially cooked bacon, and a plate of greasy hash browns. Mmm, mmm, mmm. What better way to start off the day than by loading up on carbohydrates, nitrates, and grease?

The bartender, Jonesy, filled my cup with lukewarm coffee. I topped it off with a dollop of room temperature milk. The pale liquid tenaciously floated on the surface rather than deign to mix in with the tepid brew.

"You want some gravy over those hash browns?" Jonesy asked as he placed a plate of artery-clogging calories before me.

"What? And wreck my diet? Don't be silly." I picked up a questionable-looking fork and dug in, taking comfort in the knowledge that my stomach was about to be well coated.

Jonesy poured himself a cup of joe. Then he pulled a couple of aspirin from his pocket, threw back his head, and downed them. It didn't require the keen observation skills of a detective to conclude the guy was hungover. Even the tattooed crescent moon on his arm appeared slightly askew, as if it had also been on a bender.

"So, how was *your* weekend?" I genially inquired.

"Rough," Jonesy admitted, and began to suck on a Marlboro. "I spent it running the trapline all the way from here up to the Blackfeet rez."

"The trapline?" I discarded a slice of bacon that had barely kissed the griddle.

"That's what I call hitting an entire string of bars. I like to see what all the other joints are up to. It helps give me new ideas for keeping my customers happy."

I took a gander at the bleary-eyed crew. They were so happy, they could barely keep their butts from sliding off the stools.

"I don't know, Jonesy. This gang looks pretty content. I don't think you have to worry too much about stocking up on Citron Absolute or putting out a bunch of fancy hor d'oeuvres."

"Maybe not. But I still consider it part of my job to get out there and check up on what's going on."

What it sounded like was a good excuse to guzzle all the booze that he could and charge it to the Ox as a business expense.

"Actually, you should be glad that I was out running the line this weekend. I came across something that I think will interest you."

"Oh yeah? What's that?" I turned the ketchup bottle over and pounded on the bottom. Congealed red paste plopped out.

"It was at the last place I landed, just east of the rez. Some little tutti-frutti was dancing up on the bar."

Jonesy's eyes grew blurry, as though the tutti-frutti was still dancing up a storm in his memory.

"Thanks, Jonesy, but Mel Gibson's more my type."

That snapped Jonesy back to reality. "Sorry. I didn't mean to space out on you, but the babe was really hot."

Talk about your ego boosts. Maybe it was time I had my breakfast with a different sort of crowd.

"It was what the babe was wearing. Not that she was dressed in all that much." He chuckled at the memory while pouring me a refill, most of which landed in my saucer. "Mostly she had on this big Indian headdress that I think was made outta eagle feathers."

Now I remembered why I ate at this place. The joint was a magnet for some of the best information around. Eagle feathers can be owned only by Native Americans, and then purely for ceremonial purposes. Any other use is illegal.

"Do you recall the name of the bar?"

"Sure do; Big Bertha's Wildlife Sanctuary."

How apropos. "I take it the place lives up to its name?"

"You betcha!" Jonesy heartily acknowledged.

I gave him a healthy tip.

"Thanks. Just do me a favor. Get me the babe's name and number, in case she ends up being fired. Maybe I can convince the boss to introduce live entertainment here at the Ox. See what I mean about doing your homework?" Jonesy grinned.

I had to admit, he was more clever than I would've suspected.

"Oh, by the way, I should probably tell you that Big Bertha's is also where the local militia hangs out."

Naturally. After all, this was Montana. One would have to be naïve to assume that investigating anything here would be easy.

I made a mental note to pop into Big Bertha's on my way back to the rez tonight. After paying my bill, I headed over to the office for a meeting with my new boss, Hank Turner, who was driving clear across the state from Billings. It was a toss-up as to whether I felt flattered or insulted. On the one hand, he was squeezing this visit into an already busy schedule. On the other, he apparently felt it was necessary to check up on me.

I arrived to find Hank Turner was already there. He sat slumped behind my desk looking like a vulture patiently waiting for a carcass on which to nosh. His broad shoulders were hunched so far forward that they resembled a pair of folded wings, while his chest sagged on top of a generous paunch. Heavy saddlebags beneath his eyes attested to the fact that Turner wasn't getting much sleep these days. That made sense, considering he was in charge of the fourth-largest state in the Union and had only two agents at his disposal. Turner's thinning hair and pasty complexion made him look like a senior citizen, though the guy was only fifty-two years old. I feared that I might be looking at my own future.

Turner must have arrived at the crack of dawn, judging by the nearly empty coffeepot. I grabbed the can of Folgers, planning to brew some more. Damn! He'd used up the last of the grounds. No problem; I'd just apply a nifty little trick I'd learned from my old boss, Charlie Hickok.

I picked up the mug I'd inherited from my predecessor. White on the outside, its interior was as brown as dry Sahara mud. My guess was that it hadn't been cleaned since 1989. Add a little warm water, stir, and I instantly had myself a killer cup of reconstituted java.

"Nice mug," Turner dryly noted.

Carolton's taste definitely ran toward the risqué; the cup's exterior was covered with line drawings of bunnies mating in a variety of sexual positions.

"Thanks. I believe it's the Kama Sutra of rabbits." What the hell. Maybe it would help to enhance my reputation within the Service. At this point, there wasn't much that could make it any worse.

Turner didn't crack a smile. "Why don't you tell me what you've been up to lately?"

I first gave him the usual rundown of hunting violations and crank calls. "And I kicked around the Blackfeet reservation yesterday. I wanted to check out the area where Al Carolton had died."

Turner cocked his head and blinked his tired eyes at me once. "Did you manage to find something that no one else has been able to, so far?" he queried, his voice tinged with sarcasm.

I took a deep breath, not wanting to start off on the wrong foot in my new field station. "Do you already have some sort of problem with me that I should know about?"

The corners of Turner's mouth pulled down in dissatisfaction. "I just don't want you to run around and waste time—so let's get something straight right off.

Here in Montana, you're basically sticking your finger in the dyke and hoping the damn thing won't burst. You've got to pick the worst crimes to work on and let the rest slide by."

What he said made perfect sense. But there were still a few niggling questions that demanded an answer.

"I'm just curious as to why Carolton would have carried a rifle with him, yet never used it if he were being attacked by a bear."

"That just goes to show how little you know about the critter, Porter. Say Agent Carolton happened to stumble upon a sow while she was feeding, or with her cubs. Unless he'd had his rifle raised, aimed, and ready to fire, she'd have been on him before he could even pull the trigger. No matter how much time you think you've got, you never have half as much as you need. At forty-four miles per hour, a bear will knock you down in a split second. You're talking about an animal that runs nearly as fast as a greyhound and can beat the world's swiftest human by thirty-five yards in a hundred-yard dash. Does that help to answer your question?"

I remembered that Turner and Carolton had been close friends, and understood why Turner wasn't thrilled with my being here. Still, the information that I'd unearthed on the rez yesterday easily fell into his worst-crimes category.

"Well, the trip up there wasn't a total waste. I bumped into the tribal game officer, Matthew Running, and learned that a number of grizzly sows have been killed since early spring, none of which were reported to Fish and Wildlife."

I expected Turner to be enthusiastic about my discovery. Instead, he remained oddly silent.

"I'd like to open an investigation since it involves endangered species."

"On the rez?" Turner disdainfully remarked. "Good luck."

It wasn't the reaction I'd hoped for. "What's that supposed to mean?"

Turner hunkered down even further in the chair. "For argument's sake, let's say it's a Blackfeet Indian who's running around killing these grizzlies. Maybe he's selling the hides and claws to make a few extra bucks. Or maybe he just doesn't like the damn things and this is his way of telling us feds to go shove it. Hell, for all we know, it could be the tribal game officer himself. In any case, nobody on the rez is going to help you out on this. And you know why not? It's because all the Blackfeet are related in some way, and the one thing you don't do is to rat out your family. You with me so far?"

I nodded.

"Now, on the other hand, let's say it's a *white* guy that's sneaking onto the rez and whacking bears. Even better, you actually wind up catching him. Zippitty doo dah! Ain't life grand! Now we've got ourselves a case. That is, unless his lawyer has half a brain and demands a jury trial. Then we're left flapping bare-assed in the wind, 'cause I can tell you right now, there ain't no jury in Montana that's ever gonna convict the mope and send him off to jail. They'll think, he may be a poacher, but he's *our* poacher. In addition, at least one juror in a group of twelve fools will conclude, 'I don't like the government and I like grizzly bears even less.' Then you've got yourself a hung jury, and the poacher's acquitted. Either way, we're dead meat."

The cold coffee tasted bitter in my mouth. According to Turner, there was no hope at all—in which case, I might as well give up my badge and walk. I'd be damned if I'd do that!

"How about if the perp turns out to be Native American and *I'm* the one who catches him?" I countered.

Turner's eyes sank so deep, they came to rest on top of his saddlebags. "Well now, wouldn't *that* just be dandy? Then we can relive Custer's Last Stand all over again." He sighed and shook his head. "Listen, orders from the Puzzle Palace in D.C. are that we're to be particularly sensitive when it comes to cases that take place on the rez. So, even if someone *were* to be prosecuted and we miraculously won, the guy would wind up with suspended jail time and a fine that he'd never bother to pay."

I was well acquainted with such scenarios, having dealt with them many times myself. The head honchos seemed to take perverse pleasure in throwing logs in front of agents' cases and making our jobs all the more difficult. As the sign Carolton had nailed above the office door said, COWS MAY COME AND COWS MAY GO. BUT THE BULL IN THIS PLACE GOES ON FOREVER.

"Is that all you've got for me?" Turner questioned.

I felt like David Copperfield trying to pull a rabbit out of a hat as I rummaged around in my mental file cabinet. Then I remembered the tip I'd received this morning.

"Well, I did hear about an eagle feather headdress

that's being worn by an exotic dancer. Somebody must have sold it to her illegally."

Hank Turner perked right up. "Now that's more like it! There's a case we can sink our teeth into that'll give us some bang for our buck. A dead grizzly's only worth a misdemeanor, but selling eagle feathers will rack up a felony."

Turner was right about that. The idiot who'd sold the eagle headdress could find himself not only in jail, but prohibited from owning a firearm, leaving the country, or voting for the rest of his natural life. All because the protection of eagles and grizzlies fell under two completely separate congressional acts. The Endangered Species Act had been purposely written so that it had a lot more bark than actual bite.

"Where was the headdress spotted?"

I wondered which Turner was more interested in— the eagle feathers or the dancer. "The girl works at a bar up near the Blackfeet rez. Someplace where the local militia hangs out."

Turner stared at me a moment and then burst into laughter. "You've gotta love those bozos back in D.C. Not only does Malfunction Junction send me a woman, but a New Yorker to boot. What the hell did you do to get their dander up?"

I wasn't about to tell him, if he hadn't already heard all the stories. I responded with a shrug.

"Well, you sure must have pissed somebody off," he commented. "Shipping you out here is damn near the equivalent of painting a target on your back. The best advice I can give is to keep your head down, your mouth shut, and make as little trouble as possible."

That confirmed it. Turner *hadn't* heard much about me.

"By the way, I brought you a little housewarming gift."

Turner put a plaque on my desk: THIS JOB IS 99% BORE-DOM AND 1% WHITE-HOT FEAR.

"What say you try living by that ninety-nine percent, and the two of us should get along just fine."

"Where's the adventure in that?" I quipped.

Turner responded with a derisive snort. "Let me put it to you another way: I've got enough stress in my life. Don't go giving me any more agita. I strongly suggest you do something constructive with your time, like wading through Carolton's paperwork. I'm sure he's got a slew of cases that need to be closed."

On that note, Turner hauled himself from the chair and took his leave. No sooner had he walked out the door than I flipped the plaque facedown. While I might be temporarily forced to do paperwork, I wasn't about to put up my feet, lace my hands behind my head, and moan and groan about what couldn't be done. In fact, I was more determined than ever to leap tall buildings in a single bound.

My Superwoman persona was put on hold as I dragged out Carolton's files and began to slog through his open cases. There were the usual Indian wannabes who'd been caught with feathers stuck in their hat-brims. Yet another involved a fool who'd bred a pack of hybrid wolves, only to tire of feeding them. His solution was to turn the critters loose on the town.

One file was completely empty—*Grizzly Deaths on the Blackfeet Reservation*. Carolton must have had his rendezvous with fate before he'd been able to open an investigation. Either that or the case had been squelched. But it was a definite clue that he'd known something was going on. I was wondering just what that something might be when the phone rang.

"Rachel?" The voice sang out loud and clear over the wire. "This is Sally Crossbow. Remember me?"

"I certainly do." The Madonna of her day had made a lasting impression.

"I've been thinking. It seems awfully silly for you to go to a motel if you're coming back up to the rez. Why don't you just stay with me? I've got plenty of room and, Lord knows, I could use the practice brushing up on my people skills."

The thought of rooming with the sharp-tongued Sally was about as tempting as walking barefoot across broken glass. Sally quickly picked up on my hesitation.

"I'm afraid I was a bit short with you yesterday, and I'd like to make up for it. I believe I can be of some help. I'll be happy to give you what insight I have into the Blackfeet people and their culture. You'll need to know the proper etiquette if you plan to spend any time snooping around on the rez."

I had the distinct feeling that Sally wanted to keep an eye on me. As far as she knew, the fate of her grizzly cubs was still at stake. Even so, the situation could prove to be equally beneficial for both of us. Having Sally as an ally wasn't all that bad an idea.

"Thanks, Sally. It's very kind of you. That would be great."

Besides, I secretly admired the woman. Not only did she have the gumption to live her life as she chose, but

Sally wasn't afraid to kick ass in order to get things done. She clearly put herself on the line when it came to protecting and saving wildlife.

"I'll come by tonight, but it might be a bit late. I have to stop off at a bar on the way. Some place called Big Bertha's Wildlife Sanctuary."

"Oh dear Lord. Not *that* hellhole!"

"You know it?"

"Who doesn't? It's not the sort of place that *I* would patronize, I can tell you that much."

I figured if Sally disapproved, it must be quite the dive.

"Don't worry about what time you arrive; I stay up late myself. Just head on over when you're through—and be careful!"

Normally I'd have bristled at those last words, but I found her concern oddly touching.

I put Carolton's files away; there was no sense in pretending to examine them any further. My pulse rate had picked up, a sure sign that I was on to something. Grizzlies were being killed and I intended to get to the bottom of it, no matter *what* Turner said. Misdemeanor be damned! Somebody's life was about to be made miserable.

I headed back home to pack a few essentials. Hal was finally up and out of the house. I was glad he wasn't around; I didn't need him begging to come along.

I was ready to leave when Casanova appeared and once again deftly blocked my exit. His pushed-in Persian mug touted a well-practiced pout. I was convinced the feline was a reincarnated cross between James Cagney and some surly Parisian model.

Meow!

It was perfectly clear that I wasn't about to go anywhere until I'd given him what he wanted. I glanced at his bowl and saw that all the Tender Vittles were gone.

"All right. One more pack, but that's it."

The little fur ball supervised closely, making sure every last morsel had tumbled out of the package. Then he began to chow down, having gotten his way.

Temptation is a funny thing, and comes in all shapes and sizes. Casanova's long, silky coat seduced me now, and I reached down to run my hand along his glistening fur.

The cat promptly scratched me.

Ouch! You'd think I'd have learned by now not to be enticed by beauty. There was no question the cat had more than a touch of Sally Starlight in him.

I left a short note for Hal and hurried out the door.

Five

I drove past where the university football team, the Montana Grizzlies, was practicing in Grizzly Stadium. The grizzly is considered the state animal, with nearly every motel, gift shop, and restaurant in Montana named after it. People are so enamored of bears that they've created lovable characters like Winnie-the-Pooh, Paddington, and Smokey in their image. Even President Teddy Roosevelt had refused to shoot a bruin that some friends thoughtfully tied to a tree for him—thereby spawning the teddy bear craze. Yet when one of these critters was illegally killed, nobody had enough backbone to convict the guilty party. Talk about your sense of irony.

I took the two-lane scenic route to Big Bertha's, not wanting to arrive too early. The Mission Mountains soon appeared, rising majestically out of a thick bank of clouds like my very own Brigadoon. All was fine until I got stuck behind a chip truck chugging along at twenty-five miles an hour. Call me crazy, but to my mind that's cause for justifiable homicide.

The last truck I'd forcibly followed had kicked up a storm of gravel, cracking my windshield so that it resembled a spider's web. This monstrous vehicle was more benign: it simply splattered my pickup with mud. I flipped on the wipers and presto! A work of modern art was instantly born. I cursed the rig, attempting to see the road through my down-home Jackson Pollock.

I finally gave up and pulled into Oly's gas station, where I washed my windshield and picked up dinner—three hot dogs for a dollar. Forgoing the ketchup and mustard—I prefer to eat my food rather than wear it while careening down the road—I munched on a dog and placed the other two on the dashboard, then turned on the defroster to keep them warm. Yet another trick I'd learned from Charlie Hickok—the art of how to keep a meal from coagulating while on the run.

I'd planned my trip just right, finishing the last bite as I reached Big Bertha's. The parking lot was filled with Harleys and unwashed pickups. The billboard displayed an overweight woman in a partial state of undress. She was artfully covered by a swaggering peacock that stood with its tail feathers unfolded, while a python slithered across her breasts.

I parked and headed for the entrance, where a sign over the door sternly warned NO ASSHOLES. Then I walked inside to view a display of humanity in all its inebriated glory. Evidently plenty of leeway was allowed when it came to interpreting Big Bertha's warning.

Speakers blared a raucous tribute to the Allman Brothers, followed by a rousing medley of Lynyrd Skynyrd tunes, though it was difficult to hear the booming music above the catcalls and lecherous roars of the crowd.

The center of attention was a girl dressed up to look

like Dale Evans—only this was the porno version. The fringe on her micro-mini skirt swung seductively against her G-string, its slender triangular material decorated with amorous bulls. Tiny cowboy hats rounded out her costume, creatively covering the tips of her breasts. It was enough to make Trigger blush.

A large chalkboard on the wall detailed the upcoming schedule for Cabin Fever Days. Among the planned events were a Coors Can Snowball Toss, Nude Sumo Wrestling, Dead Chicken Bingo, and Bar Stool Racing. Ooh yeah! I'd be sure to mark those dates down on my calendar.

The temperature in the room felt more like spring break in Miami than November in Montana; it had to be a good eighty degrees. The air was laden with a scent that could best be described as pungent, laced with a dose of musk. It was a mixture of beer, body odor, booze, and I didn't want to guess what else.

Sexy Dale finished her act and the crowd dispersed to the pool tables and keno machines, allowing me enough room to sit at the end of the bar. I patiently waited for over two minutes, all the while trying to lasso the bartender's attention. I finally resorted to a more tried-and-true method.

"Yo! How about a Moose Drool over here!"

That seemed to do the trick. One instantly appeared. There were no bowls of peanuts and pretzels as munchies; the finger food consisted of beef jerky and turkey gizzards floating in two large jars. A pair of coconut shells, carved into caricatured Indian faces sucking on cheap cigars, were strung above the bar. Even the restrooms had their own unique touch. The sign over the men's room read GUNS, while the ladies' room was designated HOLSTERS.

During the lull in the entertainment, the biker on the next bar stool finally noticed I was there. Lucky me. The sum total of Biker Bob's charm was encapsulated in the phrase written across the back of his tee-shirt.

If You Can Read This, the Bitch Fell Off!

She must have gotten in one last good lick before she left, because Biker Bob sported a black eye. He finished his drink and slammed the glass down on the bar.

"Hey, Bert! Bring two more of these. One for me and one for my gal pal here," he growled, motioning toward me with his thumb.

Bert hopped to it as if we were the only ones there.

"Thanks, but I've already got a drink," I said, by way of polite refusal.

"No, what you've got is a Moose Drool. *This* is a drink," my new friend insisted. "You ever have a Montana Ditch?" He pushed one in front of me.

I resignedly shook my head.

"Yukon Jack whisky and water. If you were from around these parts, you'd know that. Hell, you haven't experienced Montana till you've had a Ditch!"

Maybe that's why I was craving a piña colada right now.

"Besides, darlin', this calls for a toast. I think I knew you in a past life." Biker Bob picked up my glass and held it to my lips.

"I guess that's why they call it a *past* life," I firmly replied and pushed it away.

Biker Bob guffawed and threw me a wink. Then he plucked a deep-fried nugget from off a plate and slathered it in sauce. The liquid dripped down his fingers as he popped the morsel into his mouth.

"So, sweetheart, if you don't wanna try a Ditch, how about giving one of our local delicacies a whirl?"

The thick, gooey sauce oozed down his hand. Maybe it was the beer, maybe it was the heat, but the mixed odor of oil and sweet sauce made me feel queasy.

My past-life Lothario pushed the plate closer. "Go ahead. Take a taste. It won't kill ya. That's what we call cowboy caviar."

"Cowboy caviar?" The greasy nuggets looked more like breaded golf balls.

Biker Bob flashed a grin that revealed he was missing more than a few teeth. "You know. Rocky Mountain oysters. Try 'em; they'll help loosen you up. It's our homegrown version of Viagra. But don't you worry none, sugar."

His stale breath licked at my ear.

"They only make me frisky on days that end in 'y.' Gotta stay firm for the ladies, you know."

That did it. I wasn't about to start gnawing on breaded and fried bull testicles. "Thanks, but the last thing I need is more bull in a man."

Suddenly the music kicked in and all-out pandemonium broke loose. My biker honey began thumping on the bar with his fists, as chimplike hoots flew from his mouth. He wasn't alone in his enthusiasm. It was as if a brushfire had been lit under every man in the room.

They started clapping in unison to that all-time classic Cher song, "Half Breed" as the focus of their unabashed fervor was hoisted onto the bar.

A girl dressed in a deerskin top and minuscule loincloth pranced about, patting a hand against her mouth while pretending to give an Indian war cry. She would have resembled every other bump-and-grind dancer but for the enormous war bonnet perched on her head. The Indian headdress transformed her into a low-rent Ziegfeld showgirl. Its long train flowed down her bare back and over her butt, in perverse imitation of a wedding veil.

The frenzy continued to build as the girl whipped off her top to reveal breasts covered only by tiny tomahawk pasties. She spun around while tearing off her loincloth, and I was certain the roof would cave in from the crowd's noise. Her G-string consisted of nothing more than a few well-placed, colorful feathers. The grand finale came as she displayed two bull's-eyes painted on her rear-end, then proceeded to slap them as though they were tom-toms.

If nothing else, Big Bertha's should have been closed down for its monumental display of bad taste—though I seemed to be the only one who thought so. In sync to the music, the air throbbed with an overload of testosterone-laden lust. Some smart businessman could have cornered the market in Rocky Mountain oysters by filming this place as a testimonial to their potency.

The performance ended as she pulled the tomahawk pasties from her breasts and threw them into the frenzied audience. The men in the crowd behaved like the perfect gentlemen they were, pummeling one another into the ground in a desperate effort to obtain them. No wonder her act had made such an impression on Jonesy. When I looked back, the girl was gone.

I quickly nabbed Bert the bartender before the crowd descended to drown their lust in booze.

"The dancer. What's her name?"

Bert flashed a smarmy smile. "Sorry, sweetheart. I hate to break it to you, but you're not her type."

Oy veh. I'd just about had it with this place. I grabbed his arm and flashed my badge in his face. "No problem. However, *you* might end up as the target of my next investigation if I don't get the information I want. Now just give me her name, bozo."

"Cherry Jubilee."

It made as much sense as anything else. "See, wasn't that easy? Now how about telling me where I can find her, while you get me another Moose Drool."

"Yeah, yeah, keep your shirt on. Here's your beer. Cherry will be out in a minute. It's nearly time for her waitressing shift."

Not only did I keep my shirt on, I also held on to my seat as the crowd converged six-deep around the bar. Orders flew for Coors, Mud Slides, and Hot Sex shooters as Biker Bob looked down at his empty plate and then back up at me in surprise.

"Why, sweetheart, you sure as hell must be feeling pretty loosey goosey right about now. You went and ate up all my gonads!"

Maybe it was time to move on, after all. Just then Cherry Jubilee reappeared, dressed in a low-cut black

leather bustier and matching hip-hugger pants decorated with fringe running down the sides of both legs.
She looked like Erin Brockovich Does Montana. Eyes
rimmed with heavy black liner gave her the appearance of a raccoon who'd hadn't slept for days. They
competed for attention with a pair of bee-stung, ruby-
red lips and a Rocky Mountain pile of teased hair.

"Hey, Bertie! Gimme two tequila shooters pronto! I
only have a ten-minute break before I gotta get to
work!" she barked.

He produced the drinks on the double, not bothering
to steer her my way.

Cherry picked up one of the glasses and, drawing
her shoulders forward, tucked it firmly between her
breasts while slipping a slice of lime in her lips.

The guy standing next to her looked like a broken-
down, gonzo rock-'n'-roller, complete with a long,
greasy ponytail. He bent over, licked Cherry's neck,
sprinkled the area with salt, and grazed her skin again
with his tongue. Then he grabbed the glass from between her breasts with his teeth, threw back his head,
and downed the tequila. Finally, Mr. Rock Star removed the slice of lime from her lips with his own to a
hearty round of applause.

But the show wasn't over yet. A chorus of lusty
cheers broke out as Cherry dropped to her knees. Mr.
Over-the-Hill Rock Star smiled benevolently at the
crowd as he lifted his shirt and lodged the second shot
of tequila between his stomach and jeans. Cherry's
tongue flicked snakelike across his pale abs. After salt-
ing his flesh, she licked the area again slowly.

Cherry looked up at her honey and grinned. He

placed a hand on her head and guided her back to his pants, where her teeth latched on to the rim of the glass, but the drink refused to budge.

"Pull harder!" the crowd roared.

Cherry gave another tug, and this time proved victorious.

"How about you and me try some of that action?" Biker Bob suggested.

"I'm saving it for my next life," I quipped, and headed over to the girl who'd aptly named herself after a dessert.

I was instantly swallowed up in a crowd that consisted of way too much denim and leather. A few deft jabs helped me along the way—until my elbow came in contact with the wrong customer.

"The last person who poked me like that found his ankles and wrists duct-taped together," rumbled a guy the size of Mount Everest, with a stomach to match.

It was at times like this that I became religious—right now I devoutly wished that Moses were here to help me part this sea of human flesh.

Nada. Zilch. Zippo. Not a body moved.

Since no miracle appeared to be forthcoming, I bellowed, "Dancer approaching!" at the top of my lungs.

Not only did a path clear, but I was pushed back toward the bar, where eager hands lifted me onto the counter. I performed a soft shoe around the beer bottles and shot glasses to a growing chorus of boos, working my way to the other end, where I jumped off and landed right next to Cherry and her boyfriend.

Both of them shot me a glance that left no doubt that my presence wasn't welcome. Tough luck for them.

"Hi. My name is Rachel Porter. I wonder if I could speak to you in private for a moment?" I asked, ignoring her snarling boyfriend.

Cherry's fingers idly wandered up to a gold chain around her neck, which bore a heart with a serrated edge. "What the hell for?"

"I just have a few questions. I'm a U.S. Fish and Wildlife agent."

"Oh yeah? What'd I do? Shoot an endangered moose or something?" she sneered, her fingers twisting the necklace first one way and then the other. "This is as private as it gets. Anything you have to say to me can be said in front of my boyfriend."

I took another look at the aging rock star. Tall and thin, he'd have been considered an anorexic if he were a girl.

"In that case, I'd like to know where you got the Indian headdress you were wearing tonight."

"*I* gave it to her. Why? What's the problem?" Mr. Rock Star asked, sticking out his bony chest.

"There isn't one yet. So how about filling me in on where *you* got it from?"

He snorted and shook his head. "Didn't I tell you this country is getting to be more and more like Nazi Germany? Soon the feds are gonna wanna implant microchips in our hands so they'll know not just *who* we are, but also *where* we are at all times."

Hoping to ease the tension, I said calmly, "I'm only asking about the headdress because I'd like to take a look at it."

"What for?" Cherry asked once again.

I gave the same response in turn. "I already told you.

Because I'm a special agent with U.S. Fish and Wildlife."

"What are you, stupid or something, bitch?" While verbally attacking his girlfriend, Mr. Rock Star never took his eyes off me. "It's 'cause Miss Fed here wants to check out the feathers to see if they're from eagles. Now go get it."

"Why should I?" Cherry sulked and straightened her bustier.

He swiveled his head to glare at her. " 'Cause I said so," he warned. Then he refocused his attention on me. "Hell, nothing tickles me more than cooperating with an agent for the federal U.S. goddamn government."

He emitted a mirthless laugh, its sound as venomous as the pulsating rattles on a snake.

Neither of us spoke until Cherry reappeared dragging the headdress behind her, its feathers touching the ground.

He took the warbonnet from Cherry and handed it to me with a mock ceremonial bow. "Here you go. Knock yourself out."

The piece was heavier than I'd imagined, making me wonder how she was able to dance and also maintain her balance. My finger slid down the middle of one feather, and I was caught by surprise. There was no groove, as there would have been if it were from an eagle. These plumes were smooth. I carefully examined the quills. A black pen mark had been drawn down the center of each feather, expertly replicating a furrow. The headdress was fashioned from turkey feathers.

Mr. Rock Star's dry laughter slithered over to bite me.

"I made it. Damn good work, huh?" he boasted.

The piece was an absolutely perfect artifake. "It's terrific. This bonnet could pass for an authentic heirloom. How did you get it to look so old?"

"That's a trade secret. But then, I don't suppose you're gonna give it away."

"I promise that I won't."

"What the hell you wanna go and tell her for?" Cherry complained.

Mr. Rock Star raised a threatening finger in front of her face and Cherry Jubilee immediately fell silent. "What did I warn you about interruptions?" His voice had turned as deadly as his laughter. "Huh? What did I warn you?" he demanded again, and grabbed hold of her arm.

"Not to do it," Cherry timidly responded, keeping her eyes focused on the floor.

"That's right. So don't fucking interrupt me again, or you know what'll happen!"

His fingers angrily dug into her flesh and tears sprang up in the girl's eyes.

"Hey, that's enough! Let her go," I said.

He grinned and released her arm, one finger at a time. There were red marks on Cherry's skin.

"Are you all right?" I asked her.

Cherry flashed me a dirty look that clearly meant, *Drop dead*! Mr. Rock Star calmly turned back to me, as if nothing at all had happened.

"What I do is stain the feathers with green tea and then rub 'em with steel wool to give them that antiqued look. As far as I know, that's not breaking any law. 'Let the buyer beware' is my philosophy."

As much as it irked me, the guy was right. "No,

there's nothing illegal about your work. In fact, I find it pretty amazing. I'd like to come by your shop some-time, if you don't mind." Maybe flattery would get me in the door, so that I could do some snooping around. Who knew what else I might find?

"I don't have a shop. I work out of my home," he replied.

"Then would it be all right if I visit you there?" I fin-gered the headdress, doing my best to give off the air of a prospective customer.

Mr. Rock Star licked his bottom lip, as if thinking it over. "Why? You interested in buying something?"

"It's possible. I take it that you make other things be-sides headdresses?"

He hesitated for a moment before reaching into his pocket. "Sure. Why not? Here's my business card."

I took the proffered card from his fingers and read, *Kyle Lungren. Member in Good Standing of the United Christian Patriots*. It bore his address and phone num-ber, beneath which was the insignia of a jagged heart. The emblem not only matched the trinket that hung from Cherry's neck, but was identical to the little gold pin affixed to his shirt pocket. Kyle Lungren flashed me a cocky grin. He was clearly a member of the local militia.

I slipped the card inside my pants pocket. "I'll give you a call and set up a time to stop by."

Lungren's grin took on a sinister edge as he raised a finger and pointed it at me like a pistol. "You be sure and do that. Don't be a stranger." His words were fol-lowed by the same nasty laugh as before.

I caught Cherry's eyes once again. They now held a

warning. *Keep your hands off my man. Kyle's mine, all mine!*

I didn't foresee any problem with that.

I pushed my way back through the bodies packed as tightly together as sides of prime beef, trying not to knock into the tables scattered about the floor. I was feeling like the proverbial pinball bouncing around inside a game machine, when someone stopped my progress by grabbing hold of my clothes.

"Hey, Red! What's the big rush? Where's the fire? Why doncha slow down? I bet you're a Big Apple babe. Am I right, or what?" shot a voice with the rat-a-tat-tat delivery of a tommy gun.

I turned around, trying to pull my shirt loose from a grip as determined as the jaws of life. Seated at a table behind me was a guy who resembled a human Chihuahua. It was a toss-up as to whether to pet him, or have him hauled off to the local pound.

Everything about the guy was diminutive, from his tiny hands to his squinty eyes and sharp, narrow chin. He couldn't have weighed more than a hundred and ten pounds. Just looking at him made me feel like a behemoth. But his clothes were the topper. This was obviously someone from back East, trying too hard to fit in.

His polyester shirt must have been created by a sixties flower child whose technique was to throw up in psychedelic colors all over the fabric. As for his snakeskin boots, more than a few pythons had been flayed to make them. But the real corker was on top of his head: an authentic Davy Crockett style raccoon cap complete with a fluffy tail. His movements were herky-jerky hyper as he fidgeted in his seat. Either the guy was high on speed, had to pee, or was your typical New Yorker. Oh God! I wondered if he thought the exact same thing about me?

"What makes you think I'm from New York?" I cautiously inquired.

His machine-gun laughter splattered the room, exposing exceptionally sharp miniature canines. "Whadda ya, kidding me? The way you're pushing through this crowd, of course! You could only have learned that on a New York subway. I'll double your weekly pay if you've been in this state over three lousy months."

There was no denying the guy was good.

"Well? What are you standing there for? Sit down! Take a load off!"

I still had to drive to Sally's, in addition to which I wondered if the guy had ever been given his rabies shots. Just watching him made me jittery.

"Come on, come on! I promise not to bite! Neither will my friend here, Rocky Raccoon." He playfully shook his cap's coonskin tail at me. "Let me buy you a beer, for chrissakes. I just need to talk to someone who doesn't always say *you betcha*. Otherwise I'm gonna friggin' shoot myself right here, and you wouldn't want to live with *that* for the rest of your life!"

The guy was outrageous, but there was something about him that I liked. Besides, we were two New Yorkers completely out of our element, and there wasn't any stronger bond than that. The only problem was, there were no other chairs at his table.

"Gimme a minute and I'll solve the problem." Leaning back, he tapped the biker sitting behind him. "Hey buddy! How'd you like to make a fast twenty?"

Five seconds later, my rear end was in the chair and the biker was standing.

"There! What did I tell you? I'm always good for my word! By the way, I'm Rory Calhoun. You know, like the actor in those old cowboy B-movies." Rory pretended to fire an imaginary pair of six-shooters. "Except that I was born and raised in Bay Ridge, Brooklyn. Now it's *your* turn. What are you doing in this lousy part of the world?"

He looked as much like Rory Calhoun as I resembled an exotic dancer. Especially since Bay Ridge was as Italian as one could get. Either his mother had had a cowboy fetish, or Mr. Calhoun was lying.

"My name is Rachel Porter and I'm a special agent with the U.S. Fish and Wildlife Service."

"No kiddin'?" Rory held on to his cap to emphasize his surprise. "A fed, huh? Congratulations. That oughta go over about as well as a fart in a church around here."

So much for counting on his undivided support. "What do *you* do for a living?"

"Hot tubs. I'm in the hot tub business."

"You're joking, right?" I started to laugh.

"No, I'm dead serious. I told you, I'm good for my word."

A scantily clad waitress approached and placed two Moose Drools on the table.

Rory pulled a humongous wallet from his back pocket and slapped a twenty on her tray. "There you go, sweetheart. Keep the change."

"Thank you, Rory," she cooed and gave him a peck on the cheek as strains of "Hey, Big Spender" reverberated in my brain. Rory was apparently well known and liked at Big Bertha's. But he hadn't finished tripping through his wallet just yet.

"See for yourself if you don't believe me. Look! Here's my business card." His elfin fingers shoved it in my hand.

Some Like It Hot. We provide the tub, you create the heat.

Beneath the logo was a drawing of a cowpoke and his horse relaxing together in a wooden tub. There was no stopping the smile that skidded across my face.

"What's so funny, huh?" Rory demanded, his eyes bulging like two oversized marbles. "You tell me, who doesn't enjoy soaking their bag of bones in a good, hot tub of swirling water? Especially these macho cowboys with asses as flat as pancakes. Whether your butt is smack in a saddle or bouncing around in one of those damn pickups, it's still gonna feel sore by the end of the day. I bet you wouldn't mind planting *your* fanny in one of my tubs, either."

"So, you're really able to make a living selling hot tubs in Montana?" I dubiously inquired.

Rory's coonskin cap had begun to slide so far down on his forehead that he could have passed for the missing link.

"No, I'm really a trust fund kid and my father is friggin' Ted Turner. Whadda ya think? Of course I make money at it. I'm rolling in dough."

Another partially clad waitress stopped by long enough to tickle Rory's cheek with his cap's coonskin tail. "Isn't he just the cutest thing you ever saw?"

Rory beamed and returned the compliment by patting her on the fanny and slipping her a couple of fives.

I tried to hand Calhoun back his business card.

"No, no! You keep it. Call me and I'll give you a good deal. I'm sure we can work something out. Maybe you can waste the prairie dogs that are building a fucking apartment complex under my yard. In fact, why don't you give me your card right now?"

I dug one out of my bag.

"Sorry, but I won't help you get rid of prairie dogs. I'm one of those people who actually protects them."

"That's okay. I'll think of something else," he responded as he scrutinized my card.

"What is it? Don't you believe I'm really a special agent?" I asked in amusement.

"Sure, I believe you. Who the hell would be crazy enough to lie about being a fed in Montana? It's not exactly on the top ten list in these parts."

It was time to go. Not only did spending time with Rory feel like mainlining espressos, but Meat Loaf's "Bat Out of Hell" was rocking the walls. My head was pounding, and I had no control over the involuntary tapping of my toes. Not a good sign.

I got up from my seat. "Thanks for the beer, Rory, but I really have to leave."

"Yeah, yeah. Me too. Hang around this place too long and you'll wind up catching a case of John Wayne-itis."

When he stood, he barely reached my shoulders—and that was with elevated heels on his boots. But Calhoun was able to burrow his way through the crowd like a total pro. The guy was a human Roto-Rooter. I quickly followed in his wake.

He flung open the door and we stepped outside, where I took a deep breath, stretched, and let the lingering residue from the crowd, the heat, and the stench drop away. The sky was so thickly littered with stars that it looked as though welding sparks had gone berserk and shot upward to burn holes in the night.

"For chrissakes! You know what drives me crazy? You can see forever in this damn place! What they need are a bunch of tall buildings to give it some sense of civilization. I'm talking Donald Trump, mother-sized towers, along with a shitload of street lamps."

"If you don't like the country, why come here in the first place? To be honest, you don't strike me as the cowboy type."

Calhoun's eyes glittered beneath his coonskin cap. "You're not exactly the cowgirl type, either. So my guess is that it's probably for the same reason you did. I burned too many bridges and didn't have a whole lotta choice. One good thing about Montana is that people pretty much leave you alone and don't ask a lotta questions. You might take a lesson from that."

He walked over to a shiny new silver Lincoln Continental and opened the door. "A word of advice: watch your back, Big Apple babe. These cowboys can be mean motherfuckers."

Then he slid into his vehicle, turned on the engine, and peeled off.

I pulled out his card and looked at it once more. There was another interesting aspect to his business that I hadn't noticed before. *Some Like It Hot* had no address.

Six

The highways and byways in Montana look different at night. Basically, you can't see much of anything, which tends to be a problem—especially when you're threading your way along a perilous mountain road. A steep drop-off threatens to swallow you on one side; on the other are kamikaze logging trucks that are not only bigger and stronger, but plain don't give a damn.

I wended my way up Mariah's Pass and climbed toward the heavens, traveling along on a Rocky Mountain high. I held my breath and made a wish as my wheels hit the Continental Divide. My 4X4 hung suspended, balanced on the earth's spine, before toppling over to the other side, where I found a curve unexpectedly yawning before me. I might have flown off the road but for the row of metal crosses that flashed out a warning, each representing a soul that had passed before its time.

I entered the rez at East Glacier. Relaxing, I allowed myself to go with the flow. My mind checked onto automatic pilot, entranced by the nearly full moon that danced high above the Rockies.

In no time at all I reached the turnoff for Sally's and approached the tunnel of trees, where my adrenaline kicked in. They were no longer gaily waving to me in welcome. Their skeletal arms now clawed at the night, and their strips of cloth had turned into raggedy shrouds. The spectral figures clustered tighter and tighter around me, until I was certain I could hear the beat of their phantom hearts. Finally, I caught sight of a halo of yellow light that emanated from Sally's house.

I tore through the final stretch of forest and breathed a sigh of relief as my Ford hit the open field, where I spotted her sculpted bears secretly frolicking in the moonlight. Streams of ghostly mist rose off their upturned metal faces as they gazed at the sky in delight. The spell was broken only when Sally opened the front door and stepped outside.

Dressed in elegant red silk pajamas, the onetime showgirl was quite a sight. Leather slippers trimmed with beaver covered her feet, while her hair hung loosely about her shoulders, gleaming luminescent as a moonbeam in the night. I'd never felt so dazzled, so intrigued, and so envious all in one heartbeat.

"I hope I'm not arriving too late," I offered by way of greeting.

"No. I'm just glad to see you got out of Big Bertha's in one piece and made it here alive."

She briskly waved me inside, where a pot of stew sat waiting on the stove. Her cabin appeared even more welcoming than it had before. A soft amber light gave the place a muted glow.

"So, did you find whatever you were looking for at Big Bertha's?"

"Yes and no," I admitted. "I'd been told one of the dancers was performing in an Indian headdress. Only it turned out to be made from turkey feathers, rather than those of an eagle."

"That's an old trick," Sally scoffed, and handed me a glass of red wine. "But it's a good way of parting tourists from their money."

"You know about it?" I asked, somewhat surprised.

"Let's just say I've done a lot of things in my life to get by." She smiled.

I was perfectly willing to let that go for now, though I filed the information away to possibly be pursued later. Sally placed two bowls of stew on a squat coffee table, where we sat cross-legged on cushions before the fire. She proceeded to grill me on each dancer's routine as we ate, along with exactly what they wore. Only after receiving a detailed report did Sally appear to be satisfied.

"It's just as I said. Any girl with a boob job can grind away and call herself a dancer these days. Tell me, where's the artistry in that?"

I nodded sympathetically, wondering if Sally was really artistically insulted, or just resentful of these girls because of their age. Sally answered my question by coquettishly drawing a lock of hair across her face like Salome's veil, and batting her eyes.

"So, what do you think? Can older women retain their beauty and charm?"

"Absolutely."

I sure as hell hoped so. I'd recently spotted a new wrinkle and had made a beeline directly to the nearest department store, where I'd bought fancy moisturizing cream and a twenty-four-dollar bar of soap. Both were guaranteed to be chockful of vitamins C and E, as well as grape extract, bee pollen, and alpha hydroxy. They had cost me a small fortune. I was beginning to consider cutting out the middleman and just shooting formaldehyde straight into my veins. At least that way I knew I'd be getting a decent preservative.

"Growing old is a bunch of crap," Sally responded, as if reading my mind.

She was right. I had a flash of my mother as she'd lain those last days in a coma. Even now I felt angry and tearful, blaming myself that she'd refused to rail against death.

"As for growing old gracefully, whoever came up with that bunk was just looking for a way to make denture cream, Metamucil, and Depends seem more palatable."

I couldn't help but laugh. "I don't see you ever growing old, Sally." How could she? The woman's spirit was as wild and ageless as the woods and mountains that surrounded her.

"Thank you, my dear. For that you get another glass of wine. I also want to show you something special."

She took the glass from my hand and headed for the kitchen. On the way back, she turned off the lights. The next thing I knew, her palm was covering my face, its skin as cool and delicate as papyrus. I took a deep whiff and imagined I could smell my mother's fragrance.

"Now lift your head toward the ceiling, and when I remove my hand, open your eyes."

I did as instructed and heard myself gasp. Hundreds of fluorescent stars were painted on the ceiling, where they twinkled like a colony of captive Tinker Bells. I was able to identify constellations, from Orion's Belt to the Big and Little Dippers.

"My husband painted that for me as a wedding gift. He said this way I'd always be surrounded by starlight, even though I gave up my last name when we got married."

Sally gazed at her own private galaxy and seemed momentarily transported back in time, before she looked at me again.

"One of the most important things you have to realize about the Blackfeet people is their tie to nature and the land. They believe wild things must be honored. So much so that it's taboo for them to kill a bear. Few outsiders know that grizzlies are the one animal whose name the Blackfeet won't even speak. Instead, tribal members refer to them as *badgers* or *the unmentionable ones*. Saying the word *grizzly* is considered bad luck."

"Why is that?" I asked.

The fire crackled as Sally took a sip of wine. The color reflected on her cheeks, giving her skin a youthful glow.

"Because bears are thought to be wise creatures with immortal powers. Think of their cycles and what they represent. It's when they disappear in the winter that snow comes. Food doesn't grow and people fall sick. But when bears awaken in the springtime, they bring with them the sun, crops, and flowers. Their appearance is a sign of rebirth."

That was all fine and dandy, except for one catch.

"Matthew Running used the word *grizzly* several times the other day. How do you explain that?"

Sally sighed and gently nudged a stray lock of hair

from her face. "Matthew is different. Many of the younger people have strayed from the old ways and no longer have any regard for Mother Earth or tradition. They've become seduced by what they think society has to offer. Rather than stay out here in their old family homes, they've flocked to the tribal seat of Browning, hoping to find something better and more exciting than what they already have. Instead, it's reservation life at its worst."

I'd heard Browning was more or less a hellhole and was curious to get Sally's take. "What makes the place so bad?"

Sally shook her head in disgust. "The best way to describe Browning is that it's akin to a refugee camp. The government moved most of the Blackfeet people off the land and into HUD housing in town years ago. Once that happened, people seemed to lose heart. They began to apply for welfare and became dependent on federal dole. Now, instead of just unemployment, we also have alcoholism, suicide, drugs, and anger. That's what happens when there's no hope. People keep going back to the government trough."

"Then why don't young people just move off the reservation?" I curiously inquired.

"Some do. But they almost always come back. Reservation life is the only way they've ever known. They can't assimilate into anything else."

"And their attitude toward bears?" I questioned, attempting to bring the subject back home.

"They don't honor the same taboos. When people lose their tie to the land, they also lose their tie to the culture."

I looked again at her stars. They danced before my eyes, and the constellation Ursus Major, the Great Bear, came into view.

"Which means they could also kill bears without any concern for tribal beliefs or restrictions," I concluded.

Sally impatiently clucked her tongue. "I don't believe that's necessarily true. They might use the word *grizzly*, but a full-blooded tribal member still wouldn't kill a bear. Most likely, it would be done by an apple."

I had absolutely no idea what Sally was talking about. "An *apple*?"

"Sorry, you wouldn't know that reference, would you? *Skinjin* and *apple* are slang terms for a half-breed. You know, red on the outside and white on the in."

Interesting. Apparently Native Americans had their own caste system, too. "You still haven't told me what makes Matthew Running so special."

Sally propped an elbow on the coffee table and rested her head in her hand. "Matthew was one of those who left the reservation for a while. He went off to college and got a degree. After that, he landed a good job, and could have stayed off the rez forever."

"Then why'd he come back?" Perhaps the wine was going to my head, but I could have sworn Sally's eyes grew misty.

"For the very reason I explained earlier. He has strong ties to the land and to his people. Besides, he felt he had an obligation."

"To what?"

"To me," she said quietly.

I waited for Sally to continue, not wanting to push her, afraid she might clam up.

"Matthew and my son grew up together, and were best friends. In fact, they were more like brothers. Which is why they were excited when they were both called upon to serve in Desert Storm."

Sally began to look her age for the very first time. Her shoulders slumped, her chest caved in, and the hollows in her cheeks grew deeper. My stomach clenched in a knot. I hadn't known Sally had a son, and it was easy enough to guess what had happened.

"Justin died in Kuwait. He was killed by friendly fire. Matthew was with him at the time. He'll never admit it, but I think he came back partly to look after me. That, and to help protect the wildlife on the rez. Matthew brings me all the roadkill he finds. That's how I'm able to feed the injured raptors and orphaned cubs."

I used that to get off the topic of her son and segue back to bears.

"Then who do you think is killing the grizzlies? Could it be the half-breeds that are living on the rez?"

Sally stared at something I was unable to see. "I'm not sure," she finally answered. "But I can tell you that a lot more grizzlies have been killed than Matthew chose to reveal the other day."

My stomach clenched another degree. "How many?"

Outrage began to blaze in Sally's eyes. "Eighteen, to be precise. And it's going to be difficult to discover who's responsible for their deaths. There's something out here in the West that's called the Law of the Three S's. Do you know what that stands for?"

I nodded, all too aware of the unofficial law of the land. "Shoot, shovel, and shut up."

"Exactly." Sally's lips compressed into a hard,

straight line, and her jaw was firmly set. "What do *you* think should be done to those who kill grizzlies?"

The crackling fire behind her made her look like an avenging angel, its flames shooting up around her arms, her shoulders and head.

"I think they should serve time in jail and pay a large fine," I cautiously answered, curious as to what she was getting at.

"Do you want to know what *I* think should be done to them?" she softly inquired.

I silently nodded.

"I'd like to see them placed in front of a firing squad, and be one of those allowed to pull the trigger. Anyone who blows a life off the face of this earth should be forced to pay with his own."

A chill crept through my bones as I wondered exactly which it was that Sally was talking about—the grizzlies or her son.

Seven

I woke up in a large, sun-filled bedroom that made my room in Hal's house seem like a hovel. I quickly washed, dressed, and headed into the kitchen. Sally wasn't yet up, so I didn't bother with breakfast, but tiptoed out the front door. Her metal bears instantly froze in position. Apparently, I'd almost caught them at play in the early morning light. I went along with the pretense and did my best to ignore them. After all, I was the guest and this was their territory.

I drove slowly out through the quiet arbor of cottonwoods. The colorful material on their pale gray limbs was still half asleep. These were the sturdy trees on which outlaws had regularly been hanged, giving rise to the term *cottonwood justice*.

The road wound down from Kiowa toward Browning, with the prairie on my left and the mountains of Glacier towering behind. The park's cliffs rose like a fortress, as if doing their best to keep Canada at bay. Before long, I began to near the town. I could tell I was almost there by the rows of tiny shacks that I passed. Each had a piece of plywood nailed into place where a window would normally have been.

Postage-stamp lots of land masqueraded as yards, littered with junked cars, propane tanks, and assorted trash and broken bottles. A large poster of the Marlboro Man had been slapped on one of the metal front doors. Torn and tattered, its image had become a tempting target for crude graffiti. I slowly drove along, careful not to sideswipe any of the stray dogs. They roamed the streets in packs, feeding on whatever they could wrap their mouths around.

I passed the housing area for single mothers, called Sesame Street. Nearby stood Death Row, a grim cement structure where senior citizens dwelt. From there, I turned onto Main. This was the twenty-four-hour, hot-to-trot spot where the local teens came to cruise. Each night car after car drove from one end of the strip to the other, turning around at the War Bonnet Motel.

An elongated one-story building stood on one side of the street. Besides having bars on its windows, the structure was surrounded by a tall, chain-link fence. Its defensive attitude struck me as similar to pioneers circling their wagons. Considering that these were the federal government's offices, the analogy made perfect sense.

I continued to the end of the street and parked in front of a tiny, nondescript building. The exterior was meant to be that of a charming wood cabin, but the brown paint peeling off its cement 'logs' betrayed the illusion. A weathered sign announced that I was about to enter the BLACKFEET FISH AND WILDLIFE GRIZZLY MANAGEMENT office. I walked in through the unlocked door and found a room that held a desk, a chair, a phone, and nothing more.

"I'm in here," called a voice.

I poked my head into the doorway of the other office and found Matthew Running already busy at work. Custer lay at his feet.

"I hope you don't mind that I'm here so early." I'd planned to arrive first, so Running would know I was no slug-about. The best way to do that was to make him think he'd kept me waiting.

"To be honest, I figured you'd have been here even earlier," he countered. "To me, this is kinda late."

Damn the man!

He looked up from his paperwork, and the hint of a smile danced about his lips. But it was *those eyes, those eyes, those eyes* that once again nailed me. It was as though Running had the ability to look straight into my soul.

I glanced around, searching for something to latch on to, refusing to give him access to my thoughts. My gaze landed on a small bookcase, allowing me an unexpected peek into the man with whom I was dealing. On the top shelf stood two books—Macchiavelli's *The Prince*, and Sun Tzu's essay *The Art of War*. But it was what sat next to them that drew my attention. Walking over, I discovered it was a miniature sandbox with a tiny wooden rake. Lying on its surface was a single grizzly claw, some military dog tags, and a gold wedding band. I took a closer look. Inscribed on one set of the metal dog tags was the name *Justin Crossbow*.

"That's my Zen meditation garden."

The voice was as smooth as liquid velvet in my ear, causing my heart to jump. I turned my head and found Matthew Running standing directly behind me. I hadn't even heard the man get up.

Running reached past me and picked up the rake. "I push the sand around whenever I need to think. Sometimes it helps my totem spirit's voice come through to me. Take now, for instance. It's telling me that I need to get something to eat."

I spun around to face him. "Are you mocking me?"

"No—although white people *do* like to romanticize Indian mysticism. But in this case, I'm serious. Let's go to the Red Crow Café and grab some breakfast. I'm starving."

Custer got up and wagged his tail.

"No, not you, Custer. The white woman." Running grinned. "You stay here and guard the place."

Custer lay back down and placed his chin on his paws, his eyes jealously following our every move.

Running pushed the doorknob's button in and closed it behind us as we left.

"Do you really think that simple lock is going to keep people out of your office?"

"I'm surprised at you, Porter. You should know that if people really want something badly enough, there's nothing on this earth that can stop them." Though his tone was neutral, his words held an underlying edge— until the hint of a smile swept it away. "Then again, they should at least have to work at it."

We pulled into a strip mall that was amazingly called Teepee Village. I cringed and wondered why the Blackfeet people hadn't risen en masse and torn the sign down. Running swung his old Chevy into a space, where it blended in with all the other unwashed pickups like one more bad-ass kid in a street gang. I'd quickly learned that in Montana the only clean pickups are those that belong to uncool "dudes."

We headed inside a storefront filled with eight booths and four tables. Every eye in the place turned our way and stared. Little wonder—I was the only white person there. Running thoughtfully headed for a booth in the back of the room.

The menu offered everything from "hangover stew" to eggs. I decided to be politically correct and order the Indian fry bread along with a side of home-made jam called wajapi. Running ordered the break-fast that I craved—eggs over easy, homefries, and bacon. He hungrily dug into his food as my own or-der was placed before me. The fry bread was a greedy cardiologist's dream. A large pool of melted butter slowly coagulated on the dough's greasy top. I took a bite and could instantly feel my arteries begin to harden.

Running noted my expression with a chuckle. "Yeah, you really impressed me by going native with your or-der. Personally, I wouldn't touch that stuff. Let's get you something you can actually eat."

He waved for the waitress and another plate of eggs and bacon instantly appeared. Hmm, talk about your perfect timing. It was almost as if they'd secretly sus-pected I would cave. Running confirmed as much by exchanging winks with the waitress.

So far he was winning this round. It was time that I stepped up to bat. I waited until we'd each polished off a cup of coffee and were on our second refill before I peppered Running with a round of questions.

"By the way, what was done with the grizzly carcasses that you found?"

Running didn't answer until he'd finished buttering a slice of toast and then slathered it with strawberry jam.

"I've never found a carcass. I haven't found anything besides some orphaned cubs running around."

I doubted that was true, and it made me wonder what other information Running might be withholding.

"It seems pretty damn convenient that you always manage to stumble upon cubs the way you do. Few people even see a grizzly *once* in their life. How would you explain it happening to you so often?"

"Just lucky, I guess."

"I don't believe that for a second," I fired back.

"Okay then. It's my totem spirit that guides me to them," Running loftily responded.

What a handy-dandy shield to hide behind.

"And what *is* your totem spirit? Some ancient warrior with a fondness for bears?"

"Not that it's any of your business, but mine happens to be a grizzly."

Running's voice came close to a growl, sending a shiver rippling through me.

"Great. Then maybe your totem spirit can fill in some gaps. I understand you've been able to ascertain that exactly eighteen grizzlies have been killed so far this season. That's quite a feat, considering there are never any carcasses."

Game, point and match! I held Running's stare without blinking. We sat in silence until Running was forced to acknowledge that I wasn't about to back down.

"It's because I receive a phone call each time," he finally conceded.

Why the hell hadn't he given me this information before?

"What does this person say when he calls?"

"He only gives a number. Nothing more. A number and then he hangs up."

"What kind of number? A phone number? A lottery number? A social security number?" I prodded.

Running placidly sipped his coffee. I'd been warned that patience was essential when working cases on the rez. It's part of the native culture to allow for *loooonnnng* periods of silence between question and answer. The only problem was that my own cultural gene was kicking me in the rear—good old New York impatience.

"Or maybe *call this number for a good time?*" I persisted, determined to get a reaction.

My tenacity paid off as Running's almond eyes perused me in amusement.

"They're just numbers, Porter. You know, like one, two, three, four, five. Each time he calls, the number goes up a notch."

"Then how do you know it's grizzlies that he's referring to? For chrissakes, it could be the number of nuts a squirrel is burying outside this guy's window that day!"

"I just know, that's all. The numbers are said as a taunt."

His totem spirit had probably told him that, as well. I was about to counter with a wisecrack when a huge man entered the Red Crow, flashed me a dirty look, and sat down in a booth with his back toward me. A circular pattern of eagle feathers was embroidered on the heavy woolen jacket, with the initials IBA woven beneath.

Running followed my gaze and quietly answered my unspoken question. "He's a member of a group called Indignant Blackfeet Arise. They meet here regularly at the Red Crow."

"Sorry to seem ignorant, but what kind of group is it?" They clearly sounded pissed off and ready to mutiny.

"Simply put, they believe the Blackfeet Nation should be allowed more autonomy than we've been given by the federal government. We're considered to be a sovereign nation, yet when you throw in the array of legalistic mumbo-jumbo we're forced to deal with, along with the gaping loopholes in treaties and agreements, we really don't have much power at all. Our tribal council is constantly being dictated to by Uncle Sam, who controls the purse strings. Those in the IBA are angry about it and have had enough of this sort of treatment."

The man must have overheard our conversation, for he stood up and lumbered toward us. Each of his footsteps carried the weight of an anvil, producing a thump that shook the floorboards. No less menacing was his scowl.

Standing well over six feet tall, his body was as solid as a tree trunk. Huge and round, his head sprouted a mane of long, heavy hair whose stiff ends touched the tops of his shoulders, while the skin on his face was as pockmarked as a peach pit.

"Hey, Running. Who'd you bring in here with you?" he demanded, making no pretense to be polite.

"This is Rachel Porter. She's with the U.S. Fish and Wildlife Service. And this esteemed gentleman is Bearhead Come-By-Night."

Bearhead sniffed at the air and then made a face, as if having caught a whiff of something rotten. "It just goes to show how little the federal government thinks of us. The new agent with the lousy Fish and Wildlife Service can't even be bothered to come up to the rez himself. Instead he sends a lowly secretary in his place. If I were you, I'd ship her back to Missoula with a message that you don't meet with the hired help. It's a damn insult!"

I did a slow burn. "You might want to rethink your strategy, Mr. Come-By-Night. It just so happens that *I'm* the new Fish and Wildlife special agent, and this is my *second* visit to the rez."

Bearhead swiveled his massive cranium in my direction and glowered. "Hell! You mean those sons-of-bitches in Washington foisted a *woman* on us?"

I could have used my own totem spirit right about then—one with a killer punch, capable of slugging this guy and knocking him out.

"First off, the Fish and Wildlife Service hasn't *foisted* me on the tribe. I'm the agent for the region. However, when an offense takes place on the rez that involves the Endangered Species Act, then it falls under my jurisdiction. That's what I'm here looking into."

"You don't say. And just what kind of offense would that be?"

"Grizzlies are being killed on your land on a steady basis. Whoever is responsible can look forward to being thrown in jail and paying a large fine," I bluffed, half-hoping the culprit turned out to be Bearhead himself.

He snorted in disgust. "You call *that* an offense? Stick around a while. We've got much bigger problems than a few dead bears to deal with. But then, what would you care if it doesn't involve a stinking animal?"

I'd already felt guilty just driving through Browning, knowing that I had a job and a decent place to live. "Look, I'm aware that the reservation has problems with unemployment, but a crime has still been committed."

"Unemployment?" Bearhead's voice boomed. "Do you think *that's* the worst thing taking place on this rez? There were thirty thousand crimes committed here last year. That's more than three offenses per tribal member. We're talking murder, rape, and robbery, not to mention drug dealing. And we aren't allowed to handle the majority of it ourselves, due to a little something known as the Native American Major Crimes Act."

Bearhead came close and got right in my face. "Instead of dealing with things in tribal court, our criminal cases require federal intervention. But of course *that's* no problem, because we've been allotted a whopping three FBI agents here in Browning to handle it all. So, just what do you think happens?"

My guess was that it wasn't going to be anything good.

"I'll tell you. Things get swept under the rug, including the fact that people on the rez have begun to vanish. It's always been said that if you want to get away with murder, just go to a reservation. Whoever coined that phrase knew what they were talking about. But then, we're just a bunch of drunken Indians, so what the hell's the big deal? Am I right?"

"I understand that Native Americans have a reason to be upset—"

Bearhead exploded. "That's another thing I love about you white people! First we were redskins, then we graduated to prairie niggers. Now we're called Native Americans. Once and for all, I am an *Indian*!" Bearhead bellowed the word as he pounded on his chest. "Why would I want to be called anything else, for chrissakes?"

I had the feeling it wouldn't have mattered what I said at this point. There was no dealing with the guy.

Bearhead leaned in closer again, until our noses nearly touched. "As for that last Fish and Wildlife agent of yours, Carolton? He probably got exactly what he deserved. In fact, maybe *you* should think twice before going into the woods all alone." He brought his lips close to my ear and malevolently whispered, "Watch out, or Old Caleb will get you!"

Bearhead pulled back with a sneer, then walked away and slammed out the door.

"I can see that making friends easily isn't one of your better qualities," Running observed dryly.

"Thanks for all your help and support," I snapped.

"You need help, Porter? That's something I wouldn't have suspected."

That did it. "I'm beginning to think you and your friend are as intolerant as the two of you accuse everyone else of being."

Running threw his hands over his heart in mock alarm. "Hey, Porter, don't take it so hard. Everyone starts at ground zero with me."

"In other words, you're just an obnoxious jerk to *every*one."

"That's one way of looking at it." Running smiled. "The other is to figure that I must be doing something right. After all, I'm one of the Indians that hasn't yet vanished."

Vanished. The word danced in the air like toxic fairy dust.

"Would you mind explaining that to me? Just what was Bearhead talking about?"

Running signaled for more coffee, and waited to speak until after it had been poured. "People on the rez are nervous about the fact that an increasing number of tribal members have been declared missing. It's almost as if they've been vaporized. A lot of people are blaming it on the grizzlies, and that may be one of the reasons bears are being killed."

"Do you mean that none of their bodies have ever been found?" I half-expected him to tell me that they'd been beamed up onto the mothership, along with all of the grizzly carcasses.

"No, some of them have turned up. But only their bones, and those were picked mighty clean. The problem is further compounded by all the Indian-upon-Indian crime on the rez."

"What do you mean?"

"One of our tribal members is found dead with a hole in the back of his head, and the FBI immediately writes it off as drug-related. But there's something else going on here, and no matter what the FBI says, it can't be that easily explained away. That's why the atmosphere on the rez is so tense right now. Sorry about what happened before, but I felt it was better just to let Bearhead blow off some steam."

"Yeah, at my expense."

"Better yours than mine," Matt retorted with a disarming grin.

I found myself secretly beginning to like Running, though I'd be damned if I'd let him know it.

"Let's go and I'll show you where I found the cubs," he suggested.

I was halfway out the door when a man rushed inside and roughly bumped against my arm.

"Sorry," he muttered, and continued past without bothering to stop.

He took a seat at the table we'd just vacated, where he sat with his shoulders drawn and his back hunched. Most surprising of all, the guy was Caucasian.

"Who's that?" I asked, after hopping into Running's pickup.

Matt flicked a toothpick in his mouth. "That's Doc Hutchins. He heads up Indian Health Services on the rez."

I took another gander at the man who sat alone, purposely choosing not to look at anyone. Pale and gaunt, he was in no way a role model for good, clean living. In fact, Hutchins's thinning hair and emaciated build gave him the air of a recuperating patient.

"He's not exactly the type of person that I'd envision running a health clinic."

Matthew shrugged. "Maybe not. But he does the job. Besides, it's not as if we have a hell of a lot of choice around here."

Running drove to my vehicle, where I grabbed my metal detector along with my investigation kit, and placed them in the back of his pickup. Then we took off.

Eight

The town of Browning became a distant grim memory as we headed toward the Rocky Mountain Front and Badger Two Medicine. Undulating primeval prairie rolled along, lazy as a sluggish river, its golden surface marred only by the occasional deep coulee.

"That's what killed Custer, you know," Running remarked as we passed by one of the ravines. "Those coulees can hide a lot of stuff. Like a group of angry Indians."

Prairie slowly transformed into mountains heavily robed in cedar and ponderosa pine. I glanced up and spotted bighorn sheep, nearly invisible against patches of ice. Above the sheep were ridges whose rocky peaks stabbed at the sky like a knife. Then I spotted a group of quaking aspen bedecked with colorful rags, much like the cottonwoods along the road to Sally's.

"I'm curious. That cloth must serve a purpose other than being purely decorative. What is it?"

Running hesitated, and I knew he was deciding just how much to tell me. "They're pieces of clothing that we tie to trees when we make a vow. I guess you could say that they're shrines."

He turned his head to look at me. A sheer drop

plunged off the road to our right, and my heart lurched sickeningly up into my throat. Running paid little heed, but continued to navigate as if by instinct.

"Some believe it's where spirits reside, and that it's bad luck for the cloth to be touched."

I said nothing as my fingers gripped the seat tighter. Running took note of my reaction and a hint of laughter slipped out.

"In other words, don't piss off a dead Indian. Or a live one either," he advised and steered clear of the edge.

"I could say the same thing for wildlife agents," I retorted, after regaining my breath.

Running swung onto a dirt road where the Chevy's tires jostled along a conspiracy of ruts, before we finally came to a stop. I retrieved my metal detector from the cargo bay as he locked the vehicle. That done, we began to walk.

Before long, we were in the midst of an evergreen forest where the trees grew thick as hairs on a bear. If Running was following a trail, it wasn't apparent. Any sign of a path was nothing more than a mere whisper. The only sound was the wind, which caused the pines to creak as they swayed. Some moaned, while others sighed in rhythm with the breeze. I didn't need Running to tell me that this was a special place. I intuitively knew as I walked across a swath covered in golden leaves. As for Running, he made no sound at all. His feet seemed to magically float above a carpet of pine needles.

Matt noticed that I intently studied the way he moved, and he chuckled. "Sorry Porter, but it's a trade secret. It's what we call Indianing."

Personally, I thought he was being a little *too* damn quiet; the last thing we needed to do was surprise a bear. But I guess my noise made up for the both of us. We finally stopped at a spot where fir trees huddled closely together.

Running's voice broke the silence. "This is one of the areas where I found a pair of cubs. They were clambering over that log when I first saw them."

I followed where his finger pointed while turning on the metal detector, and then began to scour the ground in search of a phantom bullet.

"How long ago was that?"

"Maybe three months," Running responded.

The metal detector registered no hits, as silent as the woods around us.

"What say we head to the next site where there were cubs?" he suggested.

I turned off the detector, and we walked on.

"Sally tells me that you'll be staying with her during your trips up here. She's a woman with a good heart."

"Yes. It's very generous of her to open her home to me."

"What I meant, is when it comes to animals. She's determined to do whatever is necessary to end the war against wildlife."

"You think there's a war going on here?" I questioned, curious to hear his response.

"Don't you? Eighteen grizzlies have been slaughtered on the rez so far this season. What else would you call it?"

Battle, war, slaughter, greed. Any of those words would do.

"Tell me, why is it that Blackfeet are so afraid of grizzlies that you don't even have a word for them?" I asked.

Running took his time to reply, moving silently along the ground. "Have you ever seen a grizzly after it's been skinned?"

I shook my head.

"Then let me enlighten you. It looks exactly like a man. That's why to hurt one is considered bad medicine in the Blackfeet culture. It can result in one of your relatives dying a terrible death. That gives the bears a great deal of power over us."

"Then why aren't *you* afraid to use the word *grizzly*?" It didn't matter that I'd already received Sally's version. I wanted to hear what Running had to say.

"I guess I became brainwashed by your culture," he responded. "I went to college at Berkeley and then was in the military for a while. But that was a lifetime ago."

"So why did you come back?"

"Because I can't stand the apathy in your world. Besides, this is still the best place for a half-breed."

An alarm bell went off in my mind. Sally had said the most likely candidate to kill a grizzly on the rez was someone of mixed blood.

"You're an apple?"

Running swiftly turned to face me. "Where the hell did you learn *that* expression?"

My cheeks began to burn and I could have kicked myself in embarrassment. "Sorry, I didn't mean to insult you. I'm just surprised."

"Oh yeah? And what are you, Porter? A full-blooded pedigree of some sort?"

Running looked on in annoyance as I laughed. "As a matter of fact, I couldn't be more of a mutt. I'm half Russian Jew and half Welsh."

He reluctantly smiled. "Welcome to the melting pot. I believe it's what's known as being an American."

We walked through a grove of aspen trees, whose leaves rained down upon us like a shower of burnished coins. Their delicate beauty made the next sight all the more jarring. Off by itself stood a tall ponderosa pine that looked as though Freddy Krueger had stopped by. Long slashes sliced through its reddish bark, creating a jagged jigsaw puzzle. The gouge marks rose ten feet high.

I warily approached and ran my fingers along the ragged scar tissue. These gashes were too deep to have been made by any human, they could only have been created by a creature of enormous power, determined to leave its mark.

Running reached up and grabbed what turned out to be a clump of matted fur. He held the dun colored hair toward me, and I took it from his hand.

"What you're looking at is a sort of ursine signpost. Those scratches are the work of a grizzly."

I stared in growing fear and fascination at the crazed pathways that ripped through the trunk. The hair felt coarse and dry in my hand. I'd never felt qualms about being in the woods before, but knowing that this fur came from a grizzly was enough to send my pulse soaring.

"Their claws did that?" I asked, doing my best to keep any tremor out of my voice. If ten sharpened grizzly nails could make mincemeat of a tree, what might they do to me?

"You better believe it. Those bears virtually have razor sharp pickaxes growing out of the ends of their toes."

Suddenly the slightest hint of a breeze, the merest quiver of a leaf, registered throughout my body. My senses grew so heightened that I was certain I could've heard the flapping of a bird's wings. I quickly turned, feeling piercing eyes, only to realize it was just the forest around me. It drove home the fact that I was in the middle of grizzly territory.

I was tempted to break into song, belting out Beatles hits at the top of my lungs, followed up by a rousing chorus of cowboy melodies. So what if I couldn't carry a tune? At least it would be enough to make a grizzly take notice.

I followed behind Matthew, walking closer than I had before. Old Caleb had duked it out with Hal, and killed Carolton. I had no intention of letting him grab hold of me. I was concentrating on trying to be aware of every single sound, when Running stopped short and I smacked into his back. Laid out before us was a scene of heart-wrenching violence.

Rocks were dislodged and trees knocked over, while remnants of stumps had been ripped to shreds. But what made the sight gruesome was all the blood residue and clusters of hair scattered about. The battle zone was approximately twelve feet in diameter. All that was missing was a body.

"I've never seen anything quite like this before," I muttered. "It looks as though a bomb went off."

Running had already moved inside the circle, where he knelt on the ground. "I have. Just not in this country." He motioned for me to join him. "Come and take a look at this."

He pointed to the impression of a bear track that was still intact. The imprint was of a grizzly's enormous back paw. I pulled a foot rule from my kit and measured the outline. The paw was sixteen inches in length. Nearby lay the indentation of a front track, which I measured as well. Its spread was ten inches wide. Basically, they were the size of dinner plates.

"This bear wasn't killed by an Indian," Running pronounced, with a noticeable tinge of relief in his voice.

"How can you possibly tell?"

"By the manner in which it was done. Though someone from the tribe *might* kill a grizzly, it would be an opportunistic crime. They'd shoot the bear from a truck, or maybe spotlight it at night." Running waved his hand over the land. "This attack was well planned. Whoever is responsible took the time to study the bear and its habits, search for its trail, and then probably put out a bait pile. My guess is that a snare was set that caught the bear by its paw. That's why this area is such a mess. The grizzly destroyed everything within a three-hundred-and-sixty-degree radius while attempting to escape. The killer clearly took great pleasure in torturing it."

I studied the scene. Running was right. The circular pattern meant the grizzly had either been tethered or snared. I dropped down and examined the splatters formed by blood residue. Not only did they disclose that a high-velocity weapon had been used to finish off the bear, but the patterns also revealed the direction in which the bullets had traveled.

I opened up my investigation kit and dug past the scissors, micrometer, and gauze pads to pull out the equipment I needed. Then I put on a pair of latex gloves and, using a tweezers, picked up samples of blood-encrusted leaves, which I bagged and tagged. Strands of loose hair were placed in a separate film canister. Both these items would be sent off to the forensics lab in Ashland, Oregon, for DNA analysis, just as was done with any homicide investigation.

I grabbed my camera and snapped a few photos, then turned on the metal detector.

"Don't waste your time. This guy is smart enough not to have used a weapon that's distinctive. Besides, he probably picked up all the shell casings."

Maybe so, but I was determined to nail that down for myself. I swung the metal detector back and forth across the area in which I believed the bullets had traveled. Finishing one length, I pivoted and retraced the ground again, slowly moving the detector from side to side.

Beep! Beep! Beep!

There it was—a hot hit! Bending down, I dug around and triumphantly claimed my treasure: the aluminum pop top from a soda can.

"Give up?" Running asked with a grin.

I kept right on going. Matthew didn't know me very well; I'd give up when hell froze over.

Come on, come on, come on! I silently urged.

The machine finally beeped again and I glanced at

the counter. The needle confirmed it had detected something metal, in the range of .38–.45 caliber ammo.

I reached down, remaining outwardly cool as my fingers scrupulously searched the ground for loot. Hidden under some leaves was a .40 caliber bullet. The shooter had most likely used a .44 Magnum—a hand cannon capable of blowing a hole through just about anything. I smugly held it up for Running's inspection.

"That's helpful. Everyone and his brother owns one of those guns in Montana," he jabbed.

Yeah. Including tribal members of the Blackfeet reservation.

I continued my search and the detector rewarded me with yet another cheerful beep. Though ammo wasn't indicated, I stopped and felt around. Lying under a stunted quaking aspen was a small black plastic knob with a yellow tab. I didn't bother to show Running my booty this time, but slipped the item into my pocket. Then my eyes were drawn back to take a second look. Something cylindrical had left the barest trace of a ring on the ground.

"You finished yet?"

I glanced back to where Running was casually rummaging through my investigation kit.

"All done. We can get going." Returning, I reached over, picked up the kit, and firmly shut the lid.

We took a different route back, during which Running pointed out a variety of plants and trees. He appeared to be much more relaxed now; evidently, he felt relatively certain that the deed couldn't be pinned on an Indian.

"Is that why you didn't report all the grizzly deaths

to Fish and Wildlife right away?" I abruptly asked, breaking into his Nature Channel narrative. "Because you were afraid that one of your own people might be guilty?"

Running's pace was momentarily marred by a slight hesitation. "Sorry if you find that difficult to understand, but I had to know for sure if someone from the tribe was responsible. It's all too easy for the feds to jump to the wrong conclusion these days."

Running seemed to read my thoughts when I didn't respond. "Don't worry; I wasn't about to let anyone get away with the crime, be it an Indian or a white man. But first I had to come to grips with exactly who it was that I might be dealing with."

"And now you know?"

"I don't know anything for sure yet. Let's just say that I have a better understanding."

"Is that something you'd care to share with me?"

"I'd rather not speculate until there's more to go on," Running dodged. "But I can tell you that I admire the way you worked the scene back there."

I was about to offer Running a deal—a swap of knowledge—when we rounded the trail and a freshly killed elk carcass came into view. At the same time a gust of wind caressed my skin, its touch as cold as a ghostly breath. The next moment, a loud bawl fractured the crystalline silence, reverberating in my head.

"Oh, shit!" Running muttered.

A sow stood nearby with two frightened cubs. There could be no doubt that she was a grizzly. The bruin bore the classic dished-in face and rounded ears, with a conspicuous hump rising up from between her shoulders.

The wind must have masked our scent until the very last second, catching the family by surprise when we carelessly interrupted their meal. A lump burned in the pit of my stomach as if stoked by a gang of sadistic little devils. I had the distinct feeling that we were about to pay for our lack of manners. The second pudgy baby joined in the fray with a shriek, and mama bear reacted by shaking a head the size of a garbage can lid, closely followed by hissing and rattling her teeth.

To make matters worse, my hands were occupied with the metal detector and investigation kit, while my 9mm was tucked away in my belt. Running had a 12-gauge shotgun by his side. However, the last thing I wanted was for the bear to be killed.

"I've gotta tell you that this grizzly is really ticked off," he softly warned.

I tried to take a breath, only to discover that the air around me had mysteriously disappeared. "Oh God! Don't shoot her if you don't have to!" I managed to whisper.

"She might make a bluff charge. Have you got the nerve to stand your ground and not run?"

Run? My legs were about as useful as two limp rubber bands at the moment, while my pulse pounded through my veins with the urgency of a lunatic trying to break out of an asylum.

Still, I knew I'd regret it for the rest of my life if the bear was killed without being given the chance to escape. This was a female of breeding age. Their slow reproduction rate already made some biologists call them "the walking dead"; I didn't want to contribute to that. Besides, we were in her territory. The sow was only doing what came naturally—protecting her babies and their food. She deserved the right to live. The one snafu was that I wasn't yet ready to die.

"I promise not to run," I swore, having never felt more frightened in my life. I took one more look at the magnificent creature. We locked eyes and I knew I was making the right choice.

"Okay, then. Just don't look her in the eye."

Aaargh!

"Keep your head down, turn slightly away, and try to make yourself appear small."

Running's voice rang hollow in my ears, as if he were on the other side of the forest.

"I'll only shoot if she crosses my comfort zone and it becomes absolutely necessary." He raised his shotgun and took aim.

Though I did as I was told, I couldn't stop my gaze from sliding back toward the bear.

She puffed herself up into a big round ball, having seemingly willed each hair of her coat to stand on end. The sow's muscles rippled and her brown fur glistened, its grizzled tips backlit by the morning sun. She began to swing her head even faster, now bouncing back and forth on her paws. Her hackles bristled, she began to slobber, and a deep woof left her black lips. That was followed by a roar that started out long and low, like the ominous rumble ripping through the earth before a giant quake, then built in crescendo until it shook the very air itself. The roar reached deep down past my lungs and into my stomach, where it grabbed hold of the most primitive part of my being which screamed, *You fool! Turn around and make a run for it!*

But it was already too late. The sow came barreling toward us on stiff legs as if to say, *I'm your worst nightmare—the toughest bad-ass mother that you've ever seen!*

It took every ounce of control I could muster to keep from yelling at Running, *What the hell are you waiting for? Just shoot the damn thing!*

I nearly shrieked as she charged. Those little round ears stood straight up from her skull like a pair of devil's horns, while the heat of her breath seemed to wrap itself around my feet.

This is it! my brain screamed. *This is how I die! Torn to pieces by a crazed grizzly!*

She suddenly veered away after getting within fifty feet. But the bear clearly hadn't finished teaching us a lesson. She growled, sending bolts of electricity shooting up from the ground to the top of my head.

There was no question that we were slated for death, if she so chose. I stared in morbid fascination at teeth as sharp as stilettos, and long, curving claws. This was a great white shark on four legs; a veritable killing machine.

That was the last thought I had as the sow charged yet again, speeding toward us as fast and furious as a freight train with fur. The world became a blur, and the air was charged with a thunderous pounding.

Running shouted in my ear, "Raise your arms as high as you can and yell at the bear to stop!"

I was so terrified that I didn't think how ridiculous it sounded, but automatically followed his directions.

"STOP BEAR, STOP!" I screamed at the top of my lungs.

I felt as if I'd left my body and was watching the scene, seeing a pair of psychotics yelling with their arms above their heads.

The sow came to a lurching halt, turned around, and plodded back to the carcass, where she and her babies gave us the evil eye.

"Now slowly start to back up," Running softly commanded.

I just hoped that my feet would obey. Thankfully they did, as Running began to talk to the sow in a soothing monotone.

"We apologize. We were just passing through and didn't mean to disturb you. That's your elk. You'll have no more trouble from us. We're getting out of your way."

Running repeated the chant over and over in mantra fashion until the bears were out of sight.

"Okay. You can turn around now; just keep walking."

No problem there. Now that my legs were working, I had no intention of stopping. Even when Running finally suggested we halt I kept right on going, until Matthew placed his hands firmly on my shoulders and turned me around to face him.

"Are you all right?"

"Let's see. No broken bones and I still seem to have all of my limbs," I joked, brittlely.

"Don't bullshit me, Porter."

Maybe it was his words, or knowing that it was finally all right to let down my guard, but every inch of me began to shake. Matthew wrapped me in arms that felt safe and strong.

"It's okay. You were great." His words soothed me as he kissed the top of my head. "Most men couldn't have withstood what you just did back there."

"Most men?" I asked, fishing for a more definitive compliment.

Running held me at arm's length and studied my face. There was something about him that I had yet to put my finger on. However, it was becoming increasingly clear that this man seemed to know me—perhaps better than I might have liked.

"Ninety-nine percent of them." Running released me. "It's a jolt when you realize that *everybody's* in the food chain, and you just happen to be standing in the wrong place at the wrong time."

My relief merged with a sudden rush of tears. I'd never felt more invigorated, though emotionally overwhelmed. There was no greater victory than coming face-to-face with death and walking away alive. I quickly turned aside and wiped my eyes, hoping Matthew hadn't noticed.

The scent of pine needles sweetened the air as they crunched beneath my feet, and the sky rapidly filled with unexpected flakes of snow. The flurry dusted the earth like Nature's talcum powder. We hadn't gone very far when I saw another bear track.

I instantly froze. The snow in the imprint was already beginning to melt from the heat of the creature's foot, revealing the bear had been here very recently. I hurried to catch up with Running.

"How did you guess that the bear was just bluffing and wouldn't attack us?" I asked.

Matthew stopped and thought about that for a moment, his profile perfectly chiseled against the backdrop of gloomy sky. "I've been around bears most of my life. You have to try to get inside their minds. That's the only way to figure out why they're in a particular spot, and what they're doing. Bears aren't particularly interested in killing us; they're just trying to live."

"And you've never been attacked?" Perhaps I should have spent more time watching reruns of *Gentle Ben*.

"Not once." A devilish grin teased at the corners of his mouth. "Tell you what. If you like, I'll strip down and you can search me for bite marks."

His body had felt taut as a bow when he'd held me against him, and there was no denying that my interest was piqued. I hesitated—then gave myself a mental slap.

Running's grin deepened, and I wondered if he knew what I'd been thinking.

"That's okay. I'll take your word for it," I gruffly responded. "I'm just glad that bear wasn't Old Caleb."

Running chuckled, which made me feel all the more self-conscious.

"Old Caleb doesn't really exist. He's the figment of an overactive imagination. Think of him as nothing more than a furry version of the bogeyman."

"I see. In other words, Old Caleb has no more validity than what the Blackfeet believe will happen if they harm a grizzly. After all, that's nothing but a folktale, too, isn't it?" I lightly jabbed.

Mathew shot me a dirty look. Maybe he didn't believe in the bogeyman, but I certainly did. I'd run into him too many times to deny his existence. That fact became disturbingly evident as we arrived back at Running's truck to find the lock had been picked and all the vehicle doors were wide open.

"What the hell happened here?" I asked, putting on a brave front as I threw my metal detector into the cargo bay.

Matthew quietly examined the Chevy inside and out, checking the tires, the brake lining, and gears. "It's probably nothing other than some kids who've cut school and are bored. This is the kind of thing they do as a harmless prank."

But we both seemed to sense it was something else. I held the investigation kit tight in my arms while we drove back to Browning, as if that would help keep me safe. Call it Old Caleb, the bogeyman, or what you will. I knew in my bones that evil was stalking the woods of the Blackfeet reservation.

Nine

Matthew dropped me off at my vehicle, and we agreed to meet later to develop a plan of action. I'd had enough of grizzlies for now, and decided to do something else with the rest of my day. This seemed as good a time as any to pay a visit to Kyle Lungren and the United Christian Patriots. Who knew what I might find at his place? If nothing else, I'd get to check up on the local militia. I pulled out his card and dialed the number on my cell phone.

"Kyle Lungren, minister of information for the United Christian Patriots," he answered.

"Rachel Porter, your friendly Fish and Wildlife agent," I responded. "I was wondering if I could stop by. My sister has a birthday coming up and I'd like to see what you've got that might work as a present."

"Right now?"

"Right now."

There was a slight pause before Lungren replied. "Okay. What the hell. Come on over."

I wrote down the directions and then drove south toward the town of Choteau. A two-lane road sliced with surgical precision through the high plains. There were no other cars around but for myself and some granny cowgirl in her vintage Studebaker who careened down

the blacktop at a whopping twenty-fives miles an hour.
Hell, my blood pressure accelerated faster than that. I
waited the obligatory five seconds and then zoomed
past, only to have sweet, little old granny respond by
shooting me the finger.

I drove through a few faded towns, none of which
stretched more than a city block long. Each had a post
office, a gas station, and a mom-and-pop grocery all
housed in identical one-room structures. The only
other businesses were bars and taxidermy shops. A
sign in one window boasted, YOU SNUFF 'EM, WE STUFF
'EM. I wondered how long it had taken to come up with
that snappy slogan.

Bison- and horse-dotted pastures were all that broke
the endless monotony of the drive between each village. The critters were so still they could have been
statues but for the frost of their breath. One bison stood
posed as if auditioning for the job on the back of an Indian head nickel. It wasn't long before I whizzed past a
handpainted sign, its bold blue letters proclaiming, GET
THE U.S. OUT OF THE UN!

Yep, I was officially in militia country. My suspicion
was confirmed as an old clunker sped past on the opposite side of the road. Each of its broken windows was
held in place with tape, while the license plate barely
hung on by a screw. The bumper sticker on its rear ordered "Quit Honking. I'm Reloading."

I continued to follow Lungren's directions, turning
right at an abandoned gas station and heading down a
dirt road. Soon an enormous chain-link fence came into
view, surrounding some sort of compound. Parked out
front were a bunch of broken-down, rusted cars, along

with a couple of old turquoise school buses. Either Kyle was a connoisseur of modern art, or this was a nouveau junk barricade. A sign on the gate dubbed the place NEARLY PARADISE and instructed, HONK YOUR HORN FOR ENTRY.

I did as advised and beeped. It just goes to show that you shouldn't always obey orders. A Rottweiler raced toward me and proceeded to heave his body against the gate. The dog slobbered and snarled nearly as much as the grizzly this morning. Two hostile confrontations in less than four hours—this must be my lucky day.

"Retreat, Uzi! Retreat!" The command came from somewhere beyond the gate.

The four-legged brute growled and glared at me like a serial killer, promising that we'd meet again. Then the critter ambled off into an open doorway. Why did I never manage to meet little old ladies who had lap dogs, baked chocolate chip cookies, and offered me tea? I contemplated that for a couple of minutes as I waited for someone to come greet me.

Two men finally appeared outside. One was tall and distinguished, sporting a neatly groomed goatee. He was quite the natty dresser, decked out in a heavy gray overcoat, along with stylish black pants and shoes. Call me judgmental, but the guy didn't strike me as your typical militia member—except for the plastic cooler that he carried. It was just large enough to fit a couple of beers. He never so much as glanced my way, but got into a car and drove off deeper into the compound.

Only then did the second man acknowledge my existence with a wave of his hand. He slowly approached and unlocked the gate.

"I'd be much obliged if you'd leave your vehicle where it is."

I did as he requested and walked inside. The man turned to face me after he'd closed and locked the gate.

"The name's Rafe Lungren. I'm Kyle's father," he said and extended his hand. "I'm also the founder and head of the United Christian Patriots."

His grip was strong and firm. In his early fifties, the man had the look of a biblical patriarch. Along with a muscular build, he had a heavy brow, a long white beard, and fiery blue eyes. His hair was fashionably shaggy. Lungren kept hold of my hand as his gaze measured my own.

"It's a pleasure to meet you, Mr. Lungren. My name is Rachel Porter."

"I know who you are, gal. Kyle mentioned you'd be stopping by. And please call me Rafe. You won't make me feel like such an old geezer that way." He smiled and squeezed my hand before releasing it. The skin around his blue eyes crinkled benignly, transforming him into a cross between a middle-aged Kris Kringle and a New Age prophet.

"And how about if I call you Rachel? I'll bet you're young enough to be my daughter."

Boy, did this guy know how to flatter a gal. "Sure."

"Why don't you come and join me in my office for a minute?"

Uh-oh. And just when I'd begun to think Lungren might be a nice guy. He was probably about to feed me to his psychotic dog for dinner.

I followed Lungren into a room where Cujo Jr.

growled at me from inside a wire cage. Pulling back his lips, the dog bared his dingy yellow teeth.

Rafe nodded in the dog's direction. "That's Uzi. He thinks he's a big old meany. Doncha boy?"

"Uzi, like the weapon?" I inquired.

"That's right," Rafe confirmed. "Being that he's got the speed and strength of a semiautomatic rifle."

Uzi snarled, as if daring me to disagree.

"Don't mind him. He's all riled up at the moment 'cause his girlfriend's not around anymore. We've gotta find him a suitable new mate. Only the best for my buddy Uzi," Lungren cooed to the doggy demon. "He's gonna sire us a whole new super race of guard dogs."

"What happened to his old girlfriend?" I asked against my better judgment.

Lungren sadly shook his head. "It seems he got a little carried away with that rough sex stuff and inadvertently killed her. You can't blame him, though; he's just a passionate boy with active hormones. Uzi doesn't know his own strength."

I was tempted to tell Lungren *that* defense had already been tried and shot down in court.

He sat behind his desk and motioned for me to take a chair. I preferred not to turn my back on the canine lover boy.

"Thanks, but I'd rather stand. I've been sitting in my pickup all day."

Lungren gave an understanding nod. "Of course, darlin'. Suit yourself. So you're the new Fish and Wildlife agent in the area, huh?"

He placed his feet on the desk and linked his hands

behind his head, giving the distinct impression that I was about to be interrogated.

"Yes." I offered no other information.

"So tell me. How long you been here?"

"About a month."

Lungren opened a desk drawer and my hand instinctively shifted toward my gun. But he merely removed a box of Milk Bone dog biscuits and tossed a treat to Uzi. Wonder dog crunched it to smithereens in a nanosecond.

"Well, I don't know what you mighta heard about our group, but we believe in minding our own business and not making any trouble. Live and let live is our motto. The proof is that we're letting you visit our compound here today."

"I appreciate that," I replied with a gracious smile.

He twirled a second biscuit between his fingers, and I wondered if I was about to be rewarded for good behavior.

Instead, I decided to see just how far he'd let me go. "Since you apparently have nothing to hide, would you mind if I take a look around?"

"Course not, darlin'. Be my guest."

Good answer—especially since there was plenty of stuff to examine. Stacks of material were piled sky high in cardboard boxes that littered the room. There were even video cassettes strewn in a corner. The only question was where to begin.

"The place is kind of a mess at the moment. I apologize for that. Some day we'll finally get organized, but we're so damn busy that we just haven't had a chance. Merchandise is flying in and out of here faster than we're able to keep track of it. In fact, we're working on our computer system right now." Lungren gave me a wink. "Don't tell nobody, but I don't know one end of a computer from the other."

"Do you mean that this place operates as some sort of store?"

"Absolutely! We're known worldwide. Here, this'll give you an idea of what we do. The United Christian Patriots runs a damn fine business, both by mail order and over the Internet."

Lungren tossed me a catalogue entitled *God, Glory and Guerrilla Warfare*. A man stood posed on its cover with his face hidden behind a black ski mask. An automatic rifle was cradled in one of his arms and a similarly masked child in the other. Flipping through its pages, I spotted ads for an Israeli gas mask—*a one-time-only price of $18.95!*—as well as books that not only explained how to make bombs, but advocated attacks on federal buildings.

There were survival weapons and communications gear, along with videos and audiotapes on everything from becoming a successful sniper to setting booby traps. There were even bumper stickers that asked the burning question, "Have You Cleaned Your Weapon Today?" Over two hundred pages offered everything that the consumer-driven militia member could possibly want.

I thumbed back to the first page and read, *Our goal is to help YOU survive the coming race war, prepare for the Messiah, and arm yourself against the invasion of United Nations forces.*

"We kinda like to think of ourselves as a one-stop

shop. Those folks smart enough to prepare for the un-expected don't need to shop nowhere else. Someday we're even gonna offer a vaccine against biological warfare," Lungren bragged. "I don't mind saying that we have ourselves quite a booming business."

I had no doubt. A recent government study had identified over eight hundred and fifty hate and militia groups, boasting fifty thousand hardcore members. That didn't include another one hundred and fifty thousand sympathetic followers, all of whom spent a total of over $100 million a year on survival gear.

"It looks like you've got your own militia shopping mall here," I commented. It couldn't have been more of a propaganda outlet.

"Tell you what, darlin'. I'll be happy to give you a professional discount on anything that you might see that you want," Lungren generously offered.

"Thanks. I'll keep that in mind."

I wandered over to his desk, where a framed photo captured him squatting in the bed of a pickup with his arms wrapped around the necks of two dead mountain lions. Beneath Lungren's desk, a black bearskin was being used as a throw rug. Part of it must have flipped over when he rose from his chair. A pale section of exposed skin revealed a stain that encircled the bear's rear paw, much like the dingy ring around a bathtub.

"That's Smokey there under the desk. He screwed up during the last forest fire, so I decided to replace him," Lungren joked. "I like to catch me a bear every once in a while. Though only black bears, and I always do it perfectly legal, of course."

Of course. And it was interesting how he'd made certain to state that he didn't go after grizzlies.

"In fact, I got a picture of Kyle lying bare-assed on one of those rugs around here somewhere. But don't go getting your hopes up. It was taken a long time ago."

Darn. And here I'd been longing to catch a glimpse of Kyle's bony rear end. Kneeling down, I felt the hide. The fur was coarse and scraggly, indicating the bear had been killed in the spring, shortly after emerging from his den.

Lungren took note of my examination and smiled. "I got Smokey Jr. there just this past year. Figured I'd save him the trouble of waiting till the fall to get wasted."

I flipped the bearskin right-side down with my foot. Dead or alive, the critter deserved at least that much respect. Then I examined the posters on the walls. One bore an illustration of an M-60 machine gun mounted on a tractor and posed the question, *Whose Farm Are You Going to Repossess?*

The sign next to it was even more blatant. Big bold letters blared out the message, *God Has a Plan for Homosexuals—It's Called AIDS*.

"Interesting posters. Is their philosophy part of what makes this place nearly paradise for you?" I asked.

Rafe leaned against the desk and folded his arms across his chest, a Cheshire cat grin on his face. "Very clever, darlin'. I like that. But that's right, I haven't yet told you about our little piece of heaven that we call Nearly Paradise, have I?"

I wondered what there possibly was to say, other than that it was a neo-fascist compound cashing in on

the delusions of a bunch of paranoid wackos determined to escape an imaginary apocalypse.

"No, you haven't. Does the place have some sort of
interesting history to it?" I politely inquired.

Lungren's face took on a beatific glow, and his voice
grew solemn and low. "No, what we're involved in has
nothing to do with the past, but rather with a brave,
new future. We're developing a patriotic brotherhood
on one hundred acres of fine land that have been sub-
divided into twenty-five lots. Each is being sold at five
thousand dollars an acre to folks who think in a similar
manner to us."

"By that, I take it you mean people who don't believe
in paying income tax and refuse to register their
firearms?" I brazenly hazarded a guess.

Lungren smiled in amusement. "You're on the right
track, darlin'. It's for all those citizens tired of sending
their children to those cesspools called public schools,
and who disagree with Big Brother's plan to control
every single aspect of our lives."

Oookay. Now we were getting into creepy territory.

"Just imagine! Before long, this is going to be the
safest little community in America, with home school-
ing, underground shelters, a private shooting range,
and even our very own church. And let me tell you,
these lots are selling faster than hotcakes. Think you
might be interested?" Lungren teased.

I dodged the question. "So homes have already been
built, and families are moving in?"

"Hell, yes! Well . . . to be totally accurate, not yet.
People are still living in trailers at the moment, but
houses should be going up any day now."

The drone of a plane echoed off in the distance, its hum slowly fading away.

"It sounds as if you've got your hands full with quite an undertaking."

Lungren proudly smiled. "What say I walk you around the place and give you a quick look-see on our way over to Kyle's?"

"That would be great," I agreed.

"Excuse me, Mr. Big Shot! But the only place you're going is to the store. You were supposed to already have gone and been back an hour ago!"

I turned around and saw a forty-something woman with a dark, lacquered flip. It was easy to see that at one time she'd been quite a looker, though she was now a good thirty pounds overweight. Black liner meticulously rimmed her kelly-green eyes. Each eyelash was precisely coated with a thick layer of mascara, while dark red lipstick added the final touch to her hard-edged beauty. A huge diamond ring sat perched on the woman's finger, its three carats glowing brighter than a car's high beams.

"Sorry, sugar. I guess I just got busy and forgot about it. But it's a good thing that you're here; I want you to meet Rachel Porter, the new Fish and Wildlife agent. And this is my gorgeous wife, Honey Lungren." He slipped an arm around her shoulders and gave her a loving hug.

Honey sent an indifferent nod my way, accompanied by a royal wave of her hand. Naturally, it was the paw on which she wore the ring. "Yeah, nice to meet you."

Then she refocused her attention on her husband. "As for you, we're gonna need a bunch of glass jars if you plan to can all those vegetables you've got cooking on the stove. And how many times do I have to tell you that we're nearly out of propane?

"I can't do everything around here myself!" Her hands flew into the air, as if the very thought were enough to throw her into a tizzy. "It's not as if I'm Harriet freaking Nelson, you know. Besides, I've got my *own* career to think about!"

I held my breath, waiting to see whether Rafe would explode at her berating him in public. Instead he sheepishly grinned, as if he were a bad boy who'd been caught misbehaving.

"All right, Honey. Calm down, I admit it. I was hoping *you'd* go to the store, but I'll do it right now. The only thing is, I promised to show Rachel the layout for Nearly Paradise. After all, Kyle invited her out here. I think that letting her see the place would go a long way toward maintaining good relations. None of us wants another Waco or Ruby Ridge, now, do we?"

I dutifully shook my head no.

"I was gonna take her for a tour on the way over to Kyle's trailer. But since I have to head out, you won't mind doing that for me, will you, sweetheart?"

Honey smiled, making it clear she knew a secret that he didn't. "It would be fine with me, except for one little problem. That son of yours split like a bat out of hell about thirty minutes ago."

How interesting. That wasn't long after I'd called.

"What the hell is his problem, anyway? Kyle's always going and forgetting about his appointments," she complained.

"He's just one of those real entrepreneurial spirits, is

all," Lungren deftly covered for his son. "The boy's got a lot on his mind. Sorry about that, Rachel. But at least let Honey show you around the grounds. That way your trip won't be a total loss."

Honey remained silent, agreeing to nothing. She slowly began to twist the ring on her finger and Rafe nervously eyed the action, as if afraid she might take it off. I was clearly in the midst of a strange power game. I silently laid odds that Honey would wind up the winner.

"By the way, you're looking exceptionally lovely today, sugar pie," Rafe blatantly flattered his wife. "Seeing as how your birthday's coming up, maybe you'd like a pair of matching earrings to go with that ring. How's that sound?"

The ring twisting came to an immediate stop and a smile crossed Honey's face. She leaned over and allowed Lungren to plant an affectionate buss on her cheek. He couldn't have appeared to be any more relieved.

"My wife here is very modest, so I'm going to let you in on a little secret. The idea for Nearly Paradise was all hers. It came to Honey one night while she was asleep."

"Actually, I can't take *all* the credit. It was Archangel Michael who gave me the idea. He's not only my spiritual guide, but also my adviser on more mundane matters," she loftily confided.

Evidently the Archangel was fairly savvy when it came to conjuring up real estate deals.

"Here's another thing you might not realize, what with being new around here, but Honey's a real celebrity in these parts. She's got her own biweekly radio show called *The Coming Storm*. We need a fence around this place just to keep all her fans out," Lungren proudly crowed. "Isn't that right, sugar?"

I tried to imagine a bunch of rabid admirers attempting to storm the gate while Uzi vigilantly stood guard.

Honey made a disdainful face, but it was clear that she reveled in the attention. "Yeah—well, it's a lot of work, I can tell you that. On top of which, I'm supposed to help run our mail-order business. It's a wonder I get anything done at all."

I silently thanked Archangel Michael for having just shown me the light for ensuring Honey's cooperation.

"I can only imagine how difficult it must be for you," I commiserated. "I used to work as an actress back in New York, and I don't think *I* could have pulled off doing two radio shows a week. People just don't know how rough that is. Not only do you have the pressure of trying to book interesting guests, but then there's all that time spent doing homework in order to conduct decent interviews."

Honey turned to me as though she'd unexpectedly discovered a kindred spirit. "Absolutely! That's something nobody around here is able to comprehend. A lot of responsibility comes with being a celebrity. Just look at what it did to poor Kathie Lee! We have to give a little piece of ourselves to each and every one of our fans to keep them all happy. It takes a real toll on our lives, physically, emotionally and spiritually. But try to make *him* understand that!"

We both stared at Rafe, who glanced down at his feet.

"Well, I better be heading off to the store now. You girls have yourselves a good time. And try to behave." He winked as he left.

"Don't worry about us. Just get those things I need!" Honey reprimanded.

As Rafe walked away his step held the bounce of a happy man, and I felt vaguely suspicious that he was grinning. Relationships—I'd never understand them. No wonder I was still single. Uzi added his opinion to the mix, letting loose a growl.

"As for you, I've had enough of your shenanigans!" Honey warned the pooch, throwing a withering glare his way.

Uzi instantly lay down in his cage.

"So what kind of acting did you do, anyway?" she asked, linking her arm in mine.

We were suddenly the best of friends.

"I did some commercials and was on a soap opera for a while."

Honey let out a high-pitched screech. "Oh my God! You're kidding! Which one?"

"*All My Children*. I played a reporter."

"*That's my very favorite soap in the whole wide world!*" she swooned. "I always thought that I had what it took to make it as an actress. I just never gave myself a real chance."

"But you have your own radio show. I'd say that's pretty impressive. And it sounds like you've got quite a following."

Honey sighed. "Yeah, but it isn't exactly New York."

"Maybe so. But nobody knows who *I* am. You're famous around here," I added, laying it on thick.

Honey pursed her lips. "I guess it *is* better being a someone than a has been," she agreed.

Uzi clearly wasn't the only one around here with sharp teeth.

Honey pulled a couple of pieces of comfort candy from her pocket and handed me a Hershey's Kiss. I'm such a chocolate slut, it was enough to make me temporarily forgive her.

"Tell me about your radio show," I prompted. "*The Coming Storm* sounds rather ominous. What kind of topics do you discuss?"

"Well, of course it's all about how this country is going to hell in a hand basket, what with all the coloreds and Indians demanding special privileges. Then I try to uncover the truth for my listeners about such things as what *really* happened at Waco. You *do* know about that, don't you?"

"Know what?" I asked warily.

"How the government deliberately executed those people, just because the Branch Davidians discovered Washington's secret plan to dismantle the Constitution."

Hmm. I guess I must have missed the news that particular day.

"The same with Oklahoma City. That's all a big lie. Timothy McVeigh never bombed any federal building; it was done by members of foreign intelligence agencies within the FBI. Why? To discredit the militia movement, of course. Just turn the letters of the FBI around and what do you get? The word FIB!"

I kept my mouth shut as we walked outside.

"People used to think I was crazy, but now even the

local politicians listen to my show. You wait and see: a second American Revolution is on the way. Thank God for Charlton Heston, is all I can say!"

She seemed ready to kick ass with anyone who disagreed.

We went past tar paper shacks and tin-roofed motor homes where a couple of signs had been thrust into the dirt. One read, FUTURE HOME OF THE BROTHERHOOD CHURCH while the other announced, SOON TO BE BUILT— ARMAGEDDON SHELTERS! So far, this place resembled a trashy trailer park more than a high-end housing development.

Honey abruptly stopped and turned to face me, standing so close that I wondered if I was about to be kissed. "Listen, I know you work for the government and all, but you seem like an intelligent person. So, let me ask you a question. Do you know what the most endangered species in this country of ours really is?"

I shook my head no, always willing to listen and learn.

"Well then, I'm going to tell you right here and now that it's not any damn wolf, or mangy bear, or lamb-eating bald eagle. It's the white Anglo-Saxon male!"

It took all my strength to keep a straight face. While that might be true in China, only the freshly falling flakes of snow were whiter than most of the people in Montana. A standing redneck joke was that there were never more than two black people in the state at any one time—one of whom was always in jail, while the other was just passing through. Maybe Honey Lungren was seriously unhinged.

"Just think about it. We have a civic duty to protect

our menfolk. The last thing we need is any more racial impurity in this state."

I wondered if this was the right moment to spring the fact that I was Jewish on her.

"My radio program airs every Tuesday and Thursday night at nine. You'll just love the little ditty that I use to open and close the show. I lifted it from another radio station; it's just too damn good not to use. The song is called 'Hang the Suckers High,' and warns all those elected traitors in Congress that they better stop voting against gun control. Otherwise they'll soon find themselves with their toes atwitchin', hanging from the end of a rope. It's got one hell of a catchy little tune!"

Maybe I'd save the news about my ethnic background for a more appropriate time—when I wasn't standing next to a woman whose beliefs fell to the right of Hitler. My plan of action for now was a quick change of subject and not to stop moving.

"You must have married Rafe when you were very young. You don't look old enough to be Kyle's mother." I guessed that flattery would keep her talking.

"That's 'cause I'm not. I'm his stepmother. His actual mama up and left him and Rafe years ago, when the boy was still in school. She was one of those real cheap types." Honey's lips curled up in distaste. "She took up with some low-life Indian, but don't ever let Rafe know that I told you so. It's a black mark that he's worked hard to put behind him. Unfortunately, the boy's got some of his mother's blood; he's attracted to trash, too."

"What do you mean?"

Honey shook her head in annoyance, and her hair

swayed, its flip remaining perfectly in place. "It's that girlfriend of his—some piece of garbage who calls herself Cherry Jubilee. She goes strutting around on top of bars, wearing next to nothing. If Kyle wants to have himself a whore, he should just pay for one every now and then and do it discreetly. Instead, he has the nerve to bring her here to our home. He's even moved her into his trailer! What kind of respect does that show for me and his daddy, I ask you?"

Honey's face contorted into a tight mask of rage. Full red lips protruded in an indignant pout, and her fists impotently beat at the air like two withered wings.

"That bitch makes me so damn mad! She knows I don't want her here, so now she's trying to win Rafe over to her side. What she doesn't know is that I've got final say about everything that goes on here at Nearly Paradise." Honey emitted an audible harrumph. "Since I'm a local celebrity, there's my reputation to consider. I'm not going to have it tarnished by that two-bit slut. It's just a good thing that Kyle isn't in charge. He'd most likely change the name of this place to Nearly Naked, or Nearly Nookie!"

This seemed a good time for another change of topic.

"It sounds as if Nearly Paradise is going to be quite a project. Your husband mentioned that the lots have been selling exceptionally well. How many do you have left?"

Honey removed an undisciplined lock of hair from her forehead and firmly patted it back in place. "Just give me a moment to contain myself." She took a deep breath and slowly exhaled. "Only five lots remain, and

I can tell you it's because people recognize quality when they see it."

She waved her hand imperiously at the run-down trailers that were scattered about. "It's true that we still have a long way to go, but everything takes time and money. At least people know that once they move behind our walls, they can kick back and relax. They're finally safe."

I wondered how many residents had begun to reassess that assumption after having spent some quality time with the Lungren dynasty.

"We're quite a little family here. In addition, everyone gets a jar of my butter pickles, dilly beans, and sweet 'n' sour beets when they buy a lot—though I've already warned Rafe that this is the last year I'm going to do it. But we've got so much of that crap stockpiled in our cellar that I'll give you a few jars before you leave."

Lucky me. Dilly beans. Just what I'd always wanted.

I nonchalantly gazed around, and spied a windsock off in the distance. A breeze had filled the fabric and magically brought it to life. The sock giddily waved and I saw that it marked a nearly imperceptible dirt runway. Parked next to the airstrip was the car that I'd spotted while waiting outside, but the man who'd driven it had disappeared. Then I remembered the droning sound that I'd heard. It had obviously been a plane taking off.

"Is that an airstrip over there?" I asked, pointing toward the windsock.

"What?" Honey didn't so much as look in its direction.

"The airstrip—does it belong to Nearly Paradise?" I repeated.

"Oh yeah," was the only information that she offered.

"Do you have your own airplane?" I asked, surprised.

"Uh-huh. It comes as part of the package when a new member joins our community. We guarantee that we'll fly them back here to safety, no matter where they are in the world when all hell breaks loose."

Somehow I couldn't imagine the Lungren trio risking life and limb to do that.

"I heard a plane departing earlier."

"Sure. We have supplies being flown in and out of here all the time for our mail-order business," she said dismissively.

Rafe clearly hadn't been lying when he'd said business was booming. Who'd have guessed such a little-known group would be so well financed? The year 2000 had come and gone without any nuclear wars, worldwide power outages, or invasions by alien spaceships. Surely that must have cut into their business.

"Out of curiosity, wasn't Armageddon supposed to have taken place with Y2K?" I ventured.

Honey bestowed a condescending smile upon my ignorance. "It's just a little late, is all. But it's still on the way. The time is nearly upon us when free white Christian men and women will be called upon to take up arms in a racial holy war. Even now a dark cloud is looming on the horizon, just waiting for Judgment Day. I take comfort in the words of wisdom that Commander Samuel Sherwood, of the U.S. Militia Association, recently said to his followers: *Go and look your legislator in the face, because you may be forced to blow it off one day!*"

My blood ran cold. Clearly, Honey Lungren wasn't someone to be toyed with.

"Insurrection and violence—that's a lethal combination. I'd hate to think what might happen if Nearly Paradise were to turn itself into an armed camp," I softly warned.

"Our traitor government has already made that decision for us," Honey coolly responded. "It won't be long before those in power try to implant bar code identification chips in our hands."

Honey Lungren's features turned hard and her voice dropped to a low, menacing whisper. "What will you do when they demand that *you* accept the Mark of the Beast?"

The question hung in the air like a hangman's noose. The sudden ringing of my cell phone saved me from having to answer. Plucking it off my belt, my fingers clung to the phone's hard, slim surface as though it were a life preserver.

"Excuse me, but I really have to take this call."

Honey Lungren shot me a strange look and then walked back in the direction from which we'd come. I had little time to ponder what *that* was all about as I answered the phone.

"Hello?"

"Hey, Big Apple babe! Is that you?"

I instantly recognized the caller: Rory Calhoun.

"You still up in these parts, or did you already hightail it back down to Missoula?"

"No, I'm still here."

"Good! Come by and have breakfast with me tomorrow morning. It's boring as hell in this place," the high-pitched voice complained.

Amazing! Who did this guy think I was, his own personal baby-sitter?

"Sorry, but I really don't have the time for social visits."

"Oh come on! Don't be a spoil sport," he wheedled. "I'm talking bagels and lox. Think of it as kind of welcome-to-the-land-of-log-cabin-wackos-waiting-for-the-Apocalypse-to-arrive celebration."

I immediately became suspicious. How in the hell did *he* know where I was?

"There'll also be a little creamed herring, along with some sturgeon and whitefish. I'm even getting real cream cheese—none of that low-calorie crap!"

On the other hand, I'd been dreaming about having good deli ever since landing in Montana. "I didn't think anyone north of Missoula knew what lox *was*, much less sold it."

"They don't. I'm having it flown in special from New York. This is a real blow-out I'm planning here. You're not gonna be crazy enough to pass it up, are you? Besides, trust me: you could use a friend in the area. The locals don't exactly cotton to strangers—no matter what they may have led you to believe."

Rory probably had a point. Not to mention that he'd cleverly tapped into one of my major weaknesses. All he had to do next was tempt me with good Chinese food, and I'd seriously consider making *him* my new landlord. More importantly he'd aroused my curiosity. This guy was definitely selling something more than just hot tubs, and I intended to find out what that might be.

"And what exactly do you get out of this?" I questioned.

"Someone who doesn't think it's normal to talk to cows," he joked.

"What time should I come by?"

"Let's keep it civilized. Whadda ya say to ten o'clock? That way I can still get my beauty sleep."

I was inclined to tell him to worry more about upgrading his image. He could start by ditching the polyester tie-dye shirt and Davy Crockett cap. But I practiced restraint by keeping my mouth shut as I took down directions.

Then I retraced my steps to the United Christian Patriots' ramshackle headquarters. I found Honey impatiently waiting inside with a jar of dilly beans and a tee-shirt in her hands.

"I have to get back to work now. Besides, I believe you've seen enough of Nearly Paradise. Here are some souvenirs to remember your visit by." She thrust the items at me. "I don't know what Rafe did or didn't tell you, but this was a one time look-see. So don't plan on stopping here again."

Gee, and here I'd thought we'd bonded as showbiz sisters. What had caused her sudden change of heart? Then I realized Honey must have spotted the Star of David hanging around my neck. I wore it along with a St. Christopher medal that I'd been given by a former friend in Nevada, as a way of covering all my bases. He had said that in my line of work, I needed all the help I could get. My hand instinctively edged toward the necklace, and Honey countered with a sneer. My arm dropped to my side and the tee-shirt fell onto the floor to reveal its logo: *Eliminate All Mud People*.

I placed the jar of dilly beans on Lungren's desk, leaving the shirt where it lay. "Thanks, but I don't accept gifts."

Uzi snarled as I turned to leave, and I looked back to see that Honey's hand was resting on the latch of his cage. I made no effort to hide the fact that my own fingers wrapped around the butt of my .38.

"I don't think you want to try anything stupid," I warned. If Honey thought she was going to scare me with her little bluff, I had a grizzly I'd like her to meet.

Honey's sneer shriveled and I walked out the door, where I discovered there was also a sign on this side of the gate.

PERMISSION MUST BE GRANTED TO EXIT!

Picking up a rock, I broke the flimsy lock. It was definitely time to head home and call it a day.

Ten

I pointed the Ford toward Sally's, letting my mind drift. Though I knew prejudice came in all shapes and sizes, it still surprised me no matter how well prepared I tried to be.

I thrust Honey Lungren temporarily from my thoughts by focusing on Montana's panoramic scenery, which worked its usual magic in no time at all. While I'd heard that sherbet is dandy for cleansing one's palate, it takes a dose of nature to cleanse your soul.

The newly fallen snow clung to the crevices of the Rocky Mountain Front like an intricate Spanish mantilla, adding subtle dimensions to its cliffs and peaks. One ragged summit morphed into the pearly head of a bald eagle, while another took on the visage of an enigmatic sphinx. I couldn't help but wonder how many grizzlies had already settled down for their long winter sleep, and if today's bear was the last I'd have to confront until spring.

You're not frightened, are you? taunted my ever-present demon. *You can't hide, no matter how hard you try. Run, and I'll always find you. There's no denying what you're afraid of—facing your own mortality.*

I pressed down hard on the gas pedal and sped away.

The late afternoon sun chased after me as thoughts of Matthew Running began to drift through my mind. He slid into my consciousness as effortlessly as he walked upon the land.

I found myself daydreaming about the man, and how I'd so willingly placed myself in his hands. The adrenaline rush afterward had been totally intoxicating. It was that erotic mix of flirting with danger and giving up control that was so highly seductive. Even now, I could feel myself tingling as I relived the bear attack—first visualizing it in fast forward and then in tantalizing slow motion. Finally, there had been Matthew Running wrapping his arms around me.

And that was a once-in-a-lifetime experience that would never happen again.

My reaction to Running was as irritating as an inexplicable itch. I'd been back together with Jake Santou for six months now. Granted, it was a long-distance relationship, but Santou was the man I'd been pining after for years. How could I suddenly be attracted to someone else?

I decided to bypass Browning; it could prove far too tempting to stop by Matthew's office on some lame excuse. Instead, I veered onto a back road and drove north past fields of prairie grass, tall and stiff as bristles, their wiry tips shimmering like the frosted hairs on a grizzly's back.

All was still, including my thoughts, when a sudden movement captured my attention. Glimmering in the sun was a figure that dipped and swayed like a marionette that had broken loose of its strings. I focused my gaze and scanned the area until I once again spotted

the phantom. There it was! A slender form staggered
out among the prairie grass, performing a delicate balancing act.

I brought my vehicle to a halt and lowered the window. "Are you all right?" I called out.

The figure continued to spiral and swoon. It was that
of a young girl, whose hair cascaded down her back
like a jet-black waterfall. A gray sweater and navy skirt
covered her frail limbs.

"Can you hear me?" I hollered once more.

This time the girl stopped and seemed to gaze in my
direction. Then her legs gave way and she crumpled to
the ground like a paper doll. I flung open the door and
ran to her aid, snow crunching beneath my boots.

It took less than a minute to reach the spot where the
girl lay as still as a fallen sparrow. I hooked my hands
under her arms and pulled the child to her feet. She
couldn't have weighed more than eighty pounds, and
appeared to be about twelve years old.

A steady growl filled the air, causing a flurry of shiv-
ers to rain down upon my skin. The sound was that of
a vehicle's engine, and I looked up in time to catch a
lime-green Jeep Cherokee prowling the road.

A gaunt visage stared out from behind the Cherokee's windshield. Even from this distance, there could
be no mistaking the drawn face, the hollow eyes and
sickly gray pallor. Doc Hutchins, the man I'd bumped
into at the Red Crow Café this very morning.

The vehicle continued to slowly cruise past, observing
us as though the girl and I were participants in some
strange sort of experiment. I struggled to hold the child
up with one arm and frantically wave with the other, but

the good doctor promptly sped up and took off. My eyes followed in disbelief, catching sight of the bumper sticker on his rear fender. "Look Busy! Jesus Is Coming!"

Doc Hutchins was doing a fair imitation of just that as he burned rubber and swung a hard left. The Jeep connected with the blacktop and headed south, out of the reservation.

I sincerely doubted that Doc Hutchins was running off to get more help, so I half-carried, half-dragged the girl to my vehicle. Once there, I pushed her up into the passenger seat and buckled her in. I didn't have to think twice about where to go; Sally's house was just down the road.

The sculpted bears gazed curiously as I sped by, not stopping until I'd reached the house. Their inquisitiveness was further heightened as I beeped the horn and Sally came running out.

"What's going on?" she asked, peering in at the girl.

"I found her in the field south of here. She was staggering and suddenly collapsed. Can I bring her inside?"

"Of course," Sally said briskly. "Here, let me help you carry her."

We transported her into the living room and placed her on the couch. Her skin was cold to the touch and her body shivered, as if in a state of shock.

"Dear God, what was this child thinking? How could she wander about in weather like this wearing nothing but a sweater?" Sally muttered.

Though neither of us chose to verbalize it, another question hung heavy in the air. *Doesn't she realize that she could have met up with a hungry bear?*

The girl's wan face floated like a disembodied ghost above her pillow of dark hair.

"Do you have any idea who she might be?"

Sally stared at the child before finally shaking her head. "No, but we'll find out soon enough. The important thing right now is to cover her in blankets and get some hot tea into her."

Sally bustled into the kitchen to put on the kettle, and I wrapped the shivering girl in layer upon layer of bright wool blankets. When I finished, a pair of frightened brown eyes had opened to greet me.

"Good. You're awake." I flashed a reassuring smile as Sally entered the room with a mug of tea. "Don't worry. You're safe."

"Prop her head up, Rachel," Sally instructed, and sternly looked at the girl. "Now, I don't want any argument. Just drink this down. It's herbal tea that's good for you."

The girl docilely did as instructed. My guess was that she'd probably have drunk a cup of mud, rather than face the wrath of the female drill sergeant who loomed before her.

"How do you feel now?" Sally questioned.

"Better," the child mumbled and almost instantly fell back asleep.

Part of me wondered if this was a clever ploy on the child's part to escape Sally's brusqueness. Had I thought of it, I might have been tempted to try the same tactic during *our* initial meeting. The surprising thing was how patient and tender Sally could be when it came to caring for wildlife. Too bad it didn't seem to carry over when it came to people.

I headed for the phone. "I'm going to call the tribal police and report that I found this girl. Her parents must realize that she's missing by now and are probably frantic."

As I turned to pick up the receiver, I caught sight of Sally's hand lightly hovering above the girl's head. I pretended not to notice as she softly began to stroke the dark mass of hair. Apparently Sally wasn't as tough as she liked to pretend. Perhaps it had something to do with the loss of her son. We both seemed to be dealing with a confusing jumble of emotions at the moment.

Just then Matthew Running came through the front door with Custer bounding behind him. His appearance caught me by surprise and my heart began to flicker. Damn it! I could have better prepared myself, if I'd had some warning of his arrival. As it was, I took one look at those predaceous eyes and knew I was in big trouble. I no longer wanted to pull away from their gaze, but allowed myself to sink inside them a little deeper. In turn, his eyes proceeded to swallow me whole.

Then I remembered the unknown girl who was quietly sleeping behind me. Running seemed to sense that something was amiss, and his demeanor instantly altered. The lines around his mouth grew more pronounced, and his movements were no longer fluid, but punctuated and sharp.

"What's happened?"

His voice sounded so taut that I could have trampolined off it and touched the sky.

"Rachel found a girl in a nearby field, who apparently became ill and fainted," Sally answered his question. "I've given her some tea and she's resting, but I have absolutely no idea as to who she is. Rachel was just about to call the tribal police and notify them."

"Hold off on that a second," Matthew said, and strode past me.

His hand brushed against mine and a jolt of electricity shot through my body. I instinctively knew that Running had felt the same thing.

"Why, this is Elizabeth Come-By-Night," he said in surprise. "You remember Bearhead? Well, that's his daughter."

"Lord help us. We don't need *him* getting upset." Sally raised a wary eyebrow in my direction.

I gave a slight nod, signaling that I knew perfectly well what she was talking about.

"I wonder what Elizabeth was doing all the way over here? This is a good distance from her home," Matthew said.

"Maybe she heard that I had birds and wanted to see them. Oh, dear, you don't suppose she found out about the cubs, do you?" Sally suggested.

"I sure as hell hope not. I don't think Bearhead would take too kindly to that."

Just then the girl stirred. Matthew knelt down and gently picked up her hand.

"Hey there, Elizabeth. A little birdie told me that they found you outside taking a nap. What are you doing so far from home? Did you walk over here for any special reason?"

But the child simply blinked and mutely stared at him.

"I know! You must have been trying to pick flowers

out in the snow. Or maybe you were being chased by a big snowman with a carrot for a nose?" Matthew teased.

The girl shyly shook her head, and then her eyes filled with tears. "No, nothing like that. You aren't going to punish me, are you?"

"Of course not." Matthew lightly tickled the girl. "Don't be silly. Why would I do that?"

"Because I wandered away when I wasn't supposed to," the girl whispered and buried her face in his chest.

Running responded by giving her a hug.

"I want to go home now," Elizabeth said, her voice muffled within the folds of his jacket. Custer joined in by licking her hand and the girl couldn't help but giggle.

"I think that can be arranged." Matthew picked her up in his arms and held the child as if she were his own. "How about if this pretty lady comes with us? Would that be all right, Elizabeth?" he asked and motioned toward me.

"I'm afraid *this* pretty lady is busy right now," Sally teased. "But I've got an idea: why don't you take Rachel with you, instead? Then the two of you can come back here and join me for dinner."

Matthew grinned at me, and I felt myself beginning to fall under his spell again. Even worse, I was growing to like it.

"Sure. I guess I can deal with Rachel as a substitute. Dinner sounds good, too. You know me when it comes to cooking."

"Only too well," Sally replied. "The one time he tried, I nearly ended up needing a new kitchen."

It seemed Running and I had something in common. As far as I was concerned, a kitchen was good for only two things—keeping beer cold and microwaving popcorn.

We drove off in Running's pickup with Elizabeth squeezed between us, and Custer riding shotgun in the cargo bay. The field flashed by where I'd found the girl. It looked no different than it had earlier. Elizabeth grew weary and rested her head against my arm as we sped down the road. In no time at all, she was once again asleep.

Matthew glanced over at the child and a bittersweet smile tugged at his lips. "She was lucky that you came by when you did. Otherwise, who knows what might have happened."

"I'm sure she would have been fine," I automatically responded.

"You couldn't be more wrong. Elizabeth, and all the others like her, will never be fine on this rez. Not as long as conditions stay as they are and don't improve. Wait till you see where she lives. Maybe then you'll understand that the plight of the Indian is the same as that of the grizzly. We're both just a heartbeat away from extinction."

We drove past windswept hills to the turnoff for a subdivision that was the size of a flea on the landscape. Its two short streets were dotted with tar paper shacks whose roofs were so poorly nailed on that they had to be held down by worn-out tires. The few people outside barely moved, but sat and stared vacantly off into the distance. Even dogs refused to roam these streets, preferring to hang out in Browning.

We parked in front of a dilapidated hovel like all the others, and Matthew scooped up the child in his arms.

"Come and say hello to a friend of yours." He grinned.

What a perfect way to end a fun-filled day—sparring a few rounds with Bearhead.

Running placed the girl on her feet as I knocked on a flimsy door that was immediately flung open. Bearhead looked like a man half crazed with grief. His eyes were red and his hair was a certified disaster area. It stood straight out, as though he'd been tugging on its ends. His gaze flew from me to Matthew, finally coming to rest on the child by our side. Only then did he exhale a deep, primal moan of relief. Bearhead grabbed his daughter and held her tight. That lasted for all of five seconds before he morphed into a raging madman.

"Just what in the hell have you been doing with my daughter?" he angrily demanded, shaking a clenched fist in my face.

"Excuse me, but I believe the question should be, why didn't *you* know where she was?" I retorted irritably.

"Whoa! Hold on there a second!" Matthew stepped between us, taking on the role of referee. "You want to thank Rachel instead of threatening her, Bearhead. She's the one who found Elizabeth and made sure that your daughter was safe."

Bearhead reluctantly lowered his huge paw and slowly shuffled his feet, keeping one enormous arm wrapped around the girl's shoulders. "Elizabeth was in trouble and you helped her?"

I consciously lowered my own killer hormone level

a good couple of notches. "She must not have been feeling well. I spotted her just as she fainted out in a field."

Bearhead took an embarrassed swat at his nose. "In that case, I guess my friend here is right. I owe you an apology."

He motioned for us to enter. The interior of his house proved to be just as run-down as its exterior. A few threadbare pieces of furniture were scattered about a living room whose warped wooden floor was nearly as pitted as Bearhead's face.

"Take a seat." He gestured awkwardly.

The metal folding chair squeaked protestingly beneath me. Elizabeth ran to pick up a raggedy Barbie doll as Bearhead protectively watched her every move.

"What happened?" he asked, once the girl was safely seated on the floor.

Matthew gave a noncommittal shrug. "We're not really sure. Elizabeth hasn't told us anything yet."

"Elizabeth, come over here." Bearhead's voice was stern, but the hint of a quiver betrayed his true emotion.

"Can I bring my doll?"

"Yes, Barbie can come, too. I want to talk to you."

Elizabeth looked like a tiny doll herself as she settled into the hulking man's lap.

"You had an appointment to see the doctor today after school. Did you go to the clinic like you were supposed to?"

Elizabeth nodded and began to restyle Barbie's hair.

"Are you talking about Dr. Hutchins?" I asked in surprise.

"Yes. She gets a physical once a year, the same as the

rest of the children on the rez. Why? Do you know him?"

"Only by sight." Strange. If Doc Hutchins was so interested in Elizabeth's health, then why hadn't he stopped to help?

Elizabeth pretended to give Barbie a shot. "That's what Dr. Hutchins did while I was there."

I looked over at Bearhead.

"The children all get shots this time of year to protect against the flu," he said.

"But I didn't feel so good afterward," Elizabeth confided.

Bearhead pulled a rubber band from his pocket and wrapped the child's hair up in a ponytail. "You didn't feel well, huh? And what did they give you for lunch at school?"

"Split pea soup and a bologna sandwich."

"Did you eat it?"

Elizabeth didn't respond, but continued to play with her Barbie doll.

Bearhead grunted and lifted the child off his lap. "Just as I suspected. She won't eat lunch if she doesn't like the food they serve. No wonder she fainted. It's hard to get her to eat, anyway. Look at how thin she is, and she's always trying to diet. It's all because of that Britney Spears singer. The one who's in those teen magazines. Elizabeth wants to look just like her—some scrawny white girl!"

Funny, but I could identify with that. Even Bob Dole and his dog seemed to like her.

Matthew stood up, signaling it was time to leave, and Bearhead walked us to the door.

"I want to thank you again," he grudgingly said, looming above me. "I don't know what I'd do if anything happened to my little girl, after losing her mother and my brother. I'm always worrying that some goddamn grizzly is going to try and snatch her away from me. Especially with what's been going on around here lately."

"You can't really believe that everyone who disappears on the rez has been eaten by a grizzly." Blaming everything on the bears seemed to have become an awfully convenient excuse.

"I sure as hell can," Bearhead irritably growled.

Call me a cock-eyed optimist, but I gave the critters credit for having more sense. As far as I was concerned, Bearhead had his priorities all screwy. There'd been no grizzly chasing after the girl. In addition, I didn't believe that she'd fainted from a lack of food. A more likely probability was that Elizabeth had fallen prey to narcotics. I suspected it was drug dealers rather than bears that he should have been targeting.

I kept my mouth shut until I got into Running's pickup.

"So, what's the deal with Bearhead's wife and brother? Do you also believe that they were eaten by big, bad bears?"

Matthew gave one of his noncommittal shrugs. "Who knows? His wife vanished about a year ago. Some say she ran off with another man and that Bearhead just won't admit it, preferring to believe that she's dead. As for his brother, the stories run the gamut. Some say he was killed in a hunting accident, while others swear he committed suicide by sticking a gun in his mouth and eating a bullet. Then again, there's always your phantom man-eating bear. Feel free to take your pick."

"The FBI seems to be awfully casual about all this."

"As I said before, they're pretty busy."

"Well, there's something that I haven't yet told *you* yet."

Though Running's head never moved, his almond-shaped eyes slid toward me like those of a wolf. "Oh yeah? What's that?"

I decided to play it "Indian style" and remained silent until I thought I would burst. "Hutchins drove by while I was out in the field with Elizabeth. I tried to flag him down, and he definitely saw us. But rather than stopping, he took off."

Matthew's expression remained maddeningly inscrutable. "So what are you getting at?"

Jeez! What did I have to do? Spell it out for the guy? "Elizabeth had just been to see him. Don't you find that to be odd?"

"Give yourself some credit. You look like a capable woman. Maybe he had to rush off on an emergency and figured you could handle a hungry twelve-year-old girl all by yourself."

"Oh, come on! Is that the best you can do?" I needled.

"If you're so smart, what's *your* theory, Miss High-and-mighty federal agent?"

I had to fight to keep the grin off my face. If he was trying to insult me, he'd have to do a whole lot better.

"You said yourself that there's a big drug problem here on the rez. Well, just think about it. Who has exceptionally easy access to narcotics?"

This time, Matthew turned his head and stared at me before bursting into laughter. "Doc Hutchins as a drug peddler? You've got to be kidding! He's scared of his own shadow. Just take a good look at the guy."

I bristled. "Okay. Then you tell me, why else he would run from the scene unless he were guilty of something?"

Running quickly sobered up. "Sorry, Rachel, I don't mean to poke fun. But you're dead wrong on this one. I know it in my gut. It's true that Doc Hutchins is a bit strange, but that doesn't make him a drug dealer, a pedophile, or a serial rapist."

We rode the rest of the way in silence. By the time we reached Sally's house, the moon had risen fat and round. I jumped out of the pickup and took the porch steps two at a time, only to abruptly stop, instinctively aware that Running wasn't following behind. My heart dropped, and I slowly turned to look at the man. His eyes intently studied me from where he sat in the cab of his truck, as still as a ghost in the moonlight.

An emotional cord had emerged, stretching tautly between us. It began to reel me in ever so slowly, and I allowed myself to be pulled back toward the pickup by its invisible force. I didn't stop until my arms came to rest on the driver's side window, where Matthew brought his face tantalizingly close to mine.

"I'm going to take off now. Would you mind telling Sally that I decided to skip dinner? I think we should call it a night."

"Why?" I asked, before I could stop myself.

"Because I need to take a step back in order to see

things more clearly. To do that, I have to be alone for a while."

I wondered what he was talking about—Doc Hutchins, the grizzlies, or me?

"All right."

I turned to walk inside, only to feel the touch of his hand on my arm. For a moment, I wasn't quite certain what was going on. All I knew was that my heart began to race. Then he reached out and drew me toward him. Our lips touched, and everything came to a stop. Nothing else in the world mattered—until Santou invaded my thoughts.

Only the sculpted bears bore silent witness to my indiscretion as I jerked away and raced up the steps. I don't know what frightened me more—that I'd wanted it to happen, or that I had enjoyed his kiss even more than I could have imagined. All I knew was that I had to temporarily escape the spell of the moon, the stars, and, most of all, Matthew Running.

Sally turned in surprise as I bolted inside and shut the door.

"Is something wrong? And for heaven's sake, where's Matthew?"

The blood raced to my face in blatant betrayal. Goddammit! Why did I have to be born a redhead?

Sally had eyes as sharp as her hawks', and a keen sense of cunning to match. Hal fully believed the woman to be psychic. I played with that thought as she continued to observe me. Who were we kidding? My Jewish sense of guilt was what made me so damn easy to read.

Sally poured two large glasses of wine and led me over to the fireplace. We drank in silence for a while, kept company by her personal galaxy of stars. Only when the silence became nearly unbearable did she put down her glass and turn toward me.

"Is it the fact that Matthew's half Indian that bothers you?"

"Of course not!" If anything, that was part of the attraction. I always found the lure of the unknown to be enticingly seductive.

"All right then. What's the problem?"

I looked at the woman sitting next to me and knew I could tell her just about anything.

"I'm already involved with someone else."

Sally threw back her head and a stream of laughter trilled from her lips. "Is *that* what's bothering you?"

"Well, yeah! Along with a few other piddling things like loyalty, honesty and trust," I countered, playing the good defensive linebacker.

Sally propped her elbows on her knees, rested her chin in her hands, and focused her baby blues on me. "If that's the case, then tell me about this man of yours."

I took a deep breath and opened the floodgates.

"His name is Jake Santou. He's based in New Orleans, is involved in law enforcement, and does a lot of undercover work. That's why we haven't seen very much of each other lately."

"And?"

"He drinks too much, smokes too much, and used to have a drug problem. We've had our share of trouble and the man can drive me absolutely nuts. But I love him."

"Mmm. Then what about Matthew?"

Running's image popped into my mind, along with those maddening eyes of his that could so easily see clear to my soul. "I've never met anyone quite like him."

"That's because there's no one else in the world who is. I told you that he served in Desert Storm, but I didn't mention that he trained as part of an elite military team. Matt was second-in-command of a highly specialized unit sent deep behind enemy lines to gather intelligence. He's someone who blends in so well, you don't even know that he's there. What makes Matt unique is that he possesses a special talent for reading people's hearts and their thoughts."

"Was your son in the same unit?"

Sally took a sip of wine and nodded. "He would have followed Matthew to hell and back. He began the journey with him. He just never made it home."

I wondered if she ever questioned why Running had survived in place of her son.

"I spotted a miniature sandbox in Matthew's office. It held two dog tags, a grizzly claw and a gold wedding band. Any idea why he has them in there?" Though I had every intention of remaining true blue to Santou, I couldn't help but be curious about the man.

Sally gazed into the fireplace, her face as wrinkle-free as that of a teenager. "A few of those items mean something special to him. Others are obstacles in his life. The sandbox teaches you to work around them.

Take the wedding band, for example. Matthew was divorced. He can cover the ring up with sand, but it won't change the fact that it's always going to be there. It's part of who he is. You have to learn to accept your past and to rake around the hurts, the obstacles, and all the mistakes that you've made."

"I'd just remove the ring from the sandbox and throw it away."

Sally smiled sadly. "Wouldn't it be nice if it were so easy to obliterate the past? You can't control everything that happens to you, Rachel, no matter how hard you try. You get married and divorced. Loved ones die. People don't live up to your expectations. Or perhaps you don't live up to your own. The secret is to be brave enough to leave yourself open to the things in life that are truly important."

Sally studied me as if I were one of her critters to be rehabilitated. "I get the feeling that you're afraid of losing your heart. It's probably why you've been single for so long. You've never been fearless enough to let go."

She was beginning to hit a little too close to the mark. I polished off my glass of wine and stood up.

"For all you know, I may have been married and divorced."

Sally lifted her chin and looked perceptively down her regal nose. "Uh-uh. I don't think so. You're too leery to commit to anyone."

Enough was enough. I decided to skip dinner and go to bed.

"Just realize that you could be passing up something quite special with Matt. Don't be so fast to close yourself off. There's always a reason for the things that happen to us that are beyond our control."

Maybe so, but I had every intention of keeping a tight rein on this particular one. I was heading for the bedroom door when the phone rang. Sally answered it, and then held the receiver toward me.

"It's Matt," she said, looking like the cat who'd just sliced, diced and eaten the canary.

I waited until she'd walked into the kitchen and was out of sight.

"Hello?" I answered apprehensively.

"Sorry to be phoning so late, but I just got a call from Bearhead."

Damn! The man sounded perfectly normal. It was as though nothing unusual had occurred between us at all.

"What's up?" I asked, fluctuating between disappointment and relief.

"It seems old Bearhead's had a flash of conscience, probably because you helped out his daughter today. He phoned to tell me that he'd stumbled upon a dead grizzly while hunting for elk this morning."

Hmm. That sounded more than a tad suspicious.

"He *found* it? Then why didn't he tell us about it when we were at his house earlier?"

"Why do you think? Remember, he blames them for the disappearance of his wife and brother. He probably was also afraid that we'd try to pin the deed on him."

"And what do *you* think?" I asked.

"He swears he didn't do it, and there's no reason for me not to believe him. Besides, there's more to it than that. The bear's paws and gallbladder were missing."

Paws and gallbladder? Why would anyone . . . Paws and gallbladder?

Oh dear God. Suddenly it all began to make perfect, horrible sense.

Now I knew what we were up against. I was dealing with traditional Chinese medicine and its beliefs, which have been around nearly as long as Asia itself.

Rooted in more than four thousand years of Chinese history, the trade in "medicinal" animal parts is widely practiced, with bears considered a primary staple for preventing and healing disease. Most highly prized are their gallbladders. Deemed Oriental Geritol, they're touted to cure everything from tooth decay to hemorrhoids to cancer. Galls have even become a hot-ticket item in the frenetic search for youth and vitality. Hold the Viagra! Why down a pill when you can mix some bile in a health tonic and drink the "real" thing?

Asia has decimated its own bruin population to supply a voracious three billion consumers. Only ten wild bears remain in all of South Korea. As a result, guess what country has been chosen to fill the slack? Bears in the U.S. are now viewed as walking bank accounts by poachers. And the rarer the species, the better. So grizzlies—creatures embodying strength, prowess and health—were now topping the charts.

Valued by weight, at eighteen times the market price of gold, a grizzly gall will fetch up to five thousand dollars here in the States. However, prices soar once it reaches Asia, where a gall may go for fifteen thousand bucks—unless it's from a particularly rare species of bear. Then it can garner a whopping sixty-four thousand dollars at auction. Not too shabby for a product that, when dried, looks like a fig.

And the paws not only supposedly have beneficial properties, but are also considered a chi-chi culinary delight. However, be prepared to ante up plenty of moolah when placing your order: a bowl of bear paw soup in Taiwan will run you over a thousand bucks.

"How about if I pick you up before daybreak and we head out to the site?" Matthew suggested.

I quickly agreed and hung up. Climbing into bed, I looked out the window.

An enormous poacher's moon hung in the sky. It dangled big and bright, drenching the land in ghostly white. I blinked and a shape began to take form. It moved like a poltergeist, crawling along the ground to spill in through my window. From there it continued along the floor, slipping inside my toes and invading the marrow of my bones. My blood throbbed and I shivered with fear in the night.

Meanwhile the sculpted metal bears continued to naïvely play, believing themselves safe under the moonlight.

Eleven

By the time dawn broke, I was already in Running's pickup and on the road. We were headed back to the same general area where we'd been yesterday; I just hoped that mama and her cubs had decided it was time to head for their den after yesterday's blanket of snow.

The dismal morning didn't help my frame of mind any. A dank frost replaced last night's spectral chill, while a fine mist obscured the landscape, further dampening the mood.

The atmosphere inside the truck wasn't all that much better. Silence enveloped the cab like an itchy wool sweater. I took the plunge and shattered the uncomfortable stillness.

"Listen, I'm sorry about last night."

Running might as well have been carved out of stone. "You mean you're sorry that you disagreed with me about Doc Hutchins?"

Damn! He wasn't going to make this any easier.

"No. I'm talking about my reaction to your kiss. It took me by surprise."

"Don't worry about it." He turned to me with a wry smile. "Although I admit, you did bruise my ego a bit. I didn't think I was all that bad a kisser."

I remembered the touch of his lips pressing against

mine, and the frost in my bones began to melt. "You're not." Oh shit. "It's just that I'm involved with someone."

A fleeting look of disappointment swept over his face. "Sorry. I hadn't realized." His eyes caught mine and I felt myself sink a little deeper. "Friends, then?"

"Friends," I glumly responded, and slapped on my best make-believe smile.

What the hell was wrong with me? I'd obviously sent this guy mixed signals, so why did I feel so bad now that I'd set him straight?

I wadded my conflicting emotions into a tight ball and stashed them away as we reached our destination. We parked in the same spot as before. After grabbing our gear, we began to hike in.

Matthew once again moved in rhythm with the forest. His feet barely made a sound and left no sign of his passing. There was no need to ask where we were going; I felt sure Bearhead had supplied explicit directions. Soon we came upon a scene much as we'd witnessed yesterday.

Claw marks tore wildly into nearby trees, and I stared in awe at the remaining bark. It looked like human skin that had been tattered and flayed. The adjacent ground resembled a lunar landscape, with the few pines left standing brutally whittled into tall matchsticks as if a twister had recently gone through.

"Well, now I know why bears are being snared rather than simply killed," Running remarked, his shoulders beginning to slump.

"Why's that?"

"In order to make them enraged. Fear and anger enlarge their gallbladder." Running rubbed his thumb and index finger together. "That means poachers get more money."

The mist was mischievously turning the snow into slush, eradicating all trace of whoever had been here before us. No sign of a carcass was in sight and, without a body, there was little to go on.

"Terrific. We've got no bait pile, no bear, no nothing," Running growled. "I'm beginning to think we're dealing with some sort of phantom."

"Yeah, a phantom who leaves footprints behind."

I'd caught sight of the tracks partially hidden beneath a grove of pines. The low-hanging branches had possessively protected the prints embedded in the snow.

We found two separate sets, each containing prints heading both toward the site and walking away. The boot tracks were identical, indicating that they'd been made by the same person.

"The first set shows where the perp initially entered and exited the scene," Running theorized. "The second pair must have been made when he returned for the bear. See where the snow has been flattened? The grizzly must have been pulled out by sled."

I studied the footprints more carefully. They displayed varying degrees of depth. It made sense that the suspect's tracks would have been deeper as he hauled the bear out, due to the extra weight. However, a deep set of tracks also led *into* the torn-up circle. That meant he must have carried something in with him. But what? Gut instinct told me it had to be whatever was being used to attract grizzlies. I donned a pair of latex gloves, turned on the metal detector, and went to work.

I'd covered almost every square inch of ground when the metal detector sprang to life. I reached beneath a stand of bushes to discover something far more intriguing than a bullet: a heavy band of double-layered leather that was a good three inches wide and a half inch thick. It was a Telonics radio collar that had been unbolted. Either this was the work of a poacher, or we were dealing with one hell of an ambidextrous bear. The transmitter was still encased in its waterproof fiberglass shell—but it had been smashed and broken.

This was the type of collar biologists place on tranquilized animals so that their movements can be more easily followed. A drop of blood stained the leather near an identification number. I bagged it and then searched around some more, eventually finding a red plastic ear tag. MONTANA GRIZZLY BEAR was printed on it. Whoever was stalking grizzlies must have managed to obtain their radio collar frequencies. The unfairness of the hunt made my blood boil.

"Who has the list of frequencies for radio-collared bears on the rez, and where are they kept?" I asked.

"I do, and they're in my office," Matthew replied evenly.

Though I tried to maintain a neutral expression, my stomach began to tighten. "Then can you tell me how many of the bears that were tagged are now missing?"

Running responded with one of his shrugs. "It's hard to say."

My stomach contracted a little more. "And why is that?"

"Lots of things can happen. Transmitter batteries give out. Radio collars get knocked off. Sometimes bears head into Glacier National Park and out of range. Just because you've found a radio collar doesn't mean that bears are being targeted and tracked in that manner. Some of these grizzlies could have wandered into snares all on their own."

By now, my stomach had turned into a raging inferno. "Right. And I suppose a bear just happened to pick up a rock and beat the living crap out of this transmitter, while he was at it."

Running didn't speak for a minute, but kept his head angled toward the ground. "Okay. Look, there was a break-in at my office a while back."

"Why in the hell didn't you mention that before?" I nearly shouted.

"Nothing was missing and I figured it was just the work of some rowdy kids."

"When did this happen?" I asked, my mind beginning to reel. Running knew as well as I did that the numbers could have simply been copied.

"Over a year ago," he nonchalantly responded, but his eyes clouded over.

I should have figured. He was protecting his own, and now the grizzlies were being picked off one by one.

"Look, I'd know if anyone on the rez was responsible for this," Matthew insisted.

"And do you want to tell me how? Would your totem spirit tip you off?"

"I have a string of informants." Running's voice dropped and his eyes grew hard. "Listen, Porter. Protecting these grizzlies is as important to me as it is to you."

I truly wanted to believe the man. The problem was, I didn't dare.

* * *

Running dropped me back at Sally's and we agreed to stay in touch. Right now, I had to hurry off to a bagels and lox breakfast. I headed south out of the rez toward Willow Creek.

I hadn't anticipated that Rory's directions would take me past the Lungren compound. Even more of a surprise was the vehicle that I spotted coming from its access road. I checked my rearview mirror just to make sure that I wasn't seeing things. Yep. A lime-green Jeep Cherokee with a "Look Busy! Jesus Is Coming!" bumper sticker pulled out. I watched as Doc Hutchins drove north toward the Blackfeet rez. Hmm. What had *he* been doing at Nearly Paradise? I doubted the good doctor was buying a fake Indian headdress.

I continued on, eventually catching sight of the billboard I'd been told to look for. PLEASE NEUTER YOUR PETS, WEIRD FRIENDS AND RELATIVES! I then turned onto a gravel road. There was nothing to indicate anyone lived back here, and I began to wonder if Calhoun was some sort of practical joker. So far, I saw only old missile silos, each surrounded by a chain-link fence, their nuclear warheads slumbering beneath concrete pads.

I was beginning to rhyme the name Calhoun with words like *buffoon* when a gated entry finally appeared off to my left. I drove up, pressed the monitor, and smiled sweetly for the security camera. My Ford was granted access and I proceeded in, curious as to why a guy selling hot tubs would need high-tech protection. Soon after, a house that looked like Tony Soprano's wet dream came into view.

The two-story extravaganza boasted a tall picture

window above the front door. Displayed behind it was a schmaltzy chandelier. I parked and strolled up a walkway lined with a dozen nude statues on either side. My finger hit the buzzer, which played "That's Amore." I wouldn't have been surprised to find Frank and Dean, along with the rest of the Rat Pack, waiting on the other side.

Rory opened the door to greet me, and I nearly didn't recognize him without his coonskin cap. A few thin wisps of hair had been combed across his otherwise bald pate, and blue-tinted granny glasses did their best to camouflage his bloodshot eyes.

"Hey, Big Apple! Terrific! You found the place! I never know if someone's gonna make it here, or if I'll have to dig their bones out of a ditch a coupla months from now."

Call me perverse, but I was beginning to wonder if that might not be the general idea.

"Come on in! Whadda ya standin' outside for? I've got breakfast waiting in here."

I walked in to find an interior reminiscent of one of those garish banquet halls on Long Island. In fact, I was certain I'd seen the identical decor at Joey Manzarella's Mediterranean Palace. Rory's McMansion was close to being the Palace's exact duplicate, right down to its color scheme of turquoise-blue and bullfighter-red. Every piece of furniture was covered in crushed velvet.

"I didn't get you up too early, did I?"

Rory looked temporarily baffled. "Huh? Whadda ya talkin' about?"

I nodded at the purple silk pajamas and matching robe that covered his diminutive body.

"Hey, if it's good enough for Hef, it's good enough for me. Besides, it's not like I'm in a rush to go anywhere. What am I gonna do? Slap on a lumberjack shirt and head into town for a friggin' milkshake?"

I had to agree.

"Enough small talk. Let's go eat."

Rory led me into the dining room, where the table was loaded with enough chow to feed a small crowd at the Second Avenue Deli.

"Don't be shy. Dig in!"

What the hell. I loaded my plate.

But Rory's mind was on something other than sturgeon and lox. "So, fill me in. Where do you go to eat Italian when you're back in the Big Apple?"

I almost hated to tell him that Original Ray's Pizza was as gourmet as I ever got.

"Whadda ya, kiddin' me? You've never been to Umberto's Clam House, or Café Roma for espresso and cannolis?"

I lied and said yes to keep him happy.

"Ha! What a sucker! That's nothing but tourist crap. Personally, I always preferred to go more upscale myself. You know, like Il Mulino or Rao's. Even better is Arthur Avenue in the Bronx for the real thing. Jeez, what I wouldn't give for a mouthful."

Rory looked so morose that he seemed to shrink inside his pajamas.

"Then what's stopping you? Why don't you go back for a visit?"

Rory began to fidget. "Like I told you before, I'm a businessman. I can't just take off and let everything go to hell."

Hmm. Let's see. It was ten-thirty on a Wednesday morning and Rory was still at home lounging around in his pajamas. Either he was lying, or I was in the wrong line of business.

"So where is this store of yours, anyway?"

Rory piled a thick layer of lox on an onion bagel and shoved it into his mouth. "Screw that. All I deal in is mail order."

"Then where's your factory? Or do you construct the hot tubs here?"

"Who can be bothered with that crap? I order 'em wholesale from a company in Guam."

"What?"

"Yeah. It's the American way."

But I was in for an even bigger surprise as Cherry Jubilee unexpectedly sauntered into the room, attired in a fake fur midriff top and hip-hugger acid-washed jeans. The leather fringe on her pants ran down both legs and swayed in rhythm with her hips, while her hair surpassed its Rocky Mountain high of the other night and was climbing toward Everest. But it was her face that caught my interest. Either Rocky Raccoon was doing her makeup these days, or Cherry Jubilee was sporting two prominent black eyes.

"Hey there, Whambo. What do you say?" she sneered, as if *I* were the one with the bad eye job.

"Nice set of headlights you've got there," I countered. "Did they have a sale on black eyeliner? Or is that the handiwork of your boyfriend?"

I thought I'd hit it on the mark, as Cherry's peepers began to dissolve into two muddy puddles.

"No, Kyle didn't do this. It was Little Queenie, his

bitch of a stepmother!" Cherry angrily spat, twisting her necklace so hard that I feared she might decapitate herself. "*Now* how am I going to perform at Big Bertha's?"

"You could always do your act as the Lone Ranger," Rory helpfully suggested.

"Oh, shut the hell up!" she snapped.

"Do you mind if I ask what happened?" I ventured.

I must have been living right. Cherry grabbed a bottle of Scotch, poured herself a hefty drink, and downed it.

"I was given an ultimatum by the Queen Bee to vacate the premises. It seems I'm not good enough to associate with a bunch of down-and-out losers who get off on playing with gas masks and sucking Cheez Whiz straight outta the can."

"I take it you didn't leave without a fight."

"Damn straight! I kicked that bitch's ass but good."

Maybe so, but Honey Lungren had certainly gotten in her licks. "Where was Kyle while all this was going on?"

"Who the hell knows." A pitiful sob clung to Cherry's voice. She grabbed the napkin off Rory's lap and blew her nose in it. "He took off yesterday right before this happened, and I haven't heard from him since. And all this time, I thought he was my hero!"

"Here, you'll feel better after you have a bagel with a schmear." Rory consoled and held a heavily slathered slice to her mouth.

"Will ya get that thing out of my face?" Cherry irritably slapped his hand away. "Packing fat on my hips isn't gonna help!"

It suddenly struck me that these two seemed awfully intimate—rather like an old married couple.

"How do both of you know each other, anyway?"

They exchanged a glance.

"From the bar," Rory replied a little too quickly.

Cherry chose to remain silent, having become inordinately fixated on her navel.

"You must know lots of guys from the bar, Cherry. What made you decide to come here in a pinch?"

She looked at me and smirked. "I got a thing for Rory's coonskin cap. It's got a nice big tail on it."

I just bet it did.

"Okay, girls! Now you're embarrassing me. There'll be no discussion of my physical attributes first thing in the morning. What say we play pass the peace pipe over some coffee and Danish? I had it sent all the way from Greenburg's Deli."

Cherry shot me her rendition of the evil eye. Gazing into their depths was like looking down a couple of blocked-up sewers. I knew the best thing to do to make her crazy was not to leave.

"Sure, coffee would be great. Do you mind if I use your bathroom?"

"Yeah, yeah. There's one for guests up the stairs and at the end of the hall."

Their voices drifted skyward along with me.

"What the hell is she doing at your place, anyway?" Cherry complained.

"It gets lonely out here all by myself. Next time, call ahead when you plan to get the crap beat outta you."

These two were as good as a Marx Brothers routine.

That kind of relationship took time, practice, and lots of personal history.

As I reached the top of the steps, I realized that no house tour had been offered yet. Probably just an oversight on Rory's part. That being the case, he wouldn't mind if I took a quick look-see on my own. After all, he was busy—and I was curious.

I stuck my head into the first doorway on the left. Room number one contained a king-sized bed with a mirror directly above on the ceiling. Either Calhoun liked to look at himself in bed, or all those tips at the bar were buying him some action. I stepped inside to investigate further.

Sitting on the bureau was a photo of Rory sporting a black fedora. Looming in the background was the Brooklyn Bridge. He must have been happy as hell about something; Calhoun was smiling like a lunatic. Maybe it had to do with the clothes he was wearing: a sharkskin suit rather than a tie-dyed shirt and jeans. Dangling from his right hand was a hammer, while his left arm was slung across the shoulders of someone I assumed to be a friend. Unfortunately, I'd never know for sure. The guy's head had been cut from the photo. This was both the allure and the drawback when it came to digging into a stranger's personal life. Rory had just made the leap from wacky to freaky.

I opened a drawer and methodically began to rummage through. Sometimes even *I* can't believe the things that I do. But what better way to learn about someone quickly? Rory had a predilection for silk underwear. While unusual, it wasn't something I could hold against him. Though it *did* make me feel deficient in my marked-down Kmart briefs.

There was no time to examine every single drawer, especially since Rory's private bathroom was beckoning to me. It seemed the logical commode to use, being that I was already here. Slipping in, I closed the door behind me.

The most revealing things about a person can sometimes be discovered through the items they keep in their refrigerator and medicine cabinet. My own stash clearly showed me to be an inveterate hoarder who rarely throws anything away. That's why my fridge holds food that's unidentifiable—due to the fact that it's green and furry.

As for my medicine cabinet, the FDA would have a field day. I've kept every unfinished prescription drug since 1976, probably making me responsible for the emergence of at least one super virus. So I'm always curious to see what other people keep on their shelves. It was time to dig a little deeper into Rory's psyche.

I opened the medicine cabinet. The guy was a neat freak. Every bottle, can and jar was neatly lined up, with all the labels facing out. Of course, that made my job a whole lot easier.

Let's see. On the bottom there was a can of shaving cream, some deodorant, a bottle of aspirin and a tube of Sensodyne for Rory's sensitive choppers. The middle shelf held Old Spice aftershave, disposable razors, and talcum powder. It's the very top ledge where most of the interesting items are usually placed—the drug vials.

At first glance, Rory appeared to be quite the little

pill popper. There was Bactrin, penicillin, and Zocor, along with acetaminophen, Tenormin, Valium, and Cozaar. Oddly, different names were on the vials. The most recent prescriptions had been filled in Choteau for Rory Calhoun, while others came from a pharmacy in Phoenix for a Rudy Tomasso. The oldest of the lot were for Benny Gugliani from a drugstore in Bay Ridge, New York.

Holy tamale! I knew that name from somewhere. *Come on, come on,* I goaded my memory, cursing myself for continually forgetting to take my gingko biloba. I hadn't heard it on *Entertainment Tonight*—which meant that Gugliani wasn't an actor, a network anchor, or a dot-com millionaire. Either Calhoun liked to swipe the prescription drugs of his guests, or he had a full-fledged Sybil complex. The other possibility was that he was shucking identities as easily as neckties.

I studied the plastic vial as though it were a crystal ball, hoping it would provide the answer. Finally I went back into the bedroom, where I took another gander at Rory's photo.

That was it! I remembered seeing the name in the newspapers in conjunction with a notorious case about four years ago. Gugliani was better known as Benny the Bopper, due to his penchant for knocking his victims over the head with a hammer. He'd turned government witness against the mob and was later placed in the federal witness protection program. His name must have been changed to Rudy Tomasso, after which it had somehow morphed into Rory Calhoun.

Well, whadda ya know? So much for the Guam hot tub scam; the question appeared to be, what was Benny the Bopper *really* doing these days to be making money? I grabbed the vial of Valium and went back downstairs to find out.

Rory and Cherry were still sniping at each other as though I hadn't been gone at all.

"Hey, Bopper. You got any cheese Danish there?" I casually inquired as I walked into the room.

"Yeah, sure. Help yourself," he said as Cherry continued to kvetch.

Then both stopped dead, as if on cue, and turned their heads to look at me.

"What did you say?" he warily asked.

"I hate to break up your Love Connection, but look what I found upstairs." I shook the vial of Valium at him.

Benny pounced, like a cat that had been baited with catnip. "For chrissakes! What the hell do ya think you're doing? I invite you over here for a nice breakfast and this is how you repay me? The feds are gonna kick my butt if they think I'm running around telling everyone who I am!"

Cherry added her two cents. "I told you there was something about her that I didn't like. You should learn to trust my womanly instincts."

I threw her a disgusted look. So far, her womanly instincts had successfully landed her a gig dirty dancing on top of a bar, and had helped to get her face slapped.

I turned my attention back to Benny. "I *am* a fed, remember? Now how about clueing me in as to what's going on?"

Benny thrust his face pugnaciously near mine, transforming from a hairless Chihuahua into a pit bull terrier. "Why the hell should I?"

"Because if you don't, I'll call my friends at the FBI and find out anyway. I'll also tell them that you've violated terms by keeping unlicensed weapons in your house. Oh yeah. And that you're dealing in black market pharmaceuticals," I conned, shaking the vial of Valium at him.

"What the hell are you talking about? I don't deal in any pharmaceuticals!" Benny howled. "Whadda ya trying to do? Get me thrown into prison?"

He hadn't balked at the mention of unlicensed guns. Hitting one out of two wasn't too shabby.

"Oops! I guess I'll have to say it was an honest mistake on my part *after* the FBI finishes their investigation."

"See? I *told* you she was a bitch!" Cherry snapped.

"Yeah, yeah. I know. Your womanly instincts," I countered. "Okay, Benny. Now tell me what gives."

"Unbelievable! You feds are worse than the Russki Mafia and the Colombian Cartel rolled into one!" the Bopper groused.

I stared at him without saying a word.

"Okay, okay. I testified against a coupla mob families a few years ago. It involved a Medicare scam that was being run out of Florida and New York. We netted more than twenty-seven million big ones, and I helped mastermind it," Benny said with more than a touch of pride.

"Twenty-seven million? That's quite a haul. How did you manage that?" Even I was impressed.

"Whadda ya, kidding? It was easy! There's no bigger or dumber mark than the federal government. The low-level stuff amounted to getting some garden-variety doctors to inflate their bills. But the real genius was when I brainstormed setting up a coupla sham radiology clinics. That's when the Medicare checks came rolling in."

Benny was quite the guy—a real true-blue humanitarian.

"Everything was going gangbusters until one of the Social Security numbers we used turned out to be fake, and some pencil-pushing bureaucrat caught it. Talk about your lousy breaks! After that, I was offered a deal: testify and live out my life playing cowboy in the middle of nowhere, or spend the rest of my days in jail. Who knew they'd turn out to be pretty much the same thing?"

If Benny was hoping for sympathy, he was looking in the wrong place.

"Okay, but that still doesn't explain how you and Cherry hooked up. And don't tell me it was at Big Bertha's," I warned, "because I don't buy it."

"And whadda ya gonna do if I don't feel like it?" Benny taunted. "Turn me in to the mob?"

"Hey, that's not a bad idea," I responded pleasantly.

"Real cute, Porter," Benny smirked. "I gotta tell ya, you're some piece of work."

"Thanks. I like to think so."

"Why doncha buy it, anyway?" Cherry Jubilee demanded.

"Just chalk it up to *my* womanly instincts and the fact

that I'm naturally suspicious," I replied. "Anyway, I'm sure the truth is much better, and I've always been a sucker for a good love story."

Benny used his pinkie to dislodge a piece of lox that was stuck between his teeth. "We met over at Nearly Paradise. I used to spend a lotta time there when I first landed in Montana."

"Right," I scoffed. "I can really see you fitting in with the militia crowd."

"Believe what you want, but it happens to be true." Benny sniffed, as though his feelings had been hurt. "Look at it this way: they're business people, too. Besides, there isn't anyone else to socialize with around here, unless you're a perv with a weakness for cows. Then you're in bovine heaven. I thought we might be able to do some business together."

"What were you planning? To join forces and sell hot tubs to survivalists?" Then I remembered having seen Doc Hutchins leaving Nearly Paradise earlier this morning. "Okay, then you should be able to tell me why a guy by the name of Hutchins would be hanging around the compound."

"Doc Hutchins?" Cherry piped up. "He lives there, of course."

"I figured he'd reside somewhere on the Blackfeet reservation."

"No way. Hutch has been at Nearly Paradise for years. He hates the government just as much as the Lungrens do," Cherry reported, looking mighty pleased with herself.

"And why's that?"

"It's 'cause the authorities revoked his medical license in four different states and ruined his career. After that, the only place he could get a job was running a medical clinic on some godforsaken reservation. He met Kyle at Big Bertha's not long after he moved here and immediately bought one of the lots on the compound.

I shot her a skeptical look.

"She's right, Porter," Benny chimed in. "As a matter of fact, Hutchins used to have a fly-by-night medical practice in Flushing, Queens. I know, because he was involved with our Medicare scam."

"What!"

"Don't be so naïve, Big Apple babe," the Bopper gloated, seemingly pleased at having trumped me. "Working with us was about the only way he could make any decent money, what with his license being jerked so much."

If that were true, how had he managed to land a job at a federally funded clinic? Then it hit me. "Did he happen to testify against the mob, too?"

"Good guess. His real name is Herman Bethala. Who knew we'd both end up near Choteau? Or Shithole, as I like to call it. The feds must be running outta places to put all of us. Hutchins was already living at the compound when I got here."

Benny rolled the shred of lox between his fingers and flicked it on the floor. "Now *there's* something that burns my butt. Giving that dump a name like Nearly Paradise and getting twenty-five thousand smackers a lot. That's what I call criminal! Hutchins is probably helping to steer people there and getting some kind of kickback."

"Oh, puh-lease! You're just sore 'cause Doc doesn't want to work with you anymore," Cherry tattled.

"Whoa! Hold it a minute! Were you planning to run the same kind of scam up here as you did in New York?" I incredulously asked.

"You know, Cherry, you got one helluva big mouth. You better be careful before it's permanently shut," the Bopper hissed.

"Did you hear that? This loser's threatening me! I want him arrested!" Cherry demanded, jabbing a finger in his stomach.

"Wait a second!" I commanded, getting between them. "Benny, just answer the question."

"What the hell. I'll tell ya, since it's never gonna happen anyway. Sure. Can you think of a better place for that sorta scam than on an Indian reservation, where nobody knows what the hell is going on, and doesn't give a damn?"

"In other words, Hutchins learned his lesson and you didn't," I surmised. "Obviously he's come to respect the Blackfeet people."

"Whadda ya, kidding me? You should hear how he talks about 'em, calling 'em blanket asses, teepee creepers, wagon burners—"

"Enough already. I get the picture. What do *you* think is stopping him from working with you, then?"

The Bopper munched on a cherry Danish, its red jelly staining his lips. "It's hard to say. But I know the guy. If he's not interested in what I'm offering, it's 'cause he's already involved in another sweet deal."

"Any idea as to what it might be?"

I was beginning to suspect that Hutchins was dabbling in the bear gallbladder trade. It made perfect sense: he had easy access to Asian doctors and pharmacies via the Internet and could ship the bear galls out by overnight mail.

Benny shook his head unconvincingly.

"How about you?" I asked Princess Two-Black-Eyes. Her answer was equally nonverbal.

Of course, it was just possible that the unsavory trio were in on it together. There was certainly enough money to be made, with bear galls selling for a whopping $5,600 per powdered ounce in Asia. In fact, Cherry was looking a little green around the gills, as though there might be something she was bursting to tell me.

"If you've got information, you'd better spill it now, Cherry. You don't want to be an accessory to a crime," I cajoled.

"She'll never tell you nothing," Benny bleated like a ram guarding his prize ewe. "Even if she did have a brain in that body of hers! Hell, she's still in love with militia boy. Cherry thinks of him as her knight in shining trailer-park armor. She's hoping he's gonna slay that evil stepmother of his and beg her to move back in with him."

"Shuddup, you little weasel!" Cherry angrily countered. "You're just jealous, is all!"

Hmm. Wasn't *that* interesting? We'd been talking about Doc Hutchins only to land on the topic of militia boy. I could spend the rest of my day trying to figure out *that* connection.

Cherry and Benny continued to go at each other, and I knew there was little chance of getting any more information out of them.

"Gotta go," I said, bidding adieu. I grabbed a couple of cheese Danish and a piece of cinnamon coffeecake, then slipped out the door.

Twelve

The building that housed the Indian Health Services clinic was as squat and dumpy as an overweight daschund. Inside, the facility was strewn with waiting patients exhibiting an assortment of sniffles, coughs, and fevers. That wasn't counting those burdened with broken arms, fractured legs, and aching heads. Many sat nodding off in what few chairs there were, while the rest lay curled up on the floor.

I knew that the rate of diabetes, as well as lung and heart disease, was skyrocketing on Indian reservations across the country. Still, the clinic was more crowded than I'd have imagined. The place looked like a refugee camp—only worse. IHS was poorly run and under-staffed out in the field where it counts, just like every other federal agency in the country.

"How long have you been waiting?" I asked a woman holding a colicky baby.

She looked at me with the grim eyes of a war-weary soldier. "Since yesterday. I got a number and came back this morning. It seems to be moving faster today."

I gazed at the mass of pain-riddled humanity around me. It was amazing how hope sprang eternal. I felt like a larcenous thief as I skipped to the head of the line.

The woman in charge of assigning numbers barely

acknowledged my presence. But then, she was pretty busy catching up with the latest gossip in *People* magazine.

"Hi. I was wondering if Dr. Hutchins might have a minute?" I asked and flashed my badge.

That seemed to get her attention. She looked up at me with a smirk. "Yeah. He's sitting in his office right now having a latte. Why? Did you want to join him?"

Wow. A receptionist with a sarcastic sense of humor. How unique.

"I just have a few quick questions I'd like to ask."

"A few quick questions, huh?" She leaned back and folded her arms. "Are you in diabetic shock or having a heart attack at the moment?"

I shook my head no to both.

"Well then, you're gonna have to wait just like everyone else. Take a look around. What we've got is a traffic jam. You should be able to see that the doctor is busy right now."

I didn't think she'd believe me if I suddenly pretended to faint.

"You can either take a number and wait with the others, or come back after clinic hours and try to catch him then."

"Thanks. I guess I'll try him later."

"Good choice."

But rather than leave, I decided to melt into the background and study the action. Needless to say, there wasn't a lot of activity going on. I was beginning to feel drowsy myself, when Hutchins finally emerged from an examination room with a patient. They both stepped into what I assumed to be his private office, only to reappear before long. The man left with some pills and Hutchins scurried into the other exam room to check the next patient.

"Number forty-five!" the receptionist called out, as if working at a deli.

She impatiently ushered an arthritic old woman into the newly vacant exam room. I waited until both women were out of sight and then casually sauntered into Hutchins's inner sanctum, closing the door behind me. With any luck, the good doctor would remain occupied and I'd be able to slip back out at an opportune moment. In the meantime, there was work to do.

I looked around. The walls were puke green and the paint was peeling. The space was sparsely furnished with only a desk, two chairs, and a couple of filing cabinets. The pieces were obviously secondhand, sporting surfaces that were battered and scratched. My guess was that, much like Hutchins, this was the last stop in their professional careers.

The desktop was bare but for a cup filled with cheap pens and pencils. Not a single decoration hung on the walls. There were no photos, no paintings, and certainly no framed medical diplomas. The office reeked of solitude and disappointment. Judging from the room, Hutchins—AKA Bethala—was a man without a successful past, a fulfilling present, or a promising future.

The two filing cabinets probably held patients' files. I opened the first, which proved me correct. Searching for any evidence to link Hutchins to the bear gallbladder trade, or that would indicate he was pushing drugs on the rez, I did a fast finger search through the folders. But they held little of interest, other than who had high cholesterol, hepatitis, and diabetes. It was time to move on to cabinet number two.

Naturally, this one proved to be locked. I pulled out my handy dandy Leatherman tool and jimmied the catch without any problem at all. Someday, I'd have to write the company and tell them how good their product was for breaking into secure places.

Pulling open the top drawer, I found folders categorized according to age, sex, blood type, and general state of health. Hmm. Could the IHS be involved in some sort of hush-hush study concerning health conditions on reservations? I'd learned firsthand about the federal government and secret projects, placing my own life in grave jeopardy by doing so. I hesitated a moment before taking the plunge.

What the hell. Life is short.

Yeah, but yours could be even shorter, quipped an inner voice.

I chose to ignore it and pulled out the file labeled *General Health*. Strangely enough, a page for Elizabeth Come-By-Night lay on the very top. Listed were her age, weight, and height, as well as the fact that she was in excellent health. Her last exam was dated to have been yesterday. I quickly searched through the rest of the folder, but found nothing else of interest.

Damn! So far, there was no indication that Hutchins was dealing in either bear galls or illegal drugs. The file also proved that Elizabeth hadn't been lying about her doctor's appointment. Could Running be right, after all? Perhaps Hutchins *had* been rushing off to an emergency. Still, why hadn't he bothered to make sure we were all right before speeding away?

I should have been paying more attention to my surroundings; the sound of a male voice alerted me that Hutchins was right outside the door. I managed to slip the file back in place and shut the drawer, just before the good doctor walked into the room. He looked even more wasted than I'd remembered. His sallow skin was stretched tightly across a cadaverous skull, and the teeth in his mouth were crooked and dingy.

We both jumped in surprise, but Hutchins's reaction was far more severe. The man slapped a startled hand to his chest and began to gasp. I worried that I'd prompted a heart attack, then realized I was witnessing guilt and fear. Hutchins's eyes darted furtively around the room like a trapped animal's, and he closely resembled a cornered possum as he stood with his shoulders hunched and his back pressed against the wall. What was he so nervous about?

"Sorry if I frightened you, Dr. Hutchins. But I want to ask you a few questions, and decided to wait in your office. I'm Rachel Porter, special agent with the U.S. Fish and Wildlife Service. You might not remember, but we literally bumped into each other at the Red Crow Café yesterday morning."

Maybe I shouldn't have allowed Hutchins so much time to recuperate. He promptly launched into attack mode, his anxious expression transforming into a menacing glare.

"Of course you're with the government. Who the hell else would have the gall to simply walk in here and invade my private office? After all, isn't that what you people do?"

"What do you mean?" I asked.

"That's exactly what you feds did at Waco and Ruby Ridge—invaded private property, after which you persecuted and murdered its residents. And then you wonder why a patriot like McVeigh comes along and decides to blow you all up. That's what the motto *Don't Tread on Me* means—keeping a tyrannical government at bay. You're all a bunch of jack-booted thugs who think nothing of stomping on innocent citizens' inalienable rights. Well, people are getting damned sick and tired of it. What are you doing here, anyway? Trying to plant something in my office so that you can haul me off to jail?"

Oy veh.

"Actually, I just wanted to ask why you didn't stop when I tried to wave you down yesterday. I was the woman standing out in the field."

It was as though Hutchins hadn't quite realized exactly who I was until then. Now that he did, his face grew flushed and he broke into a sweat.

"I haven't the vaguest idea what you're talking about," he stammered.

"Surely you recognized the girl that I was trying to help. After all, Elizabeth Come-By-Night *is* one of your patients."

Hutchins gave a quizzical shake of his head. But his mouth grew tightly pinched, and a nerve beneath his right eye twitched, betraying him. "You must be mistaken. I never left my office all day. And I certainly didn't see you with a sick child, or I would have come to her aid. Now, I suggest that you leave before I call the tribal police and have you brought up on charges of illegal entry."

I didn't know what was going on yet, but I'd clearly hit a nerve. "I suggest you rethink that, Dr. Bethala."

His mouth fell open, but no sound emerged.

"I'm curious as to just how much the tribal council knows about your medical background. Having your license revoked in four different states is no mean feat."

Hutchins's complexion darkened and his skeletal frame began to shake, until I could have sworn I was standing face-to-face with the Grim Reaper. Maybe I'd gone too far. Honey Lungren was already an enemy; I didn't need to have the United Christian Patriots organize a crusade against me.

"Yes, now I remember. You left the café with that tribal game officer, Mathew Running. Didn't anyone ever tell you that you should stick to your own kind? Being paid to work with these people is one thing. Socializing with them is another. That's a lesson you shouldn't take lightly. Otherwise, there are those who will have to make sure that you learn it." Hutchins's smirk wrapped around me as tight as a boa constrictor.

"Hey, doc. If you really believe that Jesus is coming, maybe *you* should begin to worry. You do realize that he was a mud person, don't you? How do you think that bodes for *your* future?"

I didn't wait to hear the answer but strode out of his office, past the profusion of bruised and broken bodies that patiently waited for help.

I suspected the United Christian Patriots worked as a funnel, picking up society's dregs and outcasts on hot-button issues like gun control and environmental restrictions. Go a little deeper and the ideology grew more dogmatic, becoming racist and hammering at the heavy hand of the federal government. Finally there were the truly hard-core, who were drawn into the funnel's very narrowest end. It was there that fanatics like McVeigh, and possibly Hutchins, popped out to wreak havoc. If they attacked, it would be when I least expected. As usual, I'd managed to land right in the middle of the vortex.

Thirteen

I was barely past the outskirts of Browning when my cell phone rang.

"Porter! Exactly what the hell do you think you're doing?"

The voice belonged to my boss, Hank Turner.

"What? No hello first?" I joked.

The response was a deep pit of silence.

"Okay, what's the problem?"

There was a long pause, followed by a heartfelt sigh. "Where do I start? First off, I just received an irate call about your activities on the reservation. It's been alleged that you're harassing the clinic doctor, disturbing his patients, and generally running amuck."

I must have stirred the pot even better than I'd thought.

"Can I ask who lodged the complaint?" I inquired, certain that I already knew.

"It was an anonymous call."

"Naturally," I chuckled.

"Would you like to know why?" Turner's voice lashed out. "It's because they're afraid you'll retaliate. It seems you were overheard making threats."

That did it! My instincts about Hutchins had to be correct. He was obviously involved with killing grizzlies for their galls. Otherwise why would he want me out of the way so badly?

"And you automatically believed these accusations?"

"Let's just say I've learned why you've been bounced around the Service so much."

"I've also solved every case I've ever worked on," I volleyed.

"That doesn't mean crap. Not if it's been the cause of all the trouble that's plagued you in the past. Either you learn to handle situations with tact, or I'm going to have to forbid you to leave the office. We need someone to do all the paperwork, anyway. I'm tempted to make you the goddamn secretary and save myself a whole world of trouble."

I wondered if male agents ever had to deal with such threats. Grizzlies weren't the only species that could've used a little more support from the powers that be within Fish and Wildlife.

"Have I made myself clear?" Turner demanded.

I bit the inside of my cheek to keep from sniping back. "Perfectly."

"All right then. But that's not the only reason I'm calling."

Oh shit. Who else had I ticked off within the last couple of hours? Then I remembered. There was that little hide-and-seek game I'd conducted at Rory Calhoun/ Benny Gugliani's place.

"The Missoula police just phoned to report that your office has been broken into."

"Is that all?" I muttered, breathing a sigh of relief.

"What the hell is that supposed to mean?" Turner

snapped. "And by the way, what exactly are you doing up north again?"

"I'm working on that eagle feather case," I quickly tap-danced. "Remember?"

"Well, you're sure taking your good ol' time solving something that should be pretty cut-and-dried. I suggest you get your butt back down to Missoula right now and find out what's going on there."

He hung up before I had a chance to say, "Roger. Over and out."

My activities on the rez would have to be put on hold for a few days. I turned the Ford around and began to head south, then placed a call to Sally. A girlish giggle greeted me as she answered the phone.

"Sally? Is that you?"

A man's laughter peppered the background, adding to the carefree atmosphere.

"Why hello, dear. Hal and his cat are here. When should we expect you for dinner?" She tittered again, and I suspected Ornish was putting the moves on her. "Sorry, but Casanova is rubbing up against my leg and tickling me."

I wondered exactly which "Casanova" she meant.

"I just found out that I need to return to Missoula right away, but I plan to be back in a couple of days."

A round of feverish whispers broke out on the other end of the wire.

"Hal says that you should take your time. He's planning to stay up here with me for a while."

Evidently Hutchins wasn't the only one who wanted me out of the way.

"Would you mind letting Matthew know that I'll call

him when I return?" Getting some distance between us probably wasn't a bad idea.

"Why don't you just call him yourself?"

"Sorry, Sally, but the reception is breaking up," I responded, and began to scratch my nails against the receiver. "Please relay the message to him for me."

I quickly hung up before she could respond. Okay, so I was a coward. But each additional contact only succeeded in drawing me that much closer to Running.

I turned the volume up on the radio, but the noise did nothing to drown out the montage of steamy images of Matthew and me that flashed through my brain. I sped down the blacktop, determined to escape them, and had very nearly succeeded, when the sun seductively gilded the few remaining leaves on a cottonwood tree so that they appeared to burst into flame.

Talk about Freud and Jung. Maybe a cigar is sometimes just a cigar, but those blazing leaves rekindled a fire that was burning inside me. I was sorely tempted to call Santou right now; maybe a little phone sex would work as a way of reconnecting. But he was deep undercover on a case, and I had no idea where to find him.

I was actually relieved to walk into the disaster that awaited me at my office. The place had been totally ransacked, but at least it took my mind off Matthew Running.

Folders were torn apart and their contents strewn everywhere. If paper were snow, the office would have been buried beneath a blizzard and declared a natural disaster. But that wasn't the worst of it; all the computer disks had been raided. The kicker was that I couldn't be certain exactly what was missing, since everything had involved Carolton's unsolved cases. There wasn't much to do other than simply clean up debris.

As I gathered a heap of papers, something sharp jabbed my finger. I carefully sifted through the wreckage until I found the culprit: a small, gold, heart-shaped pin with a serrated edge. Hmm . . . Not only had I seen one just like it hanging around Cherry Jubilee's neck, but it was an exact duplicate of the pin on Kyle Lungren's shirt pocket. Love can be vicious. Evidently, so could jewelry. I stuck the pin in my pants pocket.

By the time I headed home, I was exhausted. I'd thought it would be a relief to spend some time alone, but the house felt uncomfortably empty without Ornish and his pain-in-the-ass cat. A note lay on the kitchen table, so I picked it up and read it.

In the event that you actually come home, Casanova and I have gone up to woo Sally. She's a woman in need of a man, and it's about time we settled down.

In Ornish's own way, that was pretty romantic. At least it beat a personal ad that I'd recently spotted in the local newspaper.

Rancher looking for a good cowgirl with a good horse. Send picture of horse.

Sally was already way ahead of the game.

My stomach growled, reminding me that I had yet to eat dinner. I opened the fridge, but Hal was just as bad as I was about grocery shopping. The edibles ran from moldy Brie to an open can of Friskies chicken and liver. I settled upon a partially eaten pint of Häagen-Dazs and a bag of stale Fig Newtons. At least it covered my fruit and dairy requirements.

I was just sitting down to outguess the loser contestants on *The Weakest Link* when the doorbell rang. I instantly jumped. Sheesh—Hutchins must have gotten to me more than I'd cared to admit. I grabbed my .38, stuck it in the back of my jeans, and cautiously opened the door.

Talk about your knockout surprises! The hulking figure towering before me stood about six feet five and weighed close to three hundred pounds. Pointy alligator shoes, a diamond pinkie ring that flashed in the moonlight, flattened nose, and perfectly pomaded pompadour . . . it was none other than Vinnie Bertucci, former bodyguard and butler to con artist extraordinaire Hillard Williams. Williams was the businessman I'd busted for smuggling cocaine inside gator skin shipments down in New Orleans.

"Hey, New Yawk! How youse doin'?"

How I was doing was dumbfounded.

Vinnie stepped inside without waiting to be invited. "Nice place ya got here. Too bad I ain't working no more as a butler. It looks like you could use some help in the cleaning department."

Gee, whatever had given him *that* impression—the wads of cat hair floating about like free-form sculptures, or the piles of Tender Vittles that Casanova had swatted across the floor?

"Vinnie, what a surprise! What are you doing here in Montana?"

He took off his jacket and flexed his pecs, causing his

baby-blue Banlon shirt to tightly stretch across his muscles. It was nice to know that at least one of us had been working out.

"I'm here on vacation. I thought I might enjoy whackin' a few fish or something."

My guess was that *or something* were the operative words here.

"Anyways, I heard youse was in the area and thought I'd look ya up."

"Oh yeah? Who told you where to find me?"

"Let's just say I got friends who got friends."

Uh-huh. Most likely, they were all connected to the mob.

Vinnie lifted the open pint of chocolate chocolate-chip Häagen-Dazs off the hallway table. "I see you're still eating crap."

"Isn't it nice to know that some things never change?"

Licking his palm, Vinnie slicked an errant strand of hair back into pomaded place. "I'll betcha ten to one that's your dinner. Come on; I'm starving. Let's go grab a steak."

I took him to the Depot for a king-size meal, after which we hit the Stockman for drinks. Vinnie eye-balled a tee-shirt that hung above the bar and bore the Stockman's emblem—a longhorn steer flashing a shit-eating grin while holding a mug of beer in its hoof. But it was the logo beneath that caught his fancy.

Liquor Up Front, Poker in the Rear.

Vinnie emitted a high-pitched giggle. "That shirt is terrific. I gotta buy a coupla those to take back home to the boys. Even the guys on *The Sopranos* would love 'em!"

I took a sip of my Moose Drool.

"How the hell can you drink something with a name like that?" Vinnie's pinkie remained ever so properly curled as he picked up his Scotch and downed it.

"So Vinnie, are you still living in New Orleans?"

"Nah. That place is shot to hell. Too many damn college kids running around drunk. Anyway, I did my time down there. These days I'm back home in New Yawk with all the other Italians. I don't like living where you can't get a decent pizza."

Vinnie must have worked off whatever debt he'd had to pay, and was once again back in the mob's good graces.

"So what kind of equipment are you planning to take with you on your fishing expedition?" I asked, doing some fishing of my own.

"I thought a coupla sticks a dynamite would do it."

Just as I'd figured. "And what sort of fish are you hoping to catch?"

Vinnie rolled his eyes and ordered another Scotch. "One that won't bite me in the ass. How the hell should I know? Whatever's splashing around in the water. Why? What're youse so curious for?"

I shrugged and drank my beer. "I could use a little excitement in my life. Come on, Vinnie. What gives?"

Little Italy downed his second Scotch and gave me an affectionate shot in the arm. "You ever think about quitting this crap and making some serious money, you let me know. You're a persistent little sucker. I'll give ya that."

"Does that mean you're going to tell me?"

Vinnie must have been feeling pretty relaxed. "Okay. But it's only 'cause we're friends and go a ways back. I got your word that I can trust ya on this, right?"

"You know how it works, Vinnie. I don't get involved, as long as you're not here to kill someone or deal in illegal wildlife."

"Kill someone! That's rich," he snickered. "I'm just taking care of some unfinished business for the boys, is all. I get the job done, I get bumped up at work. Kinda like a promotion."

So far, so good. Now it was time for the million-dollar question. "And what kind of work are you doing these days?"

Vinnie paused and thought about that for a moment. "Let's just say I'm in the collection business. You know, like someone steals a chunk of cash from my employers? Well, they'd like it back. I'm here to track the guy down. I just wanna have a little talk with him, is all. I'm sure Rudy will see things my way."

"Who are you talking about?"

"A short, yappy little guy with a personality about as annoying as a gnat. Tomasso is the last name he goes by."

The steak dinner queasily rock-'n'-rolled in my stomach. Tomasso was one of the aliases living in Benny Gugliani's medicine cabinet!

"I figure the guy's gotta stick out like a sore thumb living in this friggin' state."

"What makes you think he's here?" I asked, doing my best to appear disinterested.

"I tracked him down as far as Phoenix, then I got a tip that he's living somewhere up here in the woods. You know. Kinda like the Unabomber."

"So, how much did this guy take?"

"Just outta curiosity?"

"Just out of curiosity."

"Let's say several mil."

"I see. And what happens if you can't find him?"

"That ain't an option."

The words hung in the air like dead weight.

"But don't you worry about that. It ain't your problem. Anyways, I'm stayin' at the Hilton for the next coupla days. What say we get together some more while I'm here?"

"That would be fine. The only thing is that I'm heading off for a while. I have to go down to Yellowstone on a case," I fibbed, my mind reeling with the new information about Benny Gugliani.

"What's down there?"

I hesitated.

"Hey, I tell you. You tell me. That's how it works."

"Grizzlies are being killed for their gallbladders. It's an Asian medicinal thing."

"That's disgusting," Vinnie commiserated and made a sour face. "Anyone does something like that deserves to be whacked, hacked, and dumped in the river in a barrel. They're the scum of the earth, hurting poor little animals."

I didn't bother to tell him *this* poor little animal not

only had the strength of a pile driver in each claw, but wouldn't think twice about tearing him wide open.

"Sorry that I won't be around more," I said as we parted for the night.

"That's okay. I'll catch up with ya at some point along the way." Vinnie gave me a sharp pat on the cheek and lumbered off toward the Hilton.

I felt slightly guilty about having lied, even as I wondered how much of a "coincidence" it really was that Vinnie had looked me up—and if this was the money from the Medicare scam. I went to bed with that thought.

I drifted off contemplating what the possible connection might be between Vinnie, Benny Gugliani, Doc Hutchins, and the bear gallbladder trade.

Soon I was no longer in my room but deep in grizzly country. Hawks and eagles soared lazily overhead as I hiked up a steep ravine. It was a mystical zone of grandeur where the wild things met—badger, bear, and wolverine.

In no time at all, I was standing atop a mesa and looking down upon the rest of the world. Not a sound, not a murmur destroyed the absolute silence. That is, until a resounding crash broke out and I whirled around to face a Sherman tank of hurtling fur. A grizzly was coming straight for me. The critter's muscles undulated beneath a coat that shone luminescent in the light, almost as if a ghost on four stocky legs were attacking.

Reality hit as its jaws grabbed hold of my body. Looking up, I saw a giant paw slash through the air like a machete. My pulse roared in my ears and the breath rushed from my lungs as five honed claws ripped through skin, flesh, and bone. I knew that Death had come for me.

If you act like prey, you become prey, my brain shrieked.

But I could barely think above the loud buzzing that filled the air. The sound was that of my bones crunching. Each excruciating gnash drove home the grizzly's point.

You have to decide which it will be. I either cease to exist, or you fight harder for me. The wilderness is no Disneyland and man is not the most powerful creature to walk this earth. That's what people hate more than anything else. I make them face their primeval fear.

I jerked awake with a start and found myself covered in cold sweat. I knew deep in my heart that I'd just been visited by Old Caleb. My blood rushed through my veins as I struggled to catch my breath. Then I got up and checked every corner in the room, knowing that the bogeyman never slept.

Fourteen

After that dream, I didn't wait until sunrise, but drove like a bat out of hell north, aware that I was on the trail of something big. I could feel it in my bones, in every vein, in every cell. It was as if I'd been jogging my way through this case; now I was determined to push the throttle up to full speed.

I hotfooted it straight to Benny's house. Naturally, the entrance gate was closed and locked. I planted my finger on the buzzer and didn't let up until Benny finally responded.

"You stupid backwoods moron! Get outta here before I nuke your ass back to the missing link, whoever the hell this is!"

"Rise and shine, Benny. Wipe the crud from your eyes and take a look at the monitor. It's Rachel Porter and I want to talk to you *now*!"

A stream of profanities poured through the speaker, after which the gate reluctantly swung open. Even the nude statues seemed to still be asleep as I parked and strode up the walkway. Benny was waiting to greet me, dressed in pajamas decorated with little tommy guns. You could take the boy out of the mob, but the mob remained in the boy forever. His Davy Crockett cap sat askew on his head and a sleep mask hung from his neck.

"Am I supposed to invite you in, too?"

"That would be nice."

His tiny bare feet slapped along the marble floor as I followed the sway of his coonskin tail.

"You know how early it is? My damn coffeemaker hasn't even kicked in yet!"

I flicked the machine on for him.

"You weren't completely honest with me the other day, Benny." I needed to play this just right if I hoped to get any more information.

"What the hell are you talking about now?" But his coon tail began to twitch, as if in acknowledgment of his guilt.

I cut right to the chase. "Does the name Rudy Tomasso ring a bell with you?"

Benny hunched his little shoulders and curled his fingers up by his face. "Ooh! You're really scaring me now, Porter. So you got the name off one of the vials in my medicine cabinet. Anyone ever tell you that you oughta get a life? All it proves is someone named Rudy stayed with me, and that you're a big snoop."

"Then you probably won't be interested in the fact that an old friend of mine just flew in from back East. By the way, my nickname for him is Little Italy, and he's here looking for your *pal* Rudy."

Benny turned a shade paler than his statues. "Oh shit! You know damn well *I'm* Rudy Tomasso. That's the identity the government gave me."

We were finally getting somewhere.

"You didn't happen to tell your pal where I live, did you?" Benny asked, starting to shiver like a wet Chihuahua.

"Of course not. But I think it would be smart if you called your friends at witness protection and told them to relocate you."

Benny began to hop around from foot to foot as if dancing on a bed of hot coals. "I can't! I left the damn program over a year ago!"

Brilliant. "What did you do that for?"

"It's a long story," he dodged.

"No problem; I've got time. Or should I call my friend and save him the trouble of hunting you down?" I let the threat hang in the air. "Why don't you start talking and I'll pour us some coffee?"

Benny hemmed and hawed, with his rear end hovering above a chair. I gave him a helpful push and handed him a cup of coffee. "Begin!"

"For chrissakes, who lit a fire under your ass?" he grumbled.

I pulled out my cell phone and started to punch in a series of numbers.

"All right, already! Those government morons relocated me to some stinking suburb in Phoenix after I testified. We're talking the middle of the fucking desert. What the hell was I supposed to do out there? I began to hang out at a strip club called the Sugar Shack. That's where I met Cherry.

"We hit it off and she moved into my place. Things were going great—until she scammed a bunch of cash outta me and split." Benny dumped three teaspoons of sugar into his coffee. "I didn't bother to ask *Mother, may I* when I left the witness protection program. I just packed up my bags and went after her. By the time I tracked her down in Montana, she was already working at Big Bertha's and shacked up with militia boy. So I cut her a deal."

Gee, wasn't he the nice guy. "Exactly what kind of deal are you talking about?"

"I'd let her live if she forked over all the money and gave me an intro to the United Christian Patriots."

"Why did you want an in with them?"

Benny shook his head, making it clear that I was terribly dense. "Why do you think? I had a business idea. I'd seen their catalogue and felt it had room for improvement. My plan was to sell them on retooling the image. You know, make it glossier, more upscale, very cutting edge. Sort of a hip militia version of Hammacher Schlemmer, selling everything the up-to-the-minute survivalist could possibly want."

I had to hand it to him; it was better than hawking hot tubs. "I take it they went for the idea. What was the business arrangement?"

"I'd foot all expenses and, in exchange, get a cut of the business."

Now I knew where the mob's money had gone. "And that's when you changed your name to Rory Calhoun?"

"Yeah. Who the hell's gonna live in Marlboro Country with a name like Tomasso?"

"So how's business doing?"

"It's booming! We're about to expand onto the Internet. Get a load of this—the name of the site is, jesusiscoming.com. Pretty catchy, huh? In fact, things are going so well that I plan to take the catalogue public in less than a year. That's a little stock tip for you," Benny generously offered.

"Thanks. Too bad that's never going to happen."

"Whadda ya talkin' about?" Benny wailed, and his rear end flew out of the seat.

"How should I put this?" I tapped a finger against my lips. "The state of your health depends on keeping *me* happy."

Benny's butt fell back in the chair like a lead balloon. "You really *are* a Big Apple babe. You get off on bustin' a guy's balls."

"Enough flattery; I want information. Are the Lungrens involved in the bear gallbladder trade?"

Benny dramatically wiped his brow. "Whew! And here I thought you were gonna shake me down for millions."

No, that's Vinnie's job. "I'm waiting."

"Hey, I gotta good one for you. How do ya tell the difference between a black bear and a grizzly? Black bear poop has fur and berries in it, while grizzly poop is filled with buttons, zippers, and Fish and Wildlife badges."

"You're stalling."

"Okey-dokey, Smokey. You want info? Here it is. I have no friggin' idea. What the hell do I care about that crap? You want my personal opinion? The kid could be involved in the trade. But the old man? If he's gonna do something illegal, you damn well better believe it's gonna be worth a whole lot more money than that."

"What about Hutchins?" I pressed.

"Who knows *what* that freaky deaky is into? It wouldn't surprise me if he was running a meth lab outta the clinic."

Now *that* made sense.

"What about this Italian friend of yours? Can you ditch him?" Benny asked.

"No problem. As long as you dig around and get me some rock-solid leads on who's killing grizzlies. Otherwise, your address just might slip out."

I reconnected with the blacktop before punching in Running's phone number.

"Jesus Christ, Porter! Where have you been?" His voice was short and terse.

"Didn't Sally give you my message?"

"Yeah, she did. And I left messages at both your office and Ornish's home around four o'clock this morning. But you weren't at either place." There was a slight pause before he continued. "So, what's up? Is your boyfriend in town?"

I was caught by surprise as little pinpricks of delight erupted along my spine. Matthew was jealous!

"No, some prankster broke into my office and I had to run down and check out the damage. I was probably already on the road, heading back up here when you called. Why? Is there any particular reason you were trying to reach me?"

I held my breath, secretly hoping that Running would say he couldn't live another minute without seeing me again.

"I was kicking around near the Milk River complex yesterday and discovered a snare that hadn't yet been tripped."

Shit! Wouldn't you know something good would happen the moment I left?

"What did you do?"

"I disabled it, of course. It's still early enough to head back up there and do some surveillance. Are you interested in coming along?"

"Nothing could keep me away."

"Okay, then meet me at my office on the double. We'll leave from there."

My wheels nearly flew the remaining distance to Browning. I arrived to find Running leaning against his old blue pickup, waiting for me. A covey of wings sprang to life in my stomach, where they beat in rhythm with the pounding of my heart. Matt's jet-black hair hung loose about his shoulders, and those almond eyes watched my every move. I tried hard to convince myself that I felt nothing more than anticipation over the impending hunt. But there was no denying things had changed between us since that kiss.

I reached for the passenger door handle just as Running did, and our hands touched, sparking a mini-conflagration. I couldn't have felt more flustered if I'd been standing there nude. I quickly climbed inside and closed the door—but not before catching the knowing smile that flickered across Running's lips.

I did my best to ignore the sexual tension as we rode in awkward silence. We finally reached a spot where I'd never been before. Running pulled off the road and parked close to a grove of trees.

"We'll have to hike a little farther than usual, but this is the back way into the location. No one will think to keep watch from this direction."

I quietly followed as we crossed a field as white as a

shroud. The only thing marring the tableau was a pile of weather-beaten bones. That, and the grizzly tracks stalking the ground. I shuddered, remembering my dream of Old Caleb.

"Good. The place still looks the same as it did last night," Matthew said as we arrived at the scene. "Keep an eye out while I set something up in which we can take cover."

I had every intention of maintaining a vigilant guard for both two- and four-legged critters. It didn't take long for Matthew to construct a well-camouflaged lean-to.

"Wait here. I'm going to reset the snare."

Running was a study in fluid motion as he swiftly set to work on the trap. He appeared to be an old hand at ambushes, rigging the wires so that our human predator wouldn't just be caught, but would be pulled off his feet to hang upside down. Matthew next removed his badge and placed it near the snare, as a sort of X-marks-the-spot. Having finished, he backed up while smoothing his footprints away with a branch. He caught my look of admiration and grinned.

"My badge ought to draw the perp's attention and help lure him into our trap."

"Very clever," I concurred.

"It's life's simple pleasures that make me happy," Matthew chuckled. "This is going to be quite the amusement ride for our friend. It should also give us a chance to ask him a few pointed questions before we cut him down. Let's see how much *he* likes swinging from the end of a rope."

I couldn't have agreed more. "I'll bet that it turns out

to be Kyle Lungren," I ventured, feeling pretty smug about my guess.

"Personally, I believe it's gonna be his old man. Tell you what. If I lose, I'll buy you dinner."

He smiled, and those impossibly high cheekbones trapped my heart in their very own snare. I'd never felt so confused, guilty, and excited all at once.

"But what I still can't figure out is how this guy manages to lure grizzlies in without planting a pile of blood and guts," Running said.

Still diligently on the lookout for any sign of Old Caleb, my eyes landed on an object partially hidden by brush. On the ground sat a metal cylinder that blended in with the snow—a small propane tank. The black plastic safety knob on its top resembled the one I'd found on the ground only a few days ago.

"The bears are being baited with propane." I directed Matthew's gaze toward the tank. "I've heard the smell drives them crazy. I'll bet you a Snickers bar that thing is turned on."

It was Running's turn to gaze in amazement. "Damn! You just might be right."

He tilted his head and listened for any foreign sound, ran over to shut off the valve, and quickly returned.

"So, I'm willing to pop for a sumptuous dinner and all you offer in return is a lousy candy bar?" Matthew teased as he settled down next to me.

I pulled a Snickers from my pocket and tossed it to him. "Here. I'm giving you one just because I'm a good sport."

A light layer of snow had begun to fall, caressing the

ground like a wedding veil. Matthew bit into the gooey chocolate and then held it for me to take a bite.

"Why don't you tell me about that boyfriend of yours?" he suggested.

My teeth sank into the soft, creamy bar, delighting in the first surge of caramel and sugar. "What do you want to know?"

"For one thing, why isn't he here with you?"

Good question. "With our separate careers, it seems we're never able to work it out so that we're in the same place at the same time."

"Did you ever stop to think there might be a reason for that?"

"Such as?"

"Maybe you're not really meant to be together."

My heart ached at the mere suggestion. I was about to protest, when Matthew held up a hand and stopped me.

"Shh. Listen."

All I heard at first was the wind whispering through pine needles. Then came muffled footsteps that plodded heavily through the snow. My pulse joined in the march, hammering wildly as a figure strode into view.

The man was a walking slice of the woods, dressed in camo pants and a parka so that he looked like a tree on the move.

Swish, swish. Swish, swish, the fabric of his pants legs murmured, as though conspirators were exchanging high-level secrets.

In his hand was a .30-06 shotgun, capable of firing a 220-grain open point cartridge. The ammo was particularly vile. It expands as it hits its target, making it all the more deadly should it strike a vital spot. Though the figure was tall and slender, I still couldn't be completely certain who it was—until a long strand of greasy blond hair slipped out of the parka's hood. The culprit was Kyle Lungren.

He must have picked up on my adrenaline. He stopped and suspiciously began to sniff at the air. Then, being the thief he was, his eyes were drawn to the piece of glittering metal. Lungren slowly approached Running's badge, just as Matthew had predicted. Greed overcame any sense of caution he might have otherwise had.

The next second he was no longer standing on the ground but hanging from his feet, dangling in the air like a fish on a hook. The shotgun flew out of his hands. Running and I scrambled out of the lean-to to claim our prize as Lungren's eyes bulged at us in anger and surprise.

"You goddamn filthy Indian!" he screamed, uselessly flailing his arms.

"Hey! What about me?" I inquired, feeling left out.

Matthew silently stood with his arms folded across his chest, looking every inch the modern-day Geronimo—until a geyser of laughter bubbled up, bursting his stoic bubble.

"Okay, Porter. 'Fess up! How did you know it would be Kyle?"

"He accidentally left a calling card among the debris in my office." I motioned to Lungren. "I see you forgot to wear the jagged heart pin on your jacket today."

Running looked at me curiously and I pulled the

item from my pocket. Matthew ran a finger along its serrated edge.

"Whew! This thing looks more like a weapon than jewelry. You must really attract the ladies with this, Lungren," he taunted.

"You think you know us so damn well, don't you, you fucking Injun? Well, forget it! You'll never become a white man!" Kyle spat at our feet. "That's why you hate us so much. Isn't that right, Running? You never could measure up to my daddy, no matter how hard you tried!"

I stared at the two men, wondering what the connection was between them. Up to this point, I'd been unaware that Running and Lungren even knew each other. While tempted to follow it up, I was also mindful that time was ticking away. I needed to question Kyle about the bear gallbladder trade right now if I hoped to keep the element of surprise on my side.

"Cut the crap, Lungren. I know what you've been up to."

"Oh yeah? And what's that?" he sneered. Lungren tried to grab me and I deftly stepped out of his reach.

"You've been killing grizzlies for their gallbladders. But maybe we can cut a deal. I want the names of those people you've been selling to, along with who your partners are. You give me details about the pipeline and there's a good chance I'll be able to keep you out of jail."

"Like I'd ever tell you anything, you jackbooted thug! Your government has no legal authority over me. You work for an oppressive tyranny that's anti-God and anti-gun, doing everything it can to take away our rights! Face it, Porter. You're just as scared as everyone else, 'cause you know that in the end we'll win. As for you, Running, my daddy always said you were a coward playing at being a recon soldier. But then, what else could you expect from a lousy mud person?"

I saw Matthew's hands clench and his jaw grow tight. Lungren noticed it as well, and began to laugh like a hyena. I stared, fixated by the man's distorted features, made all the more ugly tainted with hate.

"There are too many of us for you to do anything about! You're doomed! Your days are numbered!" he ranted. "As for the bear gallbladder trade? I acted alone.

"I'm just the latest in a long line of messengers. All your kind will be blown away on the day of the apocalypse! God save the United Christian Patriots!" he howled in a frenzy.

Lungren suddenly reached into the waistband of his pants, whipped out a .40-caliber handgun, and waved it around as he laughed madly. The next thing I knew, Running's hand slammed against my back and pushed me down hard to the ground.

But we weren't Lungren's target. He placed the barrel of the gun inside his mouth and put his finger on the trigger.

"No, Kyle! Don't do it!" I yelled and struggled onto my feet. I began to run toward him, only to be tackled once again.

I fell so hard that the breath rushed from my body as a shot roared out above me. Then there was nothing but silence. Except for the creak of the rope, which squeaked like a rusty metronome counting down the last moments of Kyle's life. *Tick, tock. Tick, tock.* Lungren's body swung like a pendulum until the rope eventually came to a stop, the snow below soaked with blood.

I stared in disbelief at where his head had once been. Then I turned my own head away and threw up.

Fifteen

The atmosphere in the FBI office in Browning was so tense, I thought the very air would shatter if I hiccupped. I half-expected that Running and I would be ordered to start piling sandbags around the building to fortify defenses. We had committed the ultimate sin in the West: we'd pissed off the local militia.

"What the hell did you two geniuses think you were doing?" demanded FBI agent Howard Dixon. "Talk about your royal screw-ups!"

Dixon looked much like the room—worn out and badly in need of help. His two-man crew was off investigating drug and murder charges on other parts of the reservation. That meant he'd been left alone to deal with us today.

"Look, grizzlies are being whacked. We wanted to catch the perp, and the best way to do that was to lure him into his own trap," Matthew calmly responded.

"Well, congratulations, boy-o. You did one hell of a job."

Even Dixon's dingy white shirt looked upset. Its wrinkled tail was AWOL, having escaped his pants to flap around in protest. Dixon ran a hand over his bare scalp in frustration.

"The fact is, Kyle Lungren wouldn't have committed

suicide if the bear gallbladder trade was all he was involved in," I piped up, adding my two cents. "He'd have received a slap on the wrist from the system, and you know that as well as I do. There has to be something bigger going on."

"Agent Porter is absolutely right," Running concurred. "Come on, Dixon—think about it. He acted out of desperation. He knew we were on his trail and was afraid that we'd uncover something of more consequence."

"My, my. Don't *you* two have the little support tag team going," Dixon said contemptuously. "Next you're going to tell me that he wasn't acting alone."

"You're right. That's why he did the only thing he could—he claimed that no one else was involved, and then removed himself from the equation. It's the ultimate patriotic act for these guys: it takes the heat off his cohorts and allows them to carry on with their work. The tactic makes perfect military sense," Matthew insisted.

Dixon flung a folder across his desk in disgust. "Thanks for the lesson in deep cover, Rambo. I'll be sure to confer with the two of you the next time we're about to be invaded by a foreign country. But right now, I'm trying to put a lid on the possibility of another Oklahoma City happening right here in Browning!"

"Why is it that you guys are always such assholes?" *Oops! Did I just say that?* "You'd think we handed Lungren the gun and told him to shoot himself!"

"You might as well have, hotshot," Dixon snapped, skewering me with a glare. "You presented him with the perfect opportunity to martyr himself. It's basic

Psych 101—or doesn't Fish and Wildlife hire college grads?"

"Sure, but unlike FBI recruits, we don't come off a factory line with one universal brain," I volleyed back.

"All right, that's enough!" Running intervened.

"Jesus Christ, I'd have thought at least *you* knew better, Running. You grew up in this damn place. I never imagined you'd let personal history get in the way," Dixon attacked.

"I didn't," Matthew replied between clenched teeth.

The two conducted a standoff until Dixon blinked.

"I don't have time for this crap. So here's what I want you to do: don't go home—either of you—until we get this thing sorted out. I want you both to stay at the Big Sky Motel in Cut Bank using these assumed names. It's for your own safety."

I glanced at the slip of paper. *Edith Freehold.* Now I knew Dixon didn't like me.

Running didn't fare any better. "Archie Buckmeister?"

"Yeah. It's my brother-in-law's name. You got a problem with that?" Dixon growled. "Both of you are to lay low for the next couple of days. We're flying in a few more agents to work on the case, because the next forty-eight hours are going to be crucial. We've got to reassure the Lungrens that we're doing everything possible to investigate the death of their son. That means I want the two of you available for questioning at a moment's notice."

Dixon threw Running a set of keys. "Here. I rented an unmarked vehicle for you. Make sure you're not being followed to the motel."

The significance of what had actually taken place finally began to sink in. Running and I were now walking targets for the militia. We started to head out the door, only to have Dixon's voice stop us.

"Oh yeah—and one other thing. Do us all a favor and don't get into any more trouble."

Neither of us spoke as Running drove toward Cut Bank. It was as though we'd just been banished to Elba. I wondered if this was how Benny Gugliani had felt upon being forced to move and change his name.

We checked in as Edith and Archie and received side-by-side rooms in a run-down motel that the AAA would never have recommended.

"What do you say, Edith? Feel like grabbing some dinner?" Matthew teased.

"Oh God, please don't call me that. I feel as though we're trapped in a bad rerun of *All in the Family*."

"You can't say Dixon doesn't have a sense of humor," Matthew agreed.

"I've got to take a shower or I'm going to crawl out of my skin. Give me fifteen minutes and I'll be ready."

"Sure. We can pick up a couple of toothbrushes and whatever else you need while we're out."

I'd forgotten about that. I had none of the essentials with me—makeup, hairbrush, mouthwash, deodorant. It appeared that Running was about to see me at my worst—au naturel.

I stepped into the shower and scrubbed as hard as I could, determined to wash away the horror of Kyle Lungren's death. But there was no way I could get the image of him twisting round and round on that rope out of my mind—until I glanced down at my feet and imagined that the water coming off me was tinged the color of blood. I let out a muffled scream. It was *Psycho* all over again.

My heart pounded so hard I nearly passed out. There was a reason I'd taken baths rather than showers until I was nearly thirty years old. I stared in horror as the pinkish water playfully curled around my toes.

The illusion refused to dissipate until Lungren's rope finally came to a standstill and the last of Kyle's life had hypnotically circled down the drain. I rubbed my eyes and the water ran clear again. Perhaps it was a sign that Kyle was now through with me.

I was drying off with the flimsiest of cheap towels when my cell phone rang. Sally didn't know I was back up here yet. That left either Dixon or my boss calling to scream. Unless it was Matthew checking to see if I was ready.

"Hello?" I answered, hoping it was door number three.

"I was wrong about you, Porter," a female voice hissed. "You *are* the beast. The storm is coming and you're going to pay for your sins!"

Honey Lungren hung up before I could answer. I remained standing there, nude and shivering in the cold. I turned up the room's tiny heater, but my teeth continued to chatter. Kyle Lungren was once again twisting upside down on that rope. I quickly got dressed and left the room, shutting the door firmly behind me.

Running was already in the Explorer with its heater turned on, and we drove to a McDonald's, where we ordered some comfort food—four Big Macs, two large fries, and a couple of Cokes. After that, Matthew dropped me off at a drugstore.

"Get what you need. I'll be back in a couple of minutes."

Though the owner had been ready to close shop, he reluctantly let me in. He was thoroughly pleased by the time I was through. My "essentials" had mushroomed into body lotion, shampoo, and crème rinse, along with an embarrassing amount of I-can't-live-without-it makeup.

"Christ! It looks like you've given the economy of Cut Bank quite a boost. I thought we were only staying a few days," Matthew remarked as he picked me up with my booty.

"Hey, a gal needs what a gal needs." I spotted his stash from the grocery store and snuck a peak. Inside was a box of Oreos and a bottle of red wine. "I see that you picked up your own essentials."

"Damn straight."

I knew there was a good reason why I liked this guy; I just hoped he believed in sharing. We headed back to the motel, where we had our McDinner in my room. Matthew opened the wine while I scrounged around in the bathroom and returned with two plastic cups. He poured, swirled and sniffed before taking a sip.

I was just glad for anything that helped numb the events of the day.

"So, do you want to tell me what this mysterious connection is between you and the Lungrens, or am I supposed to pretend that I haven't picked up on it?"

"What do you want to know?" Matthew mumbled between bites of his Big Mac.

I was tempted to reach over and wipe a dab of ketchup from his mouth, but decided it would be best to keep my hands to myself.

"For starters, how does Kyle's father know you were in the military?"

"Because he was my commander in Desert Storm."

I nearly dropped my fries in my lap. "You've got to be kidding me."

"It gets even better." Matthew reached over and grabbed a handful of my fries, having already polished off his own. "You don't mind, do you?"

I mourned the loss of so much as one stringy little potato. "Of course not. Help yourself." I figured it was a down payment on my share of the Oreos. "So fill me in. What's the scoop?"

Running took a moment to appraise me before dropping his bombshell. "Rafe Lungren's first wife, who was Kyle's mom, left him to marry my father."

This time my fries *did* fall out of my hand. "She's your *stepmother*? Now I know you're putting me on." This was better than a soap opera!

"That's why Kyle hated me so much. Not only did I see more of his own mother than he did, but I was closer to her than he ever was. She was never allowed back on the compound to visit him, and Kyle was prohibited from setting foot on the reservation."

Things were beginning to make more sense. "How does she feel about the situation?"

"She died a few years ago, but I know that she never regretted her choice."

"Does Rafe Lungren hate you, as well?" I asked.

Matt opened the bag of Oreos and offered them to me. I demurely took only four.

"You better believe it. Has Sally told you about her son?"

"I know that the two of you served together and that he was killed by friendly fire." I twisted the top layer off an Oreo and devoured its creamy center, after which I took tiny bites of the cookie, methodically turning it like a wheel until nothing was left.

"I don't know how friendly it was. I'll tell you something that I've never even told Sally."

The fact that I was about to learn a secret was enough to give me goose bumps.

"Justin stepped in front of me at the moment the bullet was fired. I firmly believe it came from Lungren's rifle and that the bullet was meant for me."

That helped to explain plenty.

"And Lungren was never convicted?"

"You're forgetting those two all-important words—friendly fire. Besides, I was never able to prove it. The incident was essentially covered up."

"But you're absolutely certain that Lungren was the shooter?"

"Without the shadow of a doubt." Running popped an Oreo into his mouth. "Lungren changed after Desert Storm. Don't get me wrong: he was always a bigot, but he also loved this country. Something happened in Kuwait. He came back disgusted with the government. That's when he decided there was some sort of one-world conspiracy at work, and started his own militia group."

"Funny, but the man didn't seem all that lethal to me when we met. Honey Lungren was the scary one." Her recent phone call had cemented my initial impression.

Matt's hand touched mine and I instinctively jerked. Once again, there was that electrical current that surged through me. "Don't let him fool you. Lungren's a coyote. Don't ever turn your back on the man."

Maybe it was the wine, or having Matt confide in me, that made the situation feel so intimate, but I began to babble out of sheer nervousness. "Okay, we both agree that Kyle shot himself to throw us off the trail of something. Do you have any idea what it might be?"

Running must have sensed my discomfort. He removed his hand, leaving my skin feeling preternaturally cold.

"My guess is that the group is involved big time in the illegal sale of arms. That would bring in plenty of money."

I drained my plastic cup and Matthew refilled it. Since the wine helped warm me, I drank a little more.

"Would you happen to remember the names of some of the people on the rez who are mysteriously missing, or believed to have been killed by a grizzly?"

"Sure. You've got Harley Thunder, Mary Crane, Doris Swiftdeer, Ira Blackman, and both Galen and Nancy Come-By-Night. And Helen Lungren Running." Matthew's eyes narrowed and the yellow glints sprang to life. "Why? What's your sudden interest in this?"

I looked at Running, and every cell in my body began to thrum like individual spark plugs. If I were a car,

I'd have been a Maserati raring to go. Equally disconcerting was that I could feel the same sexual tension radiating from him. I tried to cover it, but my cheeks burned like two hot plates.

"I don't know. I just have a gut feeling that there might be some sort of connection."

Though I never saw him move, Running was suddenly sitting beside me.

"And what kind of connection would that be? On the one hand, you had Kyle killing bears to supply the Asian medicinal trade. On the other end of the spectrum are a number of unsolved cases involving people who have turned up dead or missing. Of course, not a whole lot can get done when the only ones allowed to investigate are three overworked FBI agents. It's easier to bury the cases than deal with them. Still the gallbladder trade and the exploding crime rate are two totally separate issues—or am I missing something here?"

"I know it sounds crazy, but I'm certain there's a connection. Just think about it. All that's ever been found of the victims are their bones, which have been chomped on by grizzlies. Doesn't it strike you as odd that evidence continually gets destroyed in this manner? What better way for a clever serial killer to get rid of bodies and, at the same time, disguise a rash of murders?"

Matthew sighed and calmly shook his head at my theory, totally pissing me off.

"Let me get this straight. You believe there's a serial killer loose on the rez who lures in bears with the ulterior motive of having them dispose of his victims? That is, of course, when he's not just killing the critters and

taking their gallbladders to make a few extra bucks. So
who is this guy? The Hannibal Lecter of the Rockies?"

When he put it that way, my hunch *did* sound pretty
improbable.

"Why do I get the feeling that you're trying to juggle
the pieces any which way you can, so that the culprits
turn out to be the United Christian Patriots?" he asked.

It was true, though I hadn't realized it until Matthew
said it aloud. Now that he had, I was more convinced
than ever that I was on the right track.

"Listen, I discovered something that I haven't shared
with you yet. Did you know that Doc Hutchins lives on
the militia compound?"

Running shrugged. "Of course. It's common knowledge."

"Doesn't that bother you?" I asked, perplexed at his
attitude.

"It's not as if we have any choice when it comes to
medical care. All that matters is that Hutchins does his
job, and as far as I can tell, that's not a problem."

I gritted my teeth and continued. "Okay, then. How
about this? Hutchins was part of a Medicare scam involving the mob a few years ago. He agreed to testify
against them if he was placed in the federal witness
protection program. The government sent him here."

I expected Matthew to howl in indignation. Instead
he split the last of the wine between our two cups.

"I believe you, Rachel, and the whole thing sucks.
Still, you're talking about misappropriation of government funds, not some deranged psycho killing Indians
on the Blackfeet reservation."

"Then that's it? You believe Kyle was solely responsible for slaughtering all those grizzlies and no one else?"

Running leaned in close, and my pulse automatically quickened. "I didn't say that. Our case is far from over; Kyle was only a bit player. There's obviously a whole group at work. I'm also convinced the gallbladder trade is just the tip of the iceberg and that something much larger is going on. Maybe it's weapons, and maybe it's not."

He touched his cup to mine, as if he were about to make a toast. "Either way, I have no intention of dropping the ball at this point. That would mean Kyle had achieved what he'd wanted, and I'm not about to let him win. But you're pushing too hard, Rachel. You have to allow situations to develop on their own. Not everything will run on your time schedule."

Running was right. I *did* live by my own timetable—one in which the loss of a single second was totally reprehensible. There was still far too much to do. I'd been trotting through life up until my mother's death. Now, just as with this case, I intended to attack it at full gallop. I could feel my own mortality slipping away and was painfully aware that it might run out at any moment. It gave me the courage to ask a question I might not otherwise have dared.

"Matt, you said that your stepmother died. But she's on the list of those who are missing. So how do you know that she didn't just decide to walk away one day and never look back?"

Running studied me and his eyes softened, as though he understood the aching sense of emptiness that filled my soul. I felt as if I'd been deserted.

"People who love you don't leave of their own accord, Rachel. It's one of those things over which they have no control. I miss her as much as if we'd been of the same blood. But I also know that it must have been her time to go."

Although I'd buried my mother, I still held her close, hoping to ease my pain, refusing to let her spirit pass over so that she could find peace of her own.

Matthew's voice was oddly soothing as it reached inside to pluck at my heart. "Death mocks us all, Rachel. We just have to keep trying to outsmart it. The best way to do that is to enjoy the time we have left here."

Matthew polished off his wine. "Speaking of which, it's getting late. I should probably let you catch some sleep." He stood up and stretched.

I watched as he raised those strong arms above his head; I had never felt more vulnerable and alone.

Ghostly laughter broke out, reinforcing my fear. It was Kyle Lungren twisting on that rope, waiting for me to turn out the lights. And I knew, more than anything else, that I didn't want to be alone tonight.

Running was halfway out the door when I jumped up and followed. My response caught him by surprise, and he stopped and turned around. He looked at me for what felt like an eternity, saying nothing. Then his hand slowly began to travel up my spine.

"Don't leave. I'm not tired," I entreated in a low, husky whisper.

Running tested the waters further by pressing his lips against mine. All I wanted was for his arms to wrap themselves around me once more. That is, until his fingers softly began to play with my breasts.

"It's your call, Rachel."

I didn't think. I only felt, as I drew Matthew back inside the room and he closed the door. There was no need to say another word. It was perfectly clear that I was falling down the rabbit hole. Kyle Lungren withdrew into the darkness as I pressed myself tighter against Running, slipping faster and deeper into the void. Matthew pulled me down onto the bed, and we explored each other from head to toe, as I put all my misgivings on hold.

Sixteen

Rrrrring! Rrrrring!

I slowly emerged from the dark burrow I'd been curled up in, feeling all safe and snug and warm. My body still tingled after last night's erotic foray, having experienced sensations that I'd never felt before. Part of me wondered if it had all been a dream, since I now found myself alone—until I heard the water running and realized Matthew was taking a shower. The other sound was the incessant ringing of the motel phone.

"Hello?" I croaked. There was an additional sensation that I now became aware of—a steady pounding in my head.

"You sound a little hungover, chère," chortled a familiar voice. "We'll have to figure out a way to spend more time together, if being apart is driving you to drink."

I lost my breath. I struggled to regain it, gasping like a fish out of water. If I weren't already lying in bed, I'd have fallen down.

"Santou?" I sputtered in disbelief. "How did you know where to reach me?"

How else? God has obviously decided to punish you!

"My pal Dixon told me."

"Dixon?" My panicky brain searched for a reference, desperate for something to seize on to.

"You really *did* have too much to drink last night, didn't you?" Santou responded, beginning to sound concerned. "I'm sitting in the FBI office here in Browning."

"What are you doing there?" I nearly wailed.

"I was flown in to help on the Lungren case." His voice dropped to a near whisper. "I wish I was with you right now, chère. But I'm afraid that'll have to wait. So how about you jump in the shower, grab some breakfast, and head on over? We need to review what happened yesterday."

What happened yesterday? My mind suddenly went blank.

Then I heard the shower door swing open, and I was bombarded with memories of every tantalizing moment between Matthew and me last night.

"Chère? Are you all right?"

"Yes, I'm—I'm fine," I replied, struggling to snap out of my waking nightmare.

"By the way, do me a favor. Could you ring your compadre in crime and pass along the message? I'll need him here, as well."

"Sure, no problem," I automatically replied, as my heart began to race. Oh God! Running and Santou were about to come face-to-face!

"Great. Hurry on over. I can't wait to see you," Santou added in a low growl.

Matthew picked that moment to walk into the room with only a towel wrapped around his waist.

"Me, too," I responded and quickly hung up.

Running looked so good that, before Jake's call, I'd have been tempted to lure him back into bed. Judging from his smile, Matthew felt the same way. It rapidly faded as he caught sight of my expression.

"What's the matter?" he asked and sat on the edge of the bed, where his fingers gently combed my hair.

I had no choice but to tell him. "Remember I said that I'm involved with someone? What I didn't mention is that he's with the FBI. He just arrived in Browning to work on the Lungren case."

Matthew's body stiffened and his hand dropped to his side. "The guy's got great timing," he muttered.

I veered between wanting to throw my arms around him and feeling like a deceptive Jezebel. The one constant was my aching heart.

Neither of us spoke, but dressed in awkward silence as we faced away from each other. The leaden quiet continued all the way to Browning, broken only by the sipping of coffee and the munching of donuts.

We walked into the FBI office, where Dixon sat behind his desk and Santou stood anxiously waiting. I was immediately swept up by Jake's profile—the long, sharp nose, the crooked smile, and those deep-set eyes hinting at wanton pleasures. Santou's lips brushed against my cheek and he squeezed my hand, insinuating that this was only the prelude. I knew he probably planned a much more intimate reunion for later on tonight.

By now, Matthew had quietly glided over to join us. I stood like a tongue-tied dolt between the two men.

"Hi. I'm Matt Running, tribal game officer for the Blackfeet reservation." He offered Jake his hand.

The two men instinctively sized each other up.

"Jake Santou, FBI agent."

And boyfriend of that cheating, two-timing, sleep-around gal, Rachel Porter. Oh God.

Santou and Running had yet to break their handshake. Either they were about to duke it out or arm wrestle, or had discovered that they were latently gay.

Running finally broke the silence. "Santou—I seem to remember that name. Wasn't your father one of the Cajuns who worked the oil fields here years ago, during the summers?"

Jake slowly nodded as he studied Matthew's face.

"And you used to come along with him as a kid."

"That's right. How did you know?" Santou asked warily.

Matthew broke into a grin. "I believe it was my uncle who taught you to speak Piegan. Don't you remember me?"

Jake's face lit up and he pumped Matthew's hand. "Of course! In fact, it's due to your uncle that I'm here. I was brought in to work this case specifically because I speak the local language."

"But what does speaking Piegan have to do with the militia?" I asked, feeling bewildered. The way things were going, these two would become best buddies and I'd wind up being dumped.

"Nothing, really. But I've also been asked to investigate a number of reports concerning missing people on the rez."

Neither Running nor I said a word. It wasn't necessary; we felt the same way. Big Brother had arrived in the guise of the FBI and was muscling into our territory.

"Now, what say we start at the beginning and go over what happened yesterday," Santou suggested.

I only half-listened as Running gave a blow-by-blow account from the time we left his vehicle up to the point where Kyle blew off his head.

"Rachel, is there anything you'd like to add?" Jake inquired.

Yeah. I wish you'd let us get on with our work. "Not a thing."

Maybe it was the fact that I wasn't my usual rambunctious self that tipped Santou off. He waited for just the right moment to pull me aside.

"Is there some sort of problem that you want to tell me about?"

"I don't know what you mean," I dodged.

"You've barely said two words since you've been here. I don't claim to be psychic, but that's not normal for you."

"Sorry, Jake. It's just that I'm still kind of tired after yesterday."

He placed a consoling hand on my arm. "Did you have a rough night?"

I unthinkingly pulled away, startled by his question. Damn! I knew that was all Santou would need to start reassessing the situation.

"Yeah. I didn't sleep very well."

He nodded understandingly, but the barest hint of suspicion had begun to take root in his eyes. We rejoined the others and I realized that Matthew had been watching us the entire time. Even worse, both men exchanged a guarded glance and I heard Santou take a deep breath. Its ragged exhalation nicked at my heart.

"Is there anything else we need to go over, or are you done downloading me for the moment?" Running inquired.

The two men silently appraised each other, making me feel like the grand prize in a turkey shoot.

"Nah. It sounds pretty cut-and-dried, so I suppose that's it for now. Oh, except for one thing. Don't bother wasting any more of your time on that bear gallbladder case. The FBI will handle it from here since it involves Kyle Lungren as well."

What? A head of steam rose within me as fast as a stoked engine. "That's all right; I don't consider it a waste. In fact, I *prefer* to continue working the case," I immediately responded, making my position known.

Santou's smile grew thin and tight. "Then let me make myself perfectly clear: you're both to stay off the case. I don't want to go over your heads on this, but I will if necessary."

Jake had never pulled rank on me like this before. The dirty work had always been left to others. Call me paranoid, but I was sure he suspected something was going on between me and Matthew, and this was his form of punishment.

"And just why is the FBI suddenly so interested in the bear gall trade?" I challenged. "As far as I know, wildlife crime is still within my purview."

"Not when it involves the questionable death of a

militia member. Then it becomes a capital case calling for further investigation," Santou swiftly responded, coming down on me hard.

Interesting. Only a minute ago it had been cut-and-dried; now it was questionable. What did Jake think, that Matthew and I had engineered Kyle Lungren's death?

"Have *you* got a problem with that?" Santou aimed the question at Running.

"Hell no, man. Whatever you say," he replied, throwing his hands up in surrender.

That seemed to temporarily appease Jake.

"Sorry, it's just that this is a delicate situation. Listen, what say the three of us get together for dinner tonight? It's on me."

Wouldn't *that* be cozy.

"Think of it as my way of thanking you for accompanying Rachel and not letting her stumble into this thing all on her own."

I was ready to explode, but Matthew must have read my mind and beat me to the punch.

"I didn't *accompany* her anywhere, Santou. The shit that's taking place is happening on *my* reservation. As for Rachel, she's a competent professional who doesn't need *anyone's* help. Thanks for the dinner invitation, but I've already got plans for tonight. Maybe another time." Having said that, Matthew briskly walked out of the room.

"I need to get going, too. I'll talk to you later," I added, anxious to follow him outside. But Santou grabbed hold of my arm.

"Hey, wait a minute! What's the rush? You're supposed to be taking time off, remember?"

"This isn't the only case that I'm working on," I coolly reminded him. "And as far as I know, I still have a job."

Santou loosened his grip. "Okay. Then how about telling me where I can reach you early this evening?"

"I've been staying with a woman by the name of Sally Crossbow. I'll probably go to see her." I quickly scribbled down Sally's number.

Santou folded the scrap of paper and put it in his pocket as he continued to study me closely. "Are you sure everything is all right, chère?"

"Fine." *Other than having my case pulled from me.* "There are just some things I have to do," I lied, refusing to meet his eyes.

Dixon's fingers impatiently drummed on his desktop. "Do you mind wrapping this up, Santou? I didn't bring you here to socialize; we actually have work to do."

Jake held up a hand to fend him off. "Just give me another minute, Dix." Then he turned his attention back to me. "All right. Let's plan to meet tonight. I'll promise we'll sort everything out then."

"Will do." I could feel Santou's eyes suspiciously burrowing into my back as I beat a hasty retreat.

I frantically ran outside, only to find that Matthew was already in his vehicle and beginning to pull away.

"Hold on! Where are you off to?" I shouted.

But Running kept right on going. Either he hadn't heard my plea, or he chose to ignore it. There was only one thing to do—I threw myself onto the hood of his truck. I figured it was hard to ignore a woman hanging off the front of your pickup.

Running had no choice but to slam on the brakes and

reluctantly lower his window. I climbed off the hood, walked over, and firmly plunked my elbows on the ledge, not giving him a chance to speak.

"So, that's it? That's the end of our case? The FBI snarls and all you do is to obligingly roll over for them?" I jabbed, doing my best to provoke the man.

The trace of a smile flickered across his face. It was obvious that he knew what I was up to. "Yeah. You know me and Uncle Sam. I love to be his whipping boy." Matthew brought an arm up and deliberately rested it against mine, his expression one of grim determination. "I'll quit when Custer rises from his grave and takes back Little Big Horn. Until then, I have no intention of giving anything up."

I couldn't help but wonder if that included *me*, as well.

"I fully intend to find out what's happening here on the rez—especially with those FBI hotshots throwing their weight around like a couple of prizefighters. They've got hard-ons just at the thought of taking over our case." Running's eyes met mine in challenge. "So, are you interested in joining my planned insurrection? Or do you take orders from your boyfriend in there?"

A ripple of excitement surged through me—from the touch of his skin, as well as the fervor of his words. "Hey, you're the one that I'm worried about. I've already done plenty to earn *my* reputation. No way in hell am I about to quit now."

Matthew smiled and I was once again the flagrant Jezebel, reveling in a variety of enticing emotions.

"Remember when I told you that my totem spirit is a bear? Well, this case has now become personal. Anywhere in particular that you'd care to start?"

"Yeah. I need to check in with a guy by the name of Benny Gugliani. He's supposed to be digging up some information for me."

"Benny Gugliani?"

"He's another witness protection joker who was involved with Hutchins on that Medicare scam."

Running shook his head and grinned in amusement. "You just refuse to let that thing go, don't you? Kind of like my dog once he locks on to a soup bone."

I shot him a dirty look, not quite sure how to take the remark. "I can't shake the feeling that it somehow comes into play. If it turns out I'm wrong, then I'll buy *you* dinner."

"In that case, I'll come along and meet Gugliani with you."

"Thanks, but I think I should do this by myself."

"Uh-uh." Running's jaw was firmly set. "Consider it a deal breaker if we're to work this case together. Under the present circumstances, it's far too dangerous to go anywhere alone."

As much as I hated to admit it, I knew that Matt was right. I jumped into his pickup and we headed toward Willow Creek.

Benny didn't bother to question my obvious change in vehicles, but buzzed us straight through the gate without a word.

"Nice statues," Matthew commented sardonically as we went up the walkway.

"That's nothing. Wait till you get a load of the door-bell." I laughed.

But Running never had the chance. The entrance swung open before I could knock, and Vinnie Bertucci filled the doorway.

Seventeen

"Hey, New Yawk! How's by you? This is just like old times, when you used to come see me at Hillard's. Remember? I had a funny feeling you'd be dropping by. Only ain't you supposed to be in Yellowstone? Or was that Jellystone? You know, like in Yogi and Boo Boo? I always get those two places confused." A high-pitched giggle followed.

Unbelievable! How the hell did Vinnie ever find this place? Had I left a trail of breadcrumbs behind me?

"Listen, just to show there are no hard feelings, I'm willing to let bygones be bygones and invite ya in. I, for one, believe in playin' fair and square, and sharin' information with my friends whenever possible. Not like *some* people I know."

God, how I hate not having the upper hand.

"Well, come on. Don't just stand there like a coupla statues." Vinnie waved us in through the door.

The sound of pounding was the first thing to greet me. The sight of Benny tied to a chair was the second. His body jerked like a Mexican jumping bean as the chair's wooden legs banged on the floor. Benny scowled upon catching sight of me, and the little coon tail on his cap bobbed furiously.

"Good work, Porter! What the hell'd ya do? Draw the mope a map? Or did you just lead him straight to me?"

I glanced at Vinnie, feeling equally curious.

Vinnie rubbed his flattened nose. "I suppose it was a little of both. Of course, the real clue came when I caught the news about that militia freak blowing himself away. A reporter said some female Fish and Wildlife agent had been there and was now in deep shit because of it. It wasn't hard to figure out who *that* was. I thought maybe you could use some help."

"Thanks. That was very thoughtful," was all I could think of to say.

"Listen, I wouldn't take it too hard, if I were you. It sounds like the guy's gene pool needed to be discontinued anyway," Vinnie added consolingly. Then he took a closer gander at Running. "Hey, lookee here! Whadda ya know? I even get to meet a real, live Indian!"

I could always count on Vinnie to be socially suave.

"Vinnie Bertucci, meet Matthew Running, tribal game officer for the Blackfeet reservation. Matthew, this is Vinnie, an old friend of mine." Introductions over, I brought the subject back to the matter at hand. "So, Vinnie, what's going on? Why do you have Benny tied up?"

"Oh, I see you even know his real name." Vinnie carefully plucked a piece of lint from off his honest-to-God blue satin shirt. "I've been trying to persuade him real nice to give me back the money he owes. But we haven't had a meeting of the minds yet."

"I already told you, I don't have it anymore!" Benny irritably snapped.

"And I told *you* to shut the hell up with that crap!" Vinnie glowered.

He shook a massive fist in Benny's face and the Bopper immediately quieted down. It wasn't hard to understand why— Vinnie was the size of Godzilla, while the Bopper couldn't have taken on Pepe Le Pew.

"All right, that's enough. I say we cut this guy loose." Matthew made a move toward Gugliani's chair.

"Hold it right there, Tonto. You ain't on the reservation and this ain't your problem."

Running turned to me in disbelief. "*How* the hell do you know this guy?"

"Vinnie, do you mind if I take my friend into the dining room and explain it to him?"

"Sure. Just check all knives, guns, and other artillery with me before you do. I don't need to deal with some *Wagon Train* style ambush."

"Like hell I will," Matt began.

"It's okay. Just do it," I advised.

Matthew stared at me as though I were crazy.

"I trusted you on how to handle the bear the other day. Well, think of Vinnie as *my* grizzly. You're going to have to go with me on this one."

We both handed over our guns, and I produced my Speideco knife.

"Very nice," Vinnie approved. "I like a woman with good taste in weapons." Then he patted us down just to double check. "Hey, bring me back one of those cannolis from in there when you're through."

Matthew followed me into the dining room. Vinnie

was right; there was some great-looking pastry on the table. Cannolis, Napoleons, even chocolate éclairs. I almost reached for one, hoping there would be custard inside.

"*Now* do you want to tell me what's going on here?" Matthew demanded.

"I met Vinnie during a case I worked on in New Orleans. The thing is, he's got ties to the mob."

"Thanks for the hot tip. I'd gathered that already," Running dryly replied.

"It all goes back to this Medicare scam I've been telling you about. Apparently Benny ran off with a chunk of the money. Vinnie's here to get it back. But we just might be able to make this thing work for us."

"How so?"

"Vinnie's got a lot of bark and not so much bite—at least, that's what I'm hoping. I don't believe he really plans to hurt the guy, especially since I know about it. I'm going to promise Vinnie that I'll help him get his money back if, in return, he persuades Benny to talk to me."

"Rachel, you can't be serious! You can't trust either one of those goons. We need to get out of here and turn them in immediately," Running protested.

I wasn't willing to give up. "You know what Benny *did* with all that money? He invested it in a business proposition with the United Christian Patriots. I'm telling you, *he's* our key to what's taking place on the rez!"

"I still don't like it," Matthew resisted.

"Then I'm sure Santou and Dixon will be more than

happy to take this off our hands, as well. Who else do you think is going to end up working the case?"

"Okay, you win," Matthew grudgingly relented. "We'll try playing it your way for now. But the moment the situation begins to spin out of control, I'm bringing it to a stop. Is that clear?"

"Absolutely. Whatever you say."

Matthew was temporarily mollified. *Whatever you say*—isn't it amazing how men always fall for that line? I grabbed a cannoli, along with an éclair, and we walked back into the living room.

"Hey, Vinnie. Can I talk to you in private for a minute?"

"Sure," he said, looking like *Viva Zapata!* Vinnie had stuck our guns in the waistband of his pants, which were already stretched to their limit. "But I ain't leavin' this room. We can gab in the corner. What's up?"

"I'm going to be honest with you. I've also been trying to get information out of Benny. But he hasn't been very forthcoming with me, either. What say we help each other out on this?"

Vinnie took a delicate bite of his cannoli, and then daintily licked each finger. I shoved half the éclair into my mouth.

"Keep talkin'. I'm listening."

"Maybe you could give Benny a nudge and suggest it's in his best interest to tell me what I want to know. In return, I'll help you get your money back."

"You'd be willing to do that?" Vinnie asked guardedly.

"Sure. It's got nothing to do with the issues in which

I'm involved. I believe I can retrieve the money for you. The only thing is, I need to solve my case first. Also, you can't hurt Benny. Have we got a deal?"

Vinnie dislodged a piece of cannoli from a rear molar with the tip of his pinkie. "Yeah, what the hell. I'll give it a shot." He grinned. "Metaphorically speaking, of course."

"Let me have a minute with Benny before you start." Then I approached the Italian Davy Crockett. "So how's it going, Benny?"

"*How's it going?* How the hell do you *think* it's going?" he retorted, wriggling like a worm on a hook. "You know I can't get hold of that money right now. It's all invested in the catalogue and the upcoming IPO! But try getting that big lug to listen to reason. *Now* what am I supposed to do?"

"Funny you should ask. I go way back with Vinnie, and might be able to help you out of this jam."

"You'd do that for me?" Benny's eyes grew misty with gratitude. "Any favor you want is yours! Go ahead, name it."

"Terrific. How about giving me that information I requested?"

"Okay, okay. That's doable. The problem is, I haven't been able to get to it yet," he hedged. "It's not that I don't plan to, believe me! But as you can see, I've been a little tied up."

"Then you'll just have to tell me what you already know." His nickname should have been Benny the Weasel.

Vinnie now approached with a canvas duffel bag in

his hand. Opening it, he pulled out a length of piano wire, and methodically began to wrap each end around a ham-sized fist.

"Hey, Bopper. Where can I find a coupla steel buckets in this place?"

"Whadda ya want those for?" Benny asked nervously.

"For mixing concrete, of course. What else?"

It was as if a cattle prod had suddenly zapped the Bopper's ass. Benny began to talk a mile a minute.

"All right, all right! I seem to remember something."

I just bet he did.

"The militia wacks and Hutchins have tapped into some kinda unlimited resource on the rez that's bringing in big bucks. Hutchins is their main man on the project, being that he works there."

"What kind of resource are you talking about?" Matthew pressed.

"How the hell should I know? Maybe they struck oil."

I was almost tempted to let Vinnie have his way with him. No question, I needed to start dealing with a better class of criminal. That thought triggered my memory back to the distinguished-looking gentleman I'd spotted at Nearly Paradise.

"Then maybe you can tell me this. I saw Rafe Lungren with a man that I'm curious about. He's tall, dignified, well dressed, and flew out of the compound on a private plane. Do you have any idea who he might be?"

Benny perked up to the very end of his coon tail.

"Ooh, ooh! The guy's got one of those prissy little goatees that makes him look like Freud, right?"

I nodded encouragingly.

"Bingo! That's some hotshot doctor who's always flying in and outta the place. He lives somewhere on the other side of Glacier National Park."

"That's a start, but I need more specifics."

"Yeah? Well, maybe I'd think better if you loosened these ropes."

Vinnie approached with the piano wire taut in his hands.

"Okay, for chrissakes! Hold it a second, it's beginning to come back to me!" Benny squirmed in his seat. "Let's see. He lives in a fancy-schmancy town with a name that sounds like some sorta food your tribe eats for breakfast."

Oy veh. I began to run down the grocery list. "Bagels?"

"No."

"Lox?"

"Uh-uh."

"Sturgeon?"

"Nah. Doesn't sound right."

"Whitefish?"

"Yeah, that's it! And the guy's name is Robert Zarem."

Benny slumped as if he'd just finished running the New York City marathon.

I walked out of range of the Bopper's earshot.

"So, whadda ya think? Should I put this around his neck and see what else you can get?" Vinnie asked, eagerly stretching the wire.

"No, that's probably all he knows. Will you give me a few days to solve the case?"

"What about my money?" Vinnie flashed a dark look that clearly stated, *Business is business.*

"I promise to get it to you with interest." I did my best to ignore the sight of Matthew rolling his eyes.

Vinnie finally nodded. "Sure, what the hell. This ain't such a bad place to hang out for a while. Besides, I got myself some free entertainment."

I was about to ask what that might be when a one-of-a-kind voice sailed through the hallway.

"Oh, Vinnie honey! I just designed a mountain girl costume. Whadda ya think of this for dancing at the bar?"

Cherry Jubilee pranced down the stairs in a bikini top and loincloth fashioned out of black bear fur. The two swatches over her breasts swayed as she walked. A quick double take revealed them to be the critter's paws, hanging from a string around her neck. The device allowed each paw to be separately lifted, in an inspired design for exposing her breasts. By the satisfied smile on her face, she'd apparently rebounded quite well from Kyle's recent death.

Oops! I guess I'd been wrong. One glimpse of me, and her expression changed into pure hatred. Cherry lunged through space with outstretched claws.

"What the hell is *that* murdering bitch doing here? I'll kill her myself unless someone beats me to it!" she screeched.

Vinnie quickly wrapped a massive arm around her chest and pulled her back against him. The bear paws flew up in the air in surprise. It wasn't the sight of her bare breasts that lassoed my attention; rather, it was the telltale mark on one paw's inner hide. A dingy loop circled the skin, mirroring the stain on the bear rug under Rafe Lungren's desk.

A piece of the puzzle fell into place, and I knew that Rafe Lungren *was* likewise involved. He'd said it himself—he still enjoyed catching a bear every now and then. Those marks could only have been made by trapped bears struggling to escape a snare. The wire had pinched the skin, forming a pool of blood. The result was a stain that never went away.

"Please don't ask any questions right now," I whispered to Running. "Just go along with whatever I say."

Then I turned to face Cherry. "The fact is, Kyle was responsible for his own death. However, I *do* have proof that he wasn't the only one involved in the bear gallbladder trade. There's enough evidence to implicate all the others who are part of the ring. Kyle wasn't as smart as everyone thought."

"What the hell are you talking about?" Cherry furiously hissed.

"Sorry, but it's confidential information," Matthew chimed in. "I'm afraid we can't tell you anything else."

We deliberately turned away, yet remained close enough for Cherry to overhear our conversation.

"Speaking of which, we need to get that evidence out of your office. Orders are to ship it to Billings ASAP." I glanced at my watch. "Damn! It's too late to do that today. We'll have to leave the material at your place overnight and send it first thing tomorrow morning. Just make sure it's locked up safe. It's dynamite information that's too important to lose."

Benny bounced his chair over toward us. "Hey,

what's going on? Is this something *I* should know about?"

I gave him my sweetest smile. "We're saying that Rafe Lungren is looking at his last few nights of freedom. We've got enough physical evidence to lock him away behind bars for a long time, thanks to Kyle."

"Whadda ya talking about? You can't do that! What about my business deal?" Benny demanded frantically.

Matt turned the Bopper's cap around, homeboy style. "That's *your* problem, hotshot. Rafe Lungren is going down."

"You gonna believe a dirty Indian and that bitch? They're bullshitting you. They've got nothing. Don't listen to them!" Cherry insisted.

"I guess you'll just have to wait and find out. Oh, and by the way—don't pack your bags and plan to go anywhere," I advised Miss Jubilee.

I figured we'd laid enough bait to do the trick. I had no doubt that Cherry would call Lungren and warn him. Odds were that he'd be paying a visit to Matthew's office later on tonight. I promised Vinnie to stay in touch and, reclaiming our weapons, we took our leave.

"Do you want to clue me in about that game back there?" Matthew asked as we drove away in his pickup.

"I'm betting that Hutchins and Rafe Lungren are both involved in the gallbladder trade. Our little ruse should lure Lungren out of hiding."

Matthew smiled and my heart instantly flip-flopped. "Very clever. But what's your interest with this Zarem fellow?"

"He's most likely the next link in a highly organized pipeline. What better cover can you think of than for a doctor to ship bear galls overseas in packages marked medical supplies?"

Running finally seemed to be convinced. "Okay. I've got a contact in Whitefish. I'll ask him to track Zarem down and get what information he can."

"Great. In the meantime, why don't we plan to rendezvous near your office around eight o'clock tonight? That should give us plenty of time to set up surveillance."

Running pulled next to where my Ford was parked in the FBI lot, when his cell phone rang. Call it idle curiosity or downright nosiness, but I stayed put, determined to listen.

"Hey, Bearhead. What's up?"

Matthew's face abruptly turned ashen. "Don't worry. I'll get on it right away," he promised and hung up.

"What's the matter?" I asked.

"It's Elizabeth Come-By-Night. She's missing again."

Oh dear God. "Did she have any appointments after school today?" I asked, knowing it was a stupid question. Bearhead would have been sure to check that out right away after the last incident.

"No, nothing."

"Maybe she went to a girlfriend's house?" I suggested.

But Running didn't respond. Each moment felt heavy as lead until he finally spoke.

"I keep thinking about those goddamn snares up in

the mountains, hidden like a bunch of land mines. There are probably still plenty of them set and waiting to go off. Anyone roaming around in the woods could get caught in one."

I instantly pictured Bearhead's little girl trapped and frightened, in pain and all alone.

"I'm going to help Bearhead look for her, but I'll be back by eight o'clock tonight."

"I'm coming along," I said, only to have Running cut me cold.

"No, you're not. This has nothing to do with you. It's Indian business."

His words hit hard. So this was how it felt to be an outsider.

"Then what can I do to help?" I asked, not wanting to show that my feelings were hurt.

"Go to Sally's and stay out of trouble."

I closed the passenger door behind me without a word. Running took off as I stood there, having never felt more useless.

Stop being such a baby! I reprimanded myself.

But I was also worried about the girl. I couldn't help but imagine Elizabeth locked in a grizzly's jaws.

I got into my Ford and drove off, unsure of what to do next. I hadn't gone far when my thoughts were interrupted by a car flashing its lights behind me. A glance in the rearview mirror revealed that Santou was my pursuer. He caught my eye and motioned for me to pull off the road, where I sat waiting like an errant motorist as he stormed over.

"All right, chère. I thought you were going straight

to your friend's house. Where in hell have you been?" he demanded.

I gritted my teeth to keep from biting his head off. Next time around, I fully intended to be born a man.

"Why are you checking up on me?" I retorted. "I told you before, there are other cases that I'm working on."

Jake walked around, opened the passenger door, and slid onto the seat beside me. I turned, ready to lay into him, only to be caught off-guard as his hand lightly touched my cheek.

"You really don't get it, do you? I care about you, Rachel. I always have and I always will. That's why I can't just sit around while you willingly throw yourself in harm's way. You're not playing with poachers in the bayou. Nor are you wired and protected like you were in Delta country. This is hard-core crazy militia. They have one agenda and one agenda only—to overthrow the government using any means possible. The bear gallbladder trade is no more than chump change for the United Christian Patriots. What they're involved in is something far more dangerous."

"Then tell me what it is," I pressed. "I have a right to know. For chrissakes, I'm caught in the middle of this thing!"

"Which is exactly why I want you out of their reach!"

Santou immediately knew that he'd said the wrong thing; he lowered his head and his fingers plowed through a tangle of dark hair, where a renegade band of silver strands glistened like hidden treasure. It was obvious that he was struggling over just how much to tell me.

"Look, there's a worldwide market in a commodity

that's only recently made a blip on our radar screen. It's based on supply and demand, just like everything else. There's a good possibility that the United Christian Patriots are implicated in this, and that they're seriously involved in its trafficking. Does that help to answer your question?"

He had to be kidding. It didn't even begin to start.

"Then you don't deny that they're also involved in the bear gallbladder trade," I pressed, determined to verify that fact.

Santou looked at me and the muscles in his face sagged, as if he knew precisely where all this was headed.

"Don't do it, Rachel. Stay the hell out of this one. You have no idea of the hornet's nest you're about to step into."

"That's just the thing, Jake. I already have."

Santou's hooded eyes held mine, as determined as a cobra hypnotizing its prey, and I was instantly filled with guilt. I pulled my gaze away, but Jake wasn't about to let me go that easily. He pushed a strand of hair away from my eyes and replaced it with a kiss. It was enough to open the floodgates, and I fell into his arms in a rush to escape my indiscretion. This was the man who had come to embody my dreams and desires, someone who accepted my rash decisions and mistakes. He was my lover, my confidant, and my best friend. But most of all, Santou was my sanctuary in the face of despair and frustration.

"What's wrong, chère? Is there something you want to tell me?"

I swallowed my tears and shook my head. Jake's inborn Cajun melancholy spilled over, filling the entire cab. It was clear that he strongly suspected I had betrayed him. A slight dip tugged at the corners of his lips, revealing an endless well of sadness. The last thing I wanted was to add to that. Yet I was afraid I already had.

"Listen, chère. I know you've been going through a hard time lately, what with your mother's recent death. It's also true that I haven't always been there for you. We've both got careers that demand way too much of our time. But I want you to know there's no one else in my life. Nor do I ever want there to be. There's a bond between us that's stronger than either of us realizes. Please don't jeopardize that by getting caught up in something fleeting. I don't want to lose you, Rachel. You mean far too much to me."

I could barely breathe, let alone speak, as though a heavy weight were pressing on my chest. He was right. My mother's death had hit me harder than I'd have ever imagined—forcing me to reassess my life. I had decisions to make—what was important and what wasn't, who I wanted to be with, and how to spend whatever time I had left. I clearly knew that I didn't want to spend it alone.

I remained mute, neither confirming nor denying his suspicions. Santou finally grew tired of the wait. His fingers lingered on my throat as he leaned over and kissed me.

"I need to get back to Dixon. We've got things of a sensitive nature in the works."

"Jake, just give me a hint as to what it involves," I pleaded. "Come on. I deserve at least that."

Santou's shoulders drooped ever so slightly. One more push and I felt sure he would cave.

"Just satisfy my curiosity and I'll stay out of your way."

Santou's eyes homed in on mine. "All right, then. I'll tell you this much. We suspect the United Christian Patriots have become a source for viruses to be used in biological warfare. If so, they could be selling the stuff to any number of terrorist groups around the world for big bucks. Is that enough information to satisfy you?"

I had to admit, it was pretty damn good. It also tied in with something that Rafe Lungren had let slip—that his catalogue planned to offer a vaccine to be used against biological warfare.

"Do you mind if I get back to work now?"

I silently shook my head.

"All right, then. Drive straight to your friend's house and stay there. Do it for my sake, if for no other reason." With that, Santou got back in his car and drove away.

Is that enough information to satisfy you?

As the words played over and over in my mind, I silently answered Santou's question—of course not. I took a deep breath and slowly exhaled. No matter what else, one thing was undeniable: the FBI was determined to take over what was rapidly developing into a high-profile case, using Kyle Lungren's suicide to push Matt and me out of the way. And though I still loved Santou, I was damned if I'd let that happen.

Eighteen

I slowly drove toward Sally's house, chafing at both Santou's and Running's instructions. *Get out of the way, go home, play it safe.* The more I thought about it, the angrier I became. Equally frustrating was that nagging doubt had begun to take seed inside me. There was something about Santou's theory that just didn't make sense.

I decided to turn my thoughts to trying to figure out the puzzle. The first step was to go back over the information I'd gleaned from Benny. He'd claimed that a valuable resource was being exploited on the Blackfeet reservation. Then I replayed what Santou had told me. The commodity had a worldwide market based on supply and demand. I racked my brain, trying to figure out what was on reservation land that could be so highly prized, aside from those items I already knew about—untapped oil and gas, along with bear galls.

My mind wandered as I drove, determined to solve the enigma, when a grizzly materialized off in the distance, silhouetted by the late afternoon sun. He lifted his massive head and sniffed the air. Then the griz turned his attention in my direction and looked directly at me.

Though I knew I was perfectly safe, an acrid taste

filled my mouth and a primal chill zoomed up my spine. The reaction was one of pure, unequivocal fear when faced with such a powerful creature. It came from man's ongoing struggle to stay alive, and the fact that only the fittest would survive.

Zap!

It was as if I'd been struck by a mental bolt of lightning. My fingers turned clammy and I broke into a cold sweat as I realized what the reservation had as an endless commodity! Remembering Elizabeth Come-By-Night's disappearance, I immediately felt sick. There was only one way to discover if I was on the right track. I swerved around and raced back toward the Indian Health Services clinic, convinced that the answer lay with Doc Hutchins—and determined to prove my theory correct.

The place was closed and shuttered, which I'd expected since it was Sunday. Still, I couldn't afford to take the chance of being discovered if I hoped to find proof of a potentially horrifying crime.

I waited and watched, patient as a trapdoor spider, not making a move until I was fully certain no one was around. Then I snuck to the back of the building in search of a window to jimmy. The security in this place was pathetic; I easily pried one open and climbed inside.

I could have sworn I heard the rustlings of spectral patients as I slid to the floor and walked down the hallway. Ghostly echoes of their groans kept pace with my steps. I quickly headed for Hutchins's office, fearing what I would find.

The puke-green walls looked exactly the same, only

now I felt as sick as their color. The fact that the room was an empty slate only added to the villainy that I suspected was going on.

Tread lightly, leave no prints.

Hutchins had done just that, if he were truly guilty of crimes almost too unbelievable to be imagined. I headed straight for the locked cabinet and picked it open. This time, I began to go through each separate folder with the utmost diligence. If there was something to be found, I wasn't going to miss it.

Once again, I pulled out the file labeled *General Health*, but Elizabeth Come-By-Night's sheet was no longer inside.

Joshua Crane. Martha Tall Bull. Sally Crossbow.

Those were the patients whose most recent medical workups had now taken her place. Their statistics had been neatly typed up and all were declared to be in excellent physical health. My eyes focused on Sally Crossbow's name. I cursed myself for not yet having been back in touch with her; the one consoling factor was knowing that Hal was now at her house.

You're wasting precious time with useless worrying. Get back to the work at hand!

I carefully examined the other files marked *Blood Type*, *Sex*, and *Age*. Every man, woman, and child within them was listed as a "fit specimen," bearing no physical deficiencies or debilitating illnesses. I continued to thumb through folder after folder until I began to wonder if *I* might not be crazy. Nothing out of the ordinary was to be found anywhere. Who was *I* to take potshots at the militia when my own paranoia appeared to be completely out of control? If I had any brains at all, I'd skedaddle out of the building right now, while my job was still intact.

I was about ready to give up, when I saw some delinquent files between the last divider and the back of the cabinet drawer. Loosening the metal plate, I slid it forward and released them from their solitary confinement. The first manila folder was labeled *Active*. I opened it up and took a peek.

Laying on top was Elizabeth Come-By-Night's missing file. Inscribed were her weight, height, and measurements, along with age, sex, and blood type. Everything appeared to be exactly the same as before. However, an additional page had been attached to the back of her records. I flipped to the sheet and found the results of her latest blood test, along with those from a tissue exam. But of far more interest was information regarding her DNA. Then my gaze dropped to the bottom of the page, where a handwritten notation had been scribbled.

Liver requested for Y. Matsumoto.

Lungs needed by 2/12 for J. Fernando

Perfect DNA match with M. Brewster for kidney

Urgent rush on heart for A. Osala

The room began to spin and my mind shut down at the sight of the ghoulish grocery list, refusing to believe what I saw. My trembling fingers reached for the second file, labeled *Closed Cases*.

Inside was a graveyard of the dead.

Harley Thunder. Doris Swiftdeer. Ira Blackman. Helen Running.

These were the records of those people who had either died under mysterious circumstances or were still
presumed to be missing.

The file revealed not only which organs had been
taken from the victims, but also listed their recipients.

There could no longer be any doubt as to why Elizabeth was missing.

I feared I was about to black out when my cell phone
rang. The sound shot a mega-dose of adrenaline
straight to my heart. I fumbled as I tried to answer, and
nearly disconnected the caller.

"Rachel? It's Matthew."

My brain told me to speak, but no words would
come out.

"Are you there?" he asked, his voice filled with tension.

His worry helped jerk me out of my stupor. "Elizabeth? Did you find her?"

"Yes, we've got her. That's under control."

A wave of relief rushed over me to fill my limbs with
exhaustion, and a sob rose in my throat.

"The reason I'm calling is because I want to fill you
in on some information I just received. That guy you
were asking about, Robert Zarem? My contact says
he's a secretive figure who heads a small private hospital over in Whitefish. The place is a ritzy facility known
for catering to a wealthy, international clientele."

My heart stopped, knowing perfectly well what I
was about to hear.

"During the day they do a brisk plastic surgery business, but what goes on at night is a far different story."

"Tell me exactly what you've learned!"

"My informant knows a janitor who works there. He says the facility really bustles from midnight until around six A.M. The hospital has an entire floor designated just for late night surgeries. The odd thing is, there's only a skeleton staff on duty during those hours. I guess the reason is the fewer people involved, the fewer questions that can be asked."

"What about after surgery?" I asked with excitement. "Are those patients moved to another area in the hospital then?"

"Nope. They all recuperate in private rooms on that same floor. Whatever is going on is shrouded in total secrecy—and that's the problem. I haven't been able to verify what I've heard; this information is coming from an employee who could be disgruntled and has it in for the place. But there's one thing that I do know for sure. Zarem's no nip-and-tuck Dr. Look Good. The guy's a transplant surgeon."

My heart began to beat as fast as an Indy 500 race car, and I looked at the files in my hands. They held all the verification that was needed. Hutchins was an organ broker at the very least. At the very worst, he was a cold-blooded butcher dealing in modern-day cannibalism.

"Matthew, I've discovered some medical files that tie into that," I said urgently.

"Medical files? What are you talking about?" Matthew asked. "Exactly where are you?"

"I'm in Hutchins's office. I broke into the Indian Health Services clinic."

There was a moment of stunned silence, and I immediately knew I should have kept my mouth shut.

"Are you out of your goddamn mind? Get the hell out of there right now!" Running erupted.

But it was already too late. An insidious sound slithered down the hall and into the room, where it raced up my spine like fingernails on a chalkboard. An elongated, eerie creak curled around me, as if a patient had just exhaled his last dying breath. Either IHS had a very active rodent population, or I was about to receive some unwanted company.

"I'm leaving right now."

I abruptly hung up, switched off the ringer, and stood perfectly still. I remained that way for a good couple of minutes. Then I placed the phone and files on Hutchins's desk and tiptoed ever so quietly to the door. I slowly poked my head into the hallway. Everything appeared to be in order. I held my breath and listened, but heard nothing further.

You're losing it, Porter. The only things in this building are some pissed-off ghosts and your own whopping case of nerves.

I turned back into the office to gather the files, and noticed something I hadn't seen before. Perhaps it was the way the late afternoon light hit the opposite wall, but I could have sworn I detected the outline of a door.

I walked closer, wondering if my eyes were playing tricks. There it was—a separate panel painted the same color as the rest of the room, but without any doorknob. The barest sliver of space ran along the top, bottom, and sides. This had to be the entrance to some sort of hidden room. Perhaps it was a closet that had long been forgotten, or a cubbyhole where illegal narcotics were kept.

I carefully listened once more. There wasn't a sound.

Logic insisted that time was of the essence; the prudent thing to do was get out of this place right now. However, behind that door might very well lie more secrets. I had no intention of leaving until I found out.

I ran my fingers along all four of its sides, but couldn't determine how to get the damn door open. Stepping away, I rubbed my palms over my eyes, wishing I had a battering ram. Then I stared at the office wall once again.

The experience was somewhat akin to gazing at an M. C. Escher painting. A minuscule hole now appeared in the door where none had previously appeared to be. All I needed to do was trip the lock and the door should open. I dug out my Leatherman, only to discover that none of the blades would fit.

Shit! What was I supposed to do now?

What you do best, of course. Snoop around until you find something else.

That made sense. There was still one place left to look. I hotfooted it over to Hutchins's desk and pulled open the drawer. It was just possible that a set of keys might be lying inside.

But all it held was an assortment of junk, from loose paperclips to decaying rubber bands to a couple of unwrapped sour balls. Then I spotted something that just might work. Tucked away in the back were long, thin, needle-nosed scissors, with a tweezers-like apparatus on its end.

It was a mosquito hemostat clamp, used by doctors for closing off veins during surgery. I knew because my mother had been a nurse and used to have one just like it. She'd found the clamp handy for threading needles and getting into tight spaces. I walked over to the concealed door and stuck the scissors snout in the hole. Then I probed around until the tweezers clamped onto the lock. The slightest twist of my wrist, and the door clicked open. I reached in and felt along the wall until my fingers hit a switch. A quick flick, and harsh white light brusquely flooded the room.

It's strange when one's nightmares spring to life. My demons usually arrive in the dark, but death plays by its own set of rules. I found myself standing in the entrance to a makeshift morgue.

My limbs grew cold as though I were already a corpse, docilely waiting for the first bite of the knife. I imagined myself laid out on the table, a virtual market of body parts for harvest. A series of bold red lines had been drawn on my flesh, marking precisely which organs were to be taken. My eyes, kidneys, and lungs were for sale to the highest bidder. I wondered just how much a human body was worth. Then I blinked, and the illusion vanished. Only the lingering scent of antiseptic remained, tainting the air. I took a deep breath and immediately felt nauseated.

Buck up, Porter! You're the hotshot, remember? You actually think you're gonna solve this case!

I turned to find Kyle's headless ghost standing beside me.

It's all in your mind. He doesn't exist. Stop wasting time and pay attention to what's in front of you.

But Kyle's ghost doggedly followed along. I tried to calm my nerves by cataloguing everything I saw. There was a stainless steel table that was just the right size for a body. An assortment of surgical instruments was neatly arranged on the counter. Beside them were syringes, along with three small medicine vials. I walked over to examine their contents.

One contained the anticoagulant heparin, while the other was a muscle relaxant labeled Robaxin. The last bottle held liquid Valium, a popular tranquilizer. I now knew why Elizabeth Come-By-Night had been staggering out in the field. Hutchins must have injected her with a powerful cocktail in place of the flu shot she was supposed to receive. The girl had apparently managed to slip away before any further damage was done.

There could no longer be any doubt that the FBI was barking up the wrong tree. It wasn't a deadly virus that was being created, or any sort of anthrax vaccine to be sold to survivalists. The doctor had clearly made the leap from Medicare scams to the body parts Mafia.

A small refrigerator sat against the wall and I wouldn't have thought much of it but for the padlock attached to keep out nosy intruders. That was the equivalent of waving a red flag in my face. My needle-nosed clamp neatly did the trick, and I flung open the door.

Sitting on the shelf was a small cooler exactly like the one Robert Zarem had carried at Nearly Paradise. Reaching in, I pulled it toward me. Half my brain expected it to contain bear galls, neatly packed and ready for overseas shipment. The other half of my brain remained blessedly numb.

Unlatching the handles, I spread the container open wide and peered inside. It felt as if I had been struck deaf, dumb, and blind, my mind stubbornly refusing to register the contents. All I knew was that Kyle's breath began to lick hotly at my ear.

Come on, Porter! You know what you're holding in your hands. The question is, what little mud child did it come from?

Try as I might, I couldn't tear my eyes away from the unfolding nightmare. Floating inside a plastic bag of saline solution was what could only be a human heart.

I held my breath, half-expecting it to start pumping wildly. But the heart continued to slumber, as if succored by dreams of beating in a body all its own. The bag rested on a bed of dry ice, from which ghostly wisps of mist seductively rose up to embrace me. Soon I was cocooned in the web of a gentle lullaby.

This little piggy already went to market. Before long we'll need another. Who do you suppose it will be? Man, woman, or child—it makes no difference, as long as they're healthy. People are the renewable resource on the Blackfeet reservation.

The chant transformed into Kyle's ghostly laughter, which grew louder until it completely filled the room. The spell was broken when the door abruptly slammed shut behind me.

There was no time to think, much less react. Ten red-hot fingers burned into my flesh, branding me with their anger as they roughly jerked me around. I tried to prepare myself to do battle with Kyle's headless apparition, only to find I was facing something far worse: two pissed-off FBI agents. They continued to angrily glare until they saw what I held in my hands.

"Holy shit!" Dixon exclaimed, his complexion turning as green as the office walls. "Just what the hell is going on here?"

Santou caught my eye and I knew better than to betray him. "I decided to check out a hunch as to why people on the rez have been disappearing. Evidently Hutchins has been supplying the black market with body parts taken from Blackfeet Indians."

"So it wasn't a virus that was being worked on after all," Dixon muttered in disbelief.

"What made you think that was why people were missing?" I couldn't help but ask.

"High-risk experiments. We figured the Blackfeet were being used for testing purposes," Santou offered.

Dixon shot him a dirty look and promptly relieved me of the cooler, as Jake slapped a search warrant on top of the fridge.

"That piece of paper is probably the only thing that's going to save your ass, Porter," Dixon warned. "As it is, I should have you fired for disobeying a direct order."

"Oh yeah? Then what's stopping you?" I countered, unsure which angered me more—the fact that I'd screwed up and been discovered, or having to stand here while I was soundly reprimanded.

"The simple fact is that any possibility of a case would be blown if anyone learned you broke in here without a warrant!" Dixon snapped. "So, here's how it's gonna play out. You leave right now and tell no one where you've been, or what you found. As far as the world's concerned, you were never at this clinic."

"What are you talking about? I'm the one who broke this case!" I objected.

"Maybe so, but you were never supposed to have

been here in the first place. That's what you get for not following orders."

"In other words the FBI gets to take all the credit for my hard work," I growled.

"You've got it." Dixon's eyes narrowed to mere slits. "You don't have any bargaining chips to play with on this one."

"Sorry, chère, but that's the deal. Take it or leave it," Santou grimly confirmed.

No doubt about it. This was payback time in more ways than one.

"That means vamoose, Porter. Right now!" Dixon barked.

I had little choice but to exit the room. However, I'd be damned if I'd let them scavenge every scrap of evidence that I'd found. While they were occupied in the morgue, I slid the files off the desk in Hutchins's office and slipped them under my jacket, along with my cell phone. Maybe I *was* a sinking ship, but Matthew Running didn't have to go down with me. The man had earned his fair share of credit for all the work we'd already done.

I left the clinic through the front door and went to my car. Determined footsteps soon echoed behind me, as brisk as the chastising rap of a ruler. I quickly stashed the files under the front seat.

"Rachel, wait! I want to talk to you a minute."

Santou came so close that I was nearly seared by his body heat.

"I'm sorry about what just happened, but I tried to warn you to stay out of the way earlier."

I looked at the man who'd become so much a part of

my life. Jake deserved honesty, no matter what the consequence. Besides, my own conscience couldn't stand much more of this.

"We both know what's going on, Jake, so why don't we just get it over with? I admit it. I slipped up bigtime, and this is your way of getting even."

I waited for him to lash out, aware that it was well deserved. Hot tears of guilt welled up in my eyes, and I desperately wanted to ask for forgiveness. Santou stopped me by firmly pressing a finger against my lips. His touch brought my defenses crashing down. That and the look on his face, which was nearly as pained as my own.

"All we're talking about right now is what happened back there in that clinic. Okay?"

I nodded, and we both took a deep breath.

"I know you blame me for swiping cases from you in the past."

"Which you just did again," I couldn't help but jab.

"And it's something I promise to work on," Santou continued. "But this one was ours from the start."

"What in the hell are you talking about? The FBI had no idea what was really going on," I protested. "And the case still involves the smuggling of bear galls. Not only that, but people have been dying on this reservation for years. The FBI did nothing until Matt Running and I stirred things up."

The mention of Running's name caused an awkward silence.

"What made you decide to search the clinic, anyway?" I inquired, hoping to break the tension.

"Hutchins apparently tried to abduct a young girl today. Her father called our office to report that your friend, Running, had caught him. The doctor's cooling his heels in jail right now. That's what allowed us to get a search warrant. We've been suspicious of Hutchins for quite a while. It's true, we didn't know he was dealing in the illegal organ trade. But we assumed he was involved with something big."

"Then why didn't you do anything about it before now?" I asked in frustration.

"Because I operate under a different modus operandi than you, Rachel. We actually need a solid reason before we're granted permission to search private property."

The hint of a lopsided grin flitted across Santou's lips and very nearly broke my heart. We'd had our ups and downs over the years, and probably always would. But there was no denying that I loved the man. And wasn't that what relationships were all about? That belief had helped to keep my demons at bay, and to stop the darkness from entering my soul.

"Unlike you, I do my best to make cases and still remain within the confines of the law."

Santou now broke into a full-fledged smile, and I couldn't help but laugh through my tears.

"Seriously, chère. We would have uncovered it the same as you did once we got in here."

I seriously doubted that. First they would have had to discover the secret room.

"Damn, I should have figured Hutchins would be into something like this. We're aware that the illegal organ trade is a multimillion-dollar business that's expanded from Asia to Europe over to the U.S. Over seventy-five thousand Americans *alone* are on wait lists for some type of organ. There have been reports of wealthy patients willing to travel anywhere in the world to secure a transplant. Body parts are even being sold over the Internet these days!"

That remark made me wonder what Rafe Lungren's booming new business was *really* up to. "The United Christian Patriots are obviously involved in this, aren't they?"

Santou's fingers raked his hair and became entangled in the mop of curls. "You're probably right. We're gonna have to twist Hutchins for information. Maybe he'll be able to shed more light on the topic."

"That's crazy!" I exploded. "You can't wait for that. Who knows what could happen in the meantime? Rafe Lungren might go underground. More people could be killed. Why not just go and check out the compound right now?"

"For chrissakes, Rachel! Because there isn't enough evidence to obtain a search warrant yet. Lungren hasn't been caught doing anything wrong." Jake looked at me, clearly suspicious. "Just remember, you're already in double hot water for riling up the militia and sneaking into the clinic. Don't go getting any crazy ideas about invading the compound by yourself."

I kept my mouth shut, not wanting to blow my scheme. If all went according to plan, I'd catch Lungren breaking into Matthew's office tonight. *That* should give Santou the leverage he needed to search Nearly Paradise—and redeem me in the process.

"Listen, I've got to get back inside. I'll do what I can

to make sure Dixon doesn't send a negative report to your superiors."

"Thanks. I appreciate it."

Santou hesitated, and I was suddenly afraid of what he might say next.

"I love you, Rachel. I know there are things we need to work out, but I believe we're worth fighting for. I hope you feel the same way."

Santou's generosity left me speechless. I wasn't certain I'd have been as forgiving if the situation were reversed. Tears spilled down my cheeks as I now realized just how fragile true love could be, and how close I'd come to blowing it.

Jake's callused fingers wiped my tears away. "We've both made mistakes. What say we talk about them later? Meanwhile, do me a favor, chère. Go straight to your friend Sally's, and let us do our job."

Santou walked back inside as I slid into the Ford and drove off. As far as I was concerned, I'd already done their work *for* them.

I'd expected to leave Kyle Lungren's ghost behind, but wouldn't you know? Militia boy had decided to come along for the ride.

Be a good girl and let the FBI do their job, he mocked, his decapitated head balancing on his shoulders.

"Oh, shut up!" I growled.

But it was true; I felt out of the loop. Santou had only the barest sketch of a crime ring that *I'd* uncovered. He didn't even know yet about Robert Zarem and his part in the trade. That's where Matt could take credit.

In all probability, organs were going from poor to

rich, black and brown to white, female to male in a too-familiar dance of commerce. The cell phone vibrated against my hip, interrupting my thoughts. Most likely it was Matthew, wanting to know why I'd so abruptly hung up. I had every intention of telling him; we were still partners in this deal, no matter what had occurred between us. Even more to the point, we had a definite bond: we both used whatever means necessary to get our jobs done.

"Agent Porter speaking."

"Listen and don't talk," a male voice gruffly ordered. "I'm calling with a tip. I was hunting in the Milk River complex today and came upon a freshly killed grizzly. It had a radio collar around its neck."

The man proceeded to tell me exactly where the bear could be found.

"Who did you say this was?" I inquired, quickly scribbling the directions down.

"Uh-uh! You just broke the rules by asking a question. That's all the information you get." He hung up.

Damn! I hadn't even had the chance to ask if the bear was caught in a snare. I needed to get there and see what was going on. I glanced at the clock. Five P.M. Proper procedure dictated that I notify Matthew about the call; the danger was that he'd insist on coming along. By then, night would have already begun to fall. Any further delay would give a poacher enough time to sneak in and haul the carcass off before I got to the scene.

I couldn't wait. Not if I wanted to be back in Browning by eight o'clock to stake out Rafe Lungren. This latest poaching brought the number of grizzlies killed to nineteen since spring. The carnage had to stop.

I pressed the pedal to the metal and took off. I'd call Matthew once I got there.

Nineteen

A bank of dark, menacing clouds hovered overhead, indicating that snow was on the way. Equally foreboding was the evening sun that irately hung beneath. It blazed fervid as a bonfire, shooting off rays in angry sparks. The warning couldn't have been any more clear—stay away. I thrust down on the pedal even harder.

I drove along the mountain road Matt and I had traversed only yesterday and parked in the same general area. I slung a tracking device over my shoulder, turned it on, and locked the Ford. Then I slipped on the headphones, set the tracker to general scan, and holding the H-shaped antennae high in the air, began to walk.

I'd just entered the woods when I remembered that I had yet to call Matthew. Damn! I quickly removed the headgear, plucked the cell off my belt, and punched in his number. There wasn't so much as a sound. Wouldn't you know? I was apparently in a dead zone. I slowly pivoted in a three-sixty-degree turn, stopping every few inches, until I finally received a dial tone. I tried the number again and this time his voice mail answered—that is, what I could hear of it through a deafening sea of static.

"I'm at the Milk River complex checking out a tip on a dead grizzly. I'll meet you back in Browning at eight o'clock."

I hung up, unsure if Matthew would be able to decipher the message, even if he managed to receive it. But at least my conscience was clear; I'd attempted to contact him. That done, I continued on.

The forest trees began to converge, conspiring like a gang of thugs who were up to no good as they blocked out the setting sun. The wind picked up as if on cue, signaling the approach of the oncoming storm. I imagined I could hear its breeze ruffle through the pine needles in a ghostly whisper.

You're not as smart as you think! the gust jeered, and I knew that Kyle wasn't far behind.

I tried to concentrate on moving like a liquid shadow, but the scrunch of my feet resounded loudly in my ears. My limbs grew tense and a squall of prickles enveloped my flesh. I suddenly realized that I wasn't alone. The wilderness had eyes—I could feel them everywhere. They burrowed through my jacket to pierce my skin and singe my soul. Apprehension lodged like a rising moon in my throat. What would I do if confronted by a grizzly?

The next moment, the tracking device sprang to life. *Beep! Beep! Beep!*

It was the steady pulse of a mortality signal. My anonymous caller had been right: the grizzly was dead.

I continued along the trail, feeling like Hansel *and* Gretel. Each new beep took on the significance of yet another breadcrumb, as the lines on the tracking device drew closer. But still, there was no bear in sight. Despite the wind, the cold, and the fading light, I refused to leave the area without finding the grizzly.

My focus was so strong that it took a moment before I heard the alarm bell go off in my head. An imminent sense of danger commanded that I not move a muscle. I remained perfectly still and warily looked around, and then up.

Directly above me hung a wire cable strung between two trees. My heart began to pound so hard that I could scarcely breathe. I followed the deadly wire down to the ground and broke into a cold sweat. I'd walked straight into a snare. One false move and I'd be jerked into the air.

I stared at where my foot was planted within the lethal loop and began to sway. I feared I was about to faint.

Suck it up, Porter!

The sound of Kyle's laughter ringing in my ears snapped me out of my daze. I ever so carefully lifted my foot out of the wire and took a giant step backward. The bear would have to wait until I'd disarmed the trap. But as I turned, the lines on the tracking device converged tightly together. Straight ahead loomed a dense patch of quaking aspen. That had to be where the carcass was stashed!

I quickly moved toward the spot, accompanied by a string of beeps as strong as a pulsating heart. There on the ground lay a discarded radio collar. Damn, damn, *damn*! Not only had the poacher beaten me to the punch, but he'd left the collar behind as a mocking calling card.

I bent down to pick it up, when something hard struck

the back of my neck and a rush of pain swept over me like a tsunami. Every nerve ending burst into flames and my legs gave way as I fell, cursing the headphones for having muffled the approach of my assailant.

Oh, dear God! Don't let it be Old Caleb!

I forced my eyes open, but instead of four lethal paws, a man's hands floated into view as they lifted a large rock near my head.

I struggled to move, but my muscles refused to obey. It was too late, anyway. The boulder was already on a downward collision course toward me.

One last exquisite bit of pain, Kyle whispered.

The electronic beeps merged with the pounding in my brain to create a frantic cacophony. But the rock flew past me, smashing the radio collar to bits and bringing the strident racket to an abrupt end. After that, the world turned black.

I woke to a jackhammer throbbing in my head, and the cold, hard ground pressed against my skin. A deluge of tiny wet kisses showered my face, bringing to life every inch of me that ached. Even my eyelids hurt as I opened them. I found myself lying in the woods, embraced by a light blanket of falling snow. Dusk was ebbing away, having been seduced by the night and then quickly abandoned.

It didn't take long for two distinct odors to curl their way into my consciousness. The first was easy to identify—the scent of gas. My neck screamed in pain as I gingerly turned my head to the right and spotted a propane tank standing nearby. On the other side of me lay the nauseating stench of death.

I agonizingly turned again and saw that the snow to my left was drenched in blood, its surface covered with a repulsive mound of viscera. I'd been placed near a steaming pile of bear bait.

I desperately tried to move, only to discover that my ankles and wrists were tightly bound with rope. I closed my eyes, attempting to elude the constant thump of pain. But nothing could keep the reek of death from pervading my senses, nor the drip, drip, drip of fear from poisoning my brain. A warm breath unexpectedly caressed my ear, and I jerked in alarm.

"It's about time you woke up, Sleeping Beauty. I wouldn't want you to miss the show. After all, you're the star attraction."

A flashlight clicked on to reveal Rafe Lungren kneeling over me. He made absolutely certain I knew who he was by shining the flashlight on his face. Then he turned the beam outward, bathing the area around us in a golden glow. My stomach sank as his point was made. This was the spot where Kyle had shot himself.

"I didn't kill your son, Mr. Lungren. I tried to talk him out of pulling the trigger." But I knew any hope of reasoning was useless.

"Well, that just goes to show the difference in how we view things, darlin'. The way I see it, you and the people you work for drove Kyle to his death." Lungren's brow hung heavy as a cliff over his steel-blue eyes. "Kyle did what any good militia soldier does when he's caught. He neutralized himself as a source of information."

I stared at the man above me. "Your son didn't shoot himself over bear galls, did he?" I ventured. "He did it to protect something that *you're* involved in. Poaching bear gallbladders was merely secondary."

Lungren didn't say a word. He didn't need to; a flame came to life in his eyes with an abrupt flicker.

"He sacrificed himself to save your ass, and all you can call him is a good soldier?" I spat. "I hope it damn well was worth losing your only son!" I figured the best way to get Lungren talking was to make him angry.

Lungren drew himself up to his full height and towered above me like a vengeful prophet. "What do you know about loyalty, bitch? Only two-bit whores sleep with Indians!"

A gasp escaped me, and Lungren's mouth twisted into a malicious sneer.

"Did you really think you wouldn't be followed? I watched the two of you leave your motel room this morning. You deserve to die for that, if nothing else."

Helen Lungren Running's records had been among Hutchins's *Closed Cases*. Now I knew who had ordered her death.

"Just like your first wife deserved to die because she left you for a Blackfeet Indian? I *know* what you're involved in. Matthew Running believes the United Christian Patriots is selling illegal arms. But that's not what's really going on, is it?" I pushed some more. "So was Kyle's mom your first victim in the trade? And did your son die knowing what Hutchins did to her?"

Rather than erupting, Lungren knelt down once again so that his voice rang strong in my ears.

"You're a smart girl, Rachel. Bear galls used to be our major source of income until Hutchins came along. I like to think of what we're doing as a service to mankind. Look at all the lives that are being saved. Besides, it's not as if anything of importance is being sacrificed. Mud people are hardly a notch above animals."

I attempted to roll away, which brought a smile to Lungren's lips.

Shifting his weight, he drew closer. "And I knew you were laying a trap when Cherry Jubilee called. There *is* no proof of my involvement. I figured you deserved tit for tat. What better way to lure you up here than an anonymous tip about a radio-collared grizzly? Your predecessor fell for the same trick."

"*You* killed Carolton?" I blurted, kicking myself for not having been more suspicious.

"No. A grizzly did that, the same as will happen to you. I just laid out the buffet."

With any luck, a bear would come along right now and munch on the maniac hovering over me. "I didn't lie to Cherry; there's evidence that's going to put you away forever. The FBI has already caught Hutchins, and they're going through his records at the clinic right now."

Damn! The records are under the front seat of the Ford! If Lungren searches it, he'll destroy them!

"Do you really expect me to believe Hutchins would keep any papers that would implicate the United Christian Patriots in all this?" he patronizingly inquired.

"Apparently he kept more than you realize. The FBI will be picking Zarem up next," I threw out.

"You know about him?" Lungren asked in surprise.

"That's right; then it'll be your turn. In fact, the FBI already has a warrant out for your arrest," I bluffed.

"You're bullshitting, Porter," Lungren whispered in

my ear. "Zarem and Hutchins are both good soldiers. Neither of them will talk. As for the FBI, let them try to arrest me. Maybe there'll be a shoot-out at the compound, during which I'll be killed. That'll make me a martyr for the cause, just like my son. And Honey's radio show will go on fomenting violence. Every militia group in the country will rise up against the government's crimes."

"I wouldn't overrate her audience. From what I hear, the only people who listen are those with no brains."

Lungren's hand tightly encircled my throat. "Speaking of no brains, you should have had better judgment when it came to men," he hissed, his fingers digging into my flesh.

I gasped for breath, only to have a piece of duct tape slapped across my mouth.

"I'd kill you myself, but having a grizzly do it is so much better. Of course, maybe you'll get lucky and no bears will harm you. After all, you're their big protector, right? I guess we'll just have to wait and find out."

Lungren picked his rifle up off the ground, near my tracking device. The headphones were nowhere in sight.

"Happy hunting, Agent Porter," he said, and then left.

Twilight was now gone. I listened until I could no longer hear the crunch of snow beneath his boots. The sound was replaced by a silence so deep that it penetrated every molecule. It was as though I'd been swallowed up whole and had landed in the belly of the universe. The snow glittered like a sea of sequins in the night, and the moon cast sinister shadows around me.

I wriggled back and forth, eventually picking up enough speed to roll onto my side. Then I lowered my bound hands to the ground in search of a sharp object, but found nothing. Damn! I couldn't just lie here waiting to die. I continued to squirm in an attempt to loosen the ropes. Something pierced my thigh, and I remembered what was in my pocket.

I maneuvered my fingers inside, where they wrapped around the serrated heart pin I'd found on my office floor. But the pin's jagged teeth kept catching in the fabric, making the process frustratingly difficult. I suppose it was a blessing in disguise that my limbs were numb with cold; I didn't feel any pain as my fingers got nicked. It was only as I pulled the pin from my pocket that I saw the blood. I thrust my fingers into the snow and washed it off, then I placed the heart's lethal teeth against the rope and started to saw.

I was so focused on my task that the high-pitched yip of a wolf took me by surprise, and the pin jerked, cutting my fingers deeper. My flesh turned slippery, and tears of pain caused my vision to blur. I determinedly set to work again, damned if Lungren would win.

By now I'd lost all sense of feeling, forcing me to clutch the heart even tighter. But it had become slick with blood, and the pressure made it slip from my grip!

My fingers dove frantically into the freezing snow after it, but the jagged heart was nowhere to be found. I swallowed a muffled cry and stubbornly continued to grope, but the bitter cold made my fingers clumsy, and my mind grew fuzzy.

I slipped in and out of consciousness, no longer sure what was a dream and what was reality. I might have drifted off into death if a harrowing sound hadn't jarred me awake. I heard the determined tread of a creature approaching from behind, causing my pulse to race.

I lay absolutely still, knowing the slightest movement would only attract a grizzly that much sooner.

If you act like prey, you become prey. The mantra repeated itself in a sickening loop in my brain.

But rather than feeling the crunch of my bones, I heard the chilling click of a knife flicking open. Lungren must have returned!

I furtively slid my knees to my chest, planning to roll onto my back and kick Lungren to kingdom come, damned if I'd leave this world without inflicting the maximum possible injury on my attacker. I waited for just the right moment to strike, when a familiar voice floated through the night.

"I'm here, chère. It's all right," Santou whispered.

The cry buried inside me now rose to the surface, as the blade swiftly released my ankles and wrists. I was pulled onto my feet, and stood on wobbly legs as Jake's fingers ripped the tape from my mouth.

"How did you find me?" I blurted out, as Jake nervously glanced around.

"Running received your phone message and got worried when you didn't show. He passed the information on to me."

Suddenly a tiny red dot, smaller than a dime, mysteriously appeared on Santou's chest. My mind momentarily went blank, during which precious seconds were lost.

"Drop!" I yelled, and lunged to push Jake out of harm's way.

But it was too late. The bullet hit its mark. I stood in disbelief as Santou crumpled at my feet. The next instant, I was on the ground beside him.

"Jake! Are you all right?" I cried, my hands desperately trying to stop the growing pool of his blood.

"You're next, Porter," Lungren's voice targeted me from out of the darkness.

A ruby-red dot sliced through the snowy mist and landed directly on my heart, followed by the explosion of a gun. The world came to a stop as I waited for the bite of the bullet. Instead, Lungren flew out of the brush. He'd been tackled by Matthew Running, who'd appeared from nowhere, as silent as a ghost.

I rolled out of the way as Lungren landed in the gut pile, with Matt closely barreling behind. Running momentarily glanced at me, ignoring his own advice: *Never turn your back on a coyote.*

Lungren seized the opportunity to ram his rifle stock into Running's side, causing Matt to fall hard to the ground. He groaned and I feared he wouldn't make it back up. Then the tracking device once again sprang to life.

Beep! Beep! Beep!

A radio-collared grizzly was stalking the night—one that was very much alive! But I had little time to think as Lungren staggered out of the gut pile. Raising his rifle, he took aim at me.

"This is for Kyle!"

The words had barely left his mouth when a resounding roar ripped through the forest, and a sound like the thundering of horses became an enormous grizzly racing toward us.

"Matt! Old Caleb to your right!" I screamed, hoping to be heard above the crescendo of roars.

Summoning all his strength, Running leaped up and planted an explosive kick dead center in Lungren's chest. The gun misfired as Lungren was propelled directly into the creature's path. It was as if Old Caleb had been waiting for him all along. The bear grabbed the militia leader between his teeth and, lifting him off his feet, shook him like a rag doll. A dull thud echoed in the air as Lungren's body was flung against a tree.

Matthew darted to me and grabbed hold of my arm. "Run!"

"Wait! Jake's been injured!"

Running hesitated only a moment before lifting Jake up and throwing him over his shoulder; then we raced through the woods, pursued by Lungren's blood-curdling screams. We never looked back, but ran for our lives as Lungren's shrieks slowly died, replaced by the grizzly's roars which cannibalized the black night.

Epilogue

"**H**ere, drink this. It will help stop those nightmares you've been having."

I had no idea whether that was true, but I gladly took the cup of tea from Sally's hands. Old Caleb's visits had become a regular occurrence in my dreams over the past few nights.

"I caught Honey's radio program today. You should have heard it; it was one helluva doozy." Sally parted a bobby pin between her teeth, then restrained a wayward curl. "She's turning her former stepson and that dead husband of hers into a cause célèbre."

I had no doubt that Honey's ratings were soaring. She'd not only vilified the FBI for arresting Zarem and Hutchins, but even claimed that the feds and the Blackfeet were illegally trafficking in the organs of militia members! She insisted Rafe and Kyle had been killed as part of a massive cover-up.

I'd been proven wrong on one thing, however. The militia's Internet business hadn't been used to sell body parts; it was making a fortune solely through survival gear and outdoor fashions. In fact, the IPO was still on the fast track to go public. But Lungren had apparently been foolish enough to entrust Benny with all the paperwork. That allowed the Bopper to scam the militia, placing the company in his own name. I'd also learned that though most of the mob's cash had been returned, Vinnie was now a partial owner in the jesus-iscoming.com enterprise. I suppose that was one way of recouping the rest of the money.

"Are you going to see Jake today?" Sally coyly inquired.

Santou was recuperating nicely at the hospital in Great Falls. Though the bullet had penetrated the right side of his chest, it miraculously managed to miss all his major arteries. Even now, a shiver ran through me as I remembered how he'd lain unconscious on the ground, bleeding at my feet. Losing Santou would have been as bad as losing life itself. Since he was willing to forgive me my affair, I supposed I had no choice but to forgive myself. I'd acknowledged the fact that we were meant to be together over these past few days.

"Yes. It's nearly visiting hours, so I plan to head there now. I'll see you later tonight."

But I had somewhere else to go, first.

Getting into the Ford, I drove back up into grizzly country. I knew I'd never be able to sleep until I faced down the bogeyman. While I might not be able to permanently extinguish my fears, at least I could put a lid on the box, choosing when and where to open it.

I navigated the winding mountain road, parked my Ford, and began to walk the ridgeline, moving past cedar and lodgepole pines. Snow-covered peaks gazed down, chilling in their beauty. Eventually, I reached a high ridge where the valley yawned below. This would be the last hike of the season. Soon there would be too much snow.

I let the silence embalm me. The stillness slowly filled my veins and I realized it wasn't so frightening, after all. Perhaps it really *was* time to let go of the ghosts. And, with that, the permafrost that had encapsulated me for so long began to thaw.

As a magnetic presence filled the air, I realized I wasn't alone. I turned my head ever so slightly. As I feared, Old Caleb was standing there.

His dark brown fur glistened and rippled under the sun, its silver tips kissed by the frost. Regal in presence, Old Caleb stood less than fifty yards away. My hand instinctively slid toward the canister of pepper spray attached to my belt. I had no doubt this was the same bear that had killed Lungren. What would he do to me?

Old Caleb never made eye contact. Instead he continued to gaze upon his realm, as if taking one last look before heading back into the earth for his long winter sleep. Averting my eyes, I lowered my head to show that I posed no threat. Then I followed his lead and gazed down on the valley.

An enormous sense of peace came over me, even as I faced my own mortality. No matter the price, I truly believed this was the grizzlies' land to roam—country so wild that it remained untouched by the track of man. When I finally dared to look over again, the bear had vanished. I made my way back down to the Ford on shaky legs.

I opened the vehicle door and climbed inside, where yet another surprise awaited me. There on the seat was a miniature sandbox, identical to Matthew Running's. He clearly knew that my choice had been made. Arranged on its surface were a jagged gold heart, a grizzly claw, and his dog tag. The only thing missing was a wounded soul.

I gently raked the sand around them. While there was no escaping the past, it revealed that life was too short to be consumed by guilt and regret. There would always be ghosts, pain, and memories. I'd just have to figure out how to live with them.

My finger rested for a moment on the jagged gold heart. Then I turned on the engine and drove toward my future, where Santou was patiently waiting for me.

FREE BOOK!

NO PURCHASE NECESSARY!
Between July 2 and July 31, 2002,
HarperCollins Publishers will give away up to
500 copies of GATOR AIDE (0-380-79288-5) by
Jessica Speart.

Just go to www.avonmystery.com for details
and you may be an instant book winner!

(retail book value is approximately $6.99)

The Joanna Brady Mysteries by
New York Times Bestselling Author

An assassin's bullet shattered Joanna Brady's world, leaving her policeman husband to die in the Arizona desert. But the young widow fought back the only way she knew how: by bringing the killers to justice . . . and winning herself a job as Cochise County Sheriff.

DESERT HEAT
0-380-76545-4/$6.99 US/$9.99 Can

TOMBSTONE COURAGE
0-380-76546-2/$6.99 US/$9.99 Can

SHOOT/DON'T SHOOT
0-380-76548-9/$6.50 US/$8.50 Can

DEAD TO RIGHTS
0-380-72432-4/$7.50 US/$9.99 Can

SKELETON CANYON
0-380-72433-2/$7.50 US/$9.99 Can

RATTLESNAKE CROSSING
0-380-79247-8/$6.99 US/$8.99 Can

OUTLAW MOUNTAIN
0-380-79248-6/$6.99 US/$9.99 Can

DEVIL'S CLAW
0-380-79249-4/$7.50 US/$9.99 Can

And in Hardcover

PARADISE LOST
0-380-97729-X/$25.00 US/$37.95 Can

The Anna Pigeon Mysteries
by *New York Times* Bestselling Author

NEVADA BARR

LIBERTY FALLING
0-380-72827-3/$7.99 US/$10.99 Can

TRACK OF THE CAT
0-380-72164-3/$6.99 US/$9.99 Can

ILL WIND
0-380-72363-8/$7.50 US/$9.99 Can

FIRESTORM
0-380-72528-7/$7.99 US/$10.99 Can

ENDANGERED SPECIES
0-380-72583-5/$7.99 US/$10.99 Can

BLIND DESCENT
0-380-72826-5/$6.99 US/$8.99 Can

Also by Nevada Barr

BITTERSWEET
0-380-79950-2/$13.50 US/$19.50 Can